BOUND FOR TROUBLE

EM Lynley

Dreamspinner Press

Published by
DREAMSPINNER PRESS

Where Dreams Come True...
International publishers of quality gay romantic fiction since 2007

5032 Capital Circle SW
Suite 2, PMB# 279
Tallahassee, FL 32305-7886
USA
http://www.dreamspinnerpress.com/

Bound for Trouble
© 2014 EM Lynley.

Cover Art
© 2014 Paul Richmond.
http://www.paulrichmondstudio.com
Cover content is for illustrative purposes only
and any person depicted on the cover is a model.

ISBN: 978-1-62798-917-6
Digital ISBN: 978-1-62798-918-3

Printed in the United States of America
First Edition
June 2014

This paper meets the requirements of
ANSI/NISO Z39.48-1992 (Permanence of Paper).

Readers love the Delectable series
by EM LYNLEY

Gingerbread Palace

"This is a 5 Star read and highly recommend even after the holiday season. It's a heartwarming story that I'll be rereading throughout the year."
—The Novel Approach

"This book will make you cry, get mad, laugh, cry some more and I love when a book hooks your emotions like that."
—Hearts on Fire

"This was a great holiday read and as an added bonus the author includes the gingerbread recipes at the back of the book! So a sweet treat all the way around!"
—Guilty Indulgence Romance Review

An Intoxicating Crush

"This book certainly was delectable, food-wise and drink-wise and very enlightening in methods of wine making. It's a story which reminds us that good communication is the key to any successful endeavor."
—Rainbow Book Reviews

"*An Intoxicating Crush* was another excellent novel by EM Lynley. Ms. Lynley has quickly made it to my autobuy list… not only are her stories romantic but I love all of the details and information that I learn…"
—Mrs. Condit & Friends Read Books

"Ms. Lynley shows her writing skill and her expertise with this story. I always feel truly immersed into the worlds she creates with her stories."
—Top 2 Bottom Reviews

By EM LYNLEY

Bound for Trouble
Disguises
Hostile Takeover
Out of the Gate

THE DELECTABLE SERIES
Brand New Flavor
Gingerbread Palace
An Intoxicating Crush
Lighting the Way Home (with Shira Anthony)

PRECIOUS GEMS SERIES
Rarer Than Rubies
Italian Ice
Jaded

Published by DREAMSPINNER PRESS
http://www.dreamspinnerpress.com

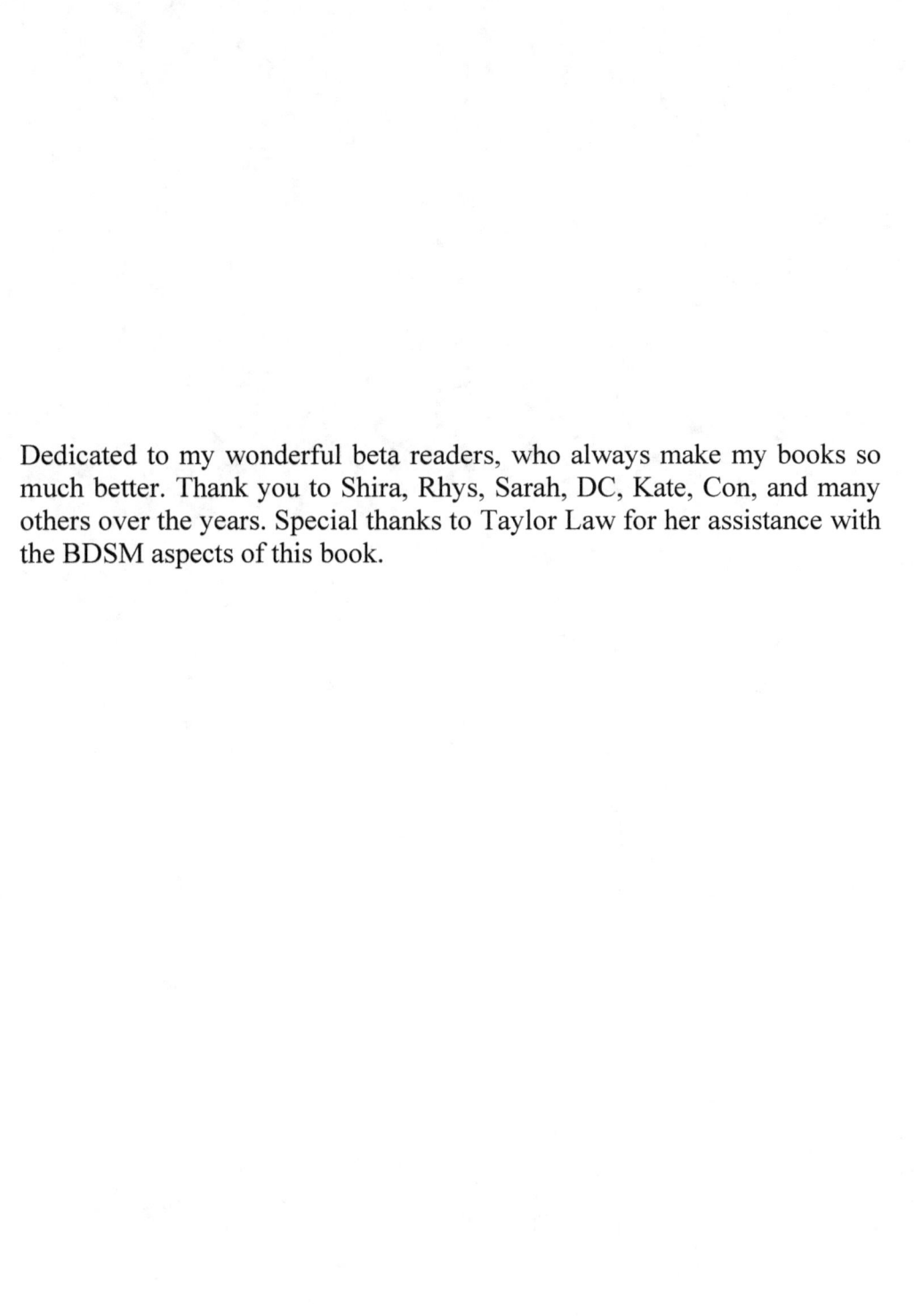

Dedicated to my wonderful beta readers, who always make my books so much better. Thank you to Shira, Rhys, Sarah, DC, Kate, Con, and many others over the years. Special thanks to Taylor Law for her assistance with the BDSM aspects of this book.

CHAPTER 1

THROUGH HIGH-POWERED binoculars, Deke watched the house from a rise about two hundred yards away, waiting, in silence. His partner, Tom Banks, was a hundred yards to the east, and a SWAT team milled just out of sight, everyone waiting for Deke's signal. He wasn't sure precisely what *he* was waiting for, but he knew it would happen soon.

It was dusk, and lights glowed from the grimy windows. He could see the shapes of people moving around inside, but the dirt and the incongruous lacy curtains obscured his view. In front of the house was an ancient, dented American pickup and two boy's bicycles, one with a shiny red seat and a pole with glittery streamers attached, and the other a sleek white mountain bike sporting bright orange wheels.

Deke would have loved a bike like that as a kid.

Serah Cartier, Deke's supervisor, settled next to him on the hill. "You positive there aren't any kids in there?"

He nodded. "They just use the bikes to deter raids," he whispered. "And that's Morales's pickup."

"All right then." She nodded.

Deke raised his hand and gave the signal. The first guys threaded silently over the hill toward the house in the dusky gloom. Deke and Banks continued to watch from the ridge with Serah.

The lead men moved to surround the house. Without warning, a huge explosion turned the entire structure into a fireball, windows shattering as the heat and force blasted them out. Everything seemed to happen in slow motion, the agents closest being blown into the air. For some reason, the entire scene was blanketed in silence. Deke wasn't sure if he was really there or just watching from a very great distance. None of it seemed real.

"Good job, Kane," a voice said over his shoulder. It was the head of the field office, Foster Ward. "They're all dead. You'll get a promotion for this one!" A large, heavy hand clapped him on the back, nearly knocking him over from the force as Ward, then Serah, started chuckling. The laughter grew louder, and soon it turned into a shout—a long, deep bellow that snapped Deke out of the scene until he discovered he had been the one shouting. He sat up, naked and drenched in sweat and tangled in the sheets in his own dark bedroom.

He ran his hands through damp hair and tried to get his frenzied breathing under control. *It's just a dream*, he reminded himself. *It's not real*. Not all of it anyway. Not the part about his boss telling him he'd be promoted for the successful operation. It hadn't been a success. It had been a nightmare. He'd fucked up, and two little kids had died in that meth lab explosion, not the drug dealers connected to a terrorist cell he'd insisted were holed up there. Morales and his accomplices had already cleared out. Deke's operation netted only some kids who'd turned an abandoned drug lab into a hideout.

Now, not only did the dream haunt him—he'd had it nearly every night in the four months since the tragedy—but his failure dogged him as well. He'd been suspended on medical leave for the first thirty days, then put on desk duty. They didn't kick you out of the Bureau right away, even for failure to get your facts straight before you sent in a SWAT team.

Blowing up kids was another matter entirely, and he was lucky he still had a job. That was mainly because he was still in a reevaluation phase, with constant psych evaluations to determine his fitness for duty. The shrink hadn't made a final determination, and if he got a thumbs-down on his psychological fitness eval, he could kiss his FBI career good-bye.

Deke sat up and stared at the empty space on the other side of the bed. He still wasn't used to being alone, still reached out for Timothy. He'd reached out a few too many times, needing support, but Timothy hadn't been able to help, and when Deke hadn't been able to move past the tragedy, Timothy moved out. He hadn't completely abandoned Deke, just moved halfway across town.

Deke glanced at the phone. *Should I?*

No.

He got out of bed and headed to the kitchen for a glass of water. His skin felt clammy, and his feet stuck to the floor. God, it needed a good scrubbing. He couldn't sleep; he might as well put the time to good use. He flipped on the lights, grabbed the pail and detergent from under the sink, and went to work. The steady back-and-forth of mopping began to settle his agitated brain.

Maybe he'd actually manage some sleep before he had to get up for work again.

Work. If you could call it that.

While he was waiting for Psych to sign off, they'd put him on the social network monitoring desk, where he couldn't hurt anyone else. He didn't even have a weapon until he was cleared again for regular duty. He now spent his days poring over Facebook and Instagram for idiots who posted photos of themselves committing crimes or spending ill-gotten gains. As boring as this was after his old job liaising with the DEA or Homeland Security and the Joint Terrorism Task Force, he actually helped bring a lot of complete idiots to justice. They weren't the same caliber of criminal he was used to dealing with—drug dealers, some weapons dealers—but Portland was safer without them on the streets.

Even the white-collar unit got more action than Deke did on his desk.

Once he spotted something suspicious, he used a variety of techniques to locate the perp; then a team of "grown-up" agents got to make the collar. Deke got a silver star on his report card for the assist, but the takedown team got the gold star—and the glory.

He wasn't sure how much longer he could endure this. If he wasn't already a little fucked-up in the head, this would surely drive him around the bend. It was the Bureau's way of easing him out when they couldn't easily fire him. He'd heard from a friend who did a stint in Tokyo that when a Japanese company wanted to get rid of someone, they put him on an impossible task or put him in a room on his own and made him feel like an outcast in the company. Japanese companies didn't like to fire people; it went against the corporate culture. Eventually, the guy would quit, and the company would save face.

Deke understood very well how successful that strategy must be. Every morning as he knotted his tie and prepared to leave his apartment, he wondered just how much longer he could keep this up. How many more days of mindless web surfing could he take before he either handed in his papers or just offed himself? Probably a good thing he didn't have his service weapon after all.

Maybe that was for the best, he thought on nights like these when the dream—the nightmare—woke him up. Tonight he'd actually had the dream twice. That only happened once in a while, but he knew it didn't bode well for his future.

CHAPTER 2

"DEKE, YOU know you're back *provisionally*," Agent Serah Cartier said as Deke settled himself into one of the uncomfortable black chairs facing her desk. It was made of the fake leather stuff that sounded like farting if you moved the wrong way, and Deke prayed he wouldn't move the wrong way. Serah leaned back in her chair and stared at him with that serious supervisory expression she must have learned in some seminar at Quantico for management types.

"I know." Deke hoped he sounded sincere enough. Certainly he was but hated the feeling he was supposed to grovel for his job. He wanted the respect of his peers and supervisors, and he acknowledged it was going to be a long time coming, after the way he'd handled the last case. He did have that nervous, butterfly-flapping-around feeling in his stomach, waiting to hear what his next assignment was going to be. He was lucky he was back here in his regular unit and not counting guns brought in on some raid.

He almost believed he belonged in another department, not here where someone might get hurt because he was around. He shook his head to dispel his own negative thoughts and turned his attention back to Serah.

"I can't justify handing you the lead on any cases for a while, so you're going to be working with me," Serah said as she stood up and slowly made her way around the desk. She was wearing a severely tailored suit, the skirt of which was probably in violation of the minimum length requirements of the Bureau. She had nice legs and liked to show them off. Not that Deke cared much, but he tried not to turn his nose up at them either. He knew how to play nice with the boss.

Serah settled herself on the edge of the desk and leaned down in Deke's direction. Her blouse probably should have had more buttons buttoned than unbuttoned, but again, that was Serah. Her large breasts swung toward Deke, her cleavage much closer to his face than he preferred as she kept talking.

"So on this next case, you're working directly under me."

Deke tried not to gulp at the way she said "under me" as if she really meant it, because there was every chance in the world that she did. She was one of those women who felt the need to go after every cock in a room and was oblivious to the fact that some guys—like Deke—were also interested in cock, and not just their own. The Bureau was pretty much "don't ask, don't tell," and it was times like these that Deke wished someone would ask because he really, *really* wanted to tell women like Serah Cartier to get their tits out of his face.

But he half-smiled and didn't react one way or the other, simply put on his own serious face and listened as she detailed the case they'd been assigned.

"There's been an ongoing investigation into Maksim Petrov's operations—cocaine and marijuana—though we've never been able to nail him on so much as a parking ticket. But we've noticed some rumblings in the area of money being funneled to weapons dealers. Not huge amounts; those are probably still going through whoever is laundering his main cash flow. But we found a few fishy PayPal transactions."

"PayPal?" This sounded like his worst nightmare. More social media cybershit.

"Yeah, something in a report you did a couple of weeks ago put them on to these. Good job. So the brass're tossing you a bone on this one, letting you follow it through." She sat on the edge of the desk and fiddled with the hem of her skirt. Her knees were just a shade too far apart. If Deke wanted, he could probably look up there.

Serah glanced down at him. Was she expecting him to look?

"Deke?"

"Yeah?" He tore his gaze away from her knee.

"You paying attention?"

"You sort of lost me at PayPal. Is this a cyber-unit investigation and I'm going to be allowed in on the kill?"

"No. Much more." Her tone turned serious, and she clamped her knees together and leaned toward Deke. "We need to find out who's sending the money and where it's coming from. Is this local, or are they just using locals to move the cash around—cutouts?"

Cutouts. Sounded like CIA stuff. But a hell of a lot more interesting than what he'd been doing for the past three months. He didn't want to bring up the psych eval, but he figured Serah would get around to it herself at some point.

"And we're partnering on this one?"

"In a manner of speaking. I'm running part of the larger investigation, reporting directly back to Ward, so you'll be doing the legwork and reporting back to me. If your leads connect to any of the other threads, I'll combine agents into a team."

"Weapons and Homeland Security?" He just wanted to make sure he understood.

"Yes. But if you don't think you can handle it, I'll give it to someone who doesn't ask so damn many stupid questions."

"I can handle this." He couldn't lose this chance.

What surprised him was that it sounded like a pretty high-profile case for his second chance. He'd expected to be given bullshit little bank robberies or something he couldn't fuck up too easily, given the fact that no one trusted him anymore.

"You get some results in this case, Deke," Serah was saying, "and you can get right back on track where you were before…." She let her voice trail off, probably knowing she didn't have to explain anything. "This is a big case—weapons-terrorism connection—and I have almost every confidence in your ability to handle it. You'll need to report to me on everything, every day, but it's mainly going to be running some undercover operatives or CIs who have intel on the suspects and very little fieldwork on your part. You'll coordinate the day-to-day, and I'll advise you on the big-picture strategy."

"I appreciate the chance—" Deke began, but she cut him off.

"Cut the crap, Kane. We both know you need a chance to *not* fuck up, and I'm basically here to babysit you." Her voice and demeanor changed dramatically, and she stood up abruptly, nearly snapping Deke's head back with the suddenness of her movement. "Ward and the big bosses threw this one at you as a way to get you to make another mistake so they can boot your ass out of the Bureau. But I'm not going to let that happen, because it's a big black mark on my ass, too, if it does. Got that?"

"Yes—"

"You just listen to me on this, and we'll be fine. Don't go getting any bright ideas without running *everything* past me. You want to shit, you ask me first. Got that?"

"Yes."

"Here's the list of the suspicious transactions." She handed him a thin folder.

He opened it and skimmed the four or five sheets of paper. A lot of transfers between $8,000 and $9,500. The threshold for reporting transactions to the Internal Revenue Service or the Treasury's Financial Crimes Enforcement Network was $10,000, and these were clearly intended to stay under the radar.

"There are several transactions each week, varying amounts, but never less than a total of $35,000... only thing that generates that much cash on a regular basis is drugs. But I don't see any connection between these and Petrov."

"That's top of your list. You've got experience with that, Deke, and some DEA connections. I have my suspicions, but it may not be Petrov at all. See which of our local usual suspects is likely to be involved in something like this. Then get into their business and see who they're connected to. We can get this from both ends, roll everyone up, and look like goddamned heroes."

Deke nodded.

"Take the files and read up on Petrov and his known associates as well as the other possibilities." She pointed to a foot-high pile of folders on a table on the opposite side of the room. "The other pile is potential CIs. You find me a few candidates we can use to get at the targets, and we'll be in business. Get back to me tomorrow by noon with the lists, and we'll decide who to start talking to."

"Y—"

"Hurry up and get started," she said, sat back down in her chair, and turned her attention to some papers on her desk. Deke had clearly been dismissed. He grabbed the folders and hurried out the door, files clutched to his chest.

BACK AT his desk, Deke stared glumly at the pile of folders he had to sort through in the next twenty-four hours. A couple of colleagues walked by and he greeted them, but neither of them seemed to have time for more than a cursory "hello" after the initial surprise of seeing Deke back at his old desk, and they kept going. Apparently, it was going to take time for his former team to trust him again. He wondered what Serah had told them about him. For all he knew, they might think he'd been in a straitjacket in the loony bin since the... incident.

He shrugged off the disappointment and reminded himself that the only way to get their respect again was to earn it, so he'd better get cracking on those files and get some results on this assignment, or he'd end up with no job. And he really did love his job. He wanted to catch bad guys, to put it in simple terms, and he used to be good at it. He'd made a mistake—a huge mistake, no arguing with that—but it didn't change the fact that he was good at his job. He needed to remember that, and hopefully, self-confidence would blossom into job performance.

Jesus, he'd been drinking too much of that Bureau psych guy's Kool-Aid.

He took a stab at the first file on the stack and couldn't concentrate, so he got up and wandered over to the kitchen to grab another cup of coffee. A third cup since lunchtime was bound to do wonders for him. He shook his head and opted for decaf, then headed back to his desk. This time he forced himself to focus and took notes on each file as he read, jotting down questions and ideas as he fleshed out the assignment and how he'd like to proceed.

He barely noticed that it had gotten dark outside—and inside—as just about everyone in the office had left. He was alone in the bullpen, but he could see Serah was still hard at work, visible through the clear glass walls of her office. He stood and stretched to ease the sore muscles in his back, disheartened to discover he'd only gotten through half the files. He was hungry, but he didn't want to leave to get anything to eat, so he had to be satisfied with a few unhealthy choices from the vending machine at the far end of the coffee room.

Back at his desk, he munched his way through pretzels and Cheetos and went back to work on the files.

Problem was he had eliminated most of the local drug guys. They were either too stupid or didn't have any record of connections with anyone remotely associated with weapons or terrorists. He'd narrowed the field down to three possibilities. He could put a CI or undercover agent in each suspect's organization while he did more research on the transactions themselves. At least he was good at that, even if he hated the work.

THE NEXT morning Serah summoned him to her office just before lunch. She was wearing a spring-y sundress, sleeveless, with a billowing skirt that showed far too much leg as she moved around the desk.

"Got any leads?"

"Narrowed the pool down to three. Petrov, Cheung, and Morales. I'd like to—"

"Forget Morales."

"But—"

"I'll put someone else on him, given the history."

Deke tried not to glare. He wasn't used to this level of micromanagement.

"Ward knows you have a hard-on for Morales after what happened in March. You're not objective."

"And if he's the one? I've got—" He stopped.

"Deke, this is for your own good. I'll get you in on the credit if we can take Morales down for anything, but I think you'll get more traction with Petrov or Cheung." She paused, but he didn't respond. "Now that we have an understanding, what's your next step?"

"I'd like to get a contact in each organization—U/C or CI—while I keep working the transactions, see where the money ends up."

"What does that matter?"

Was she testing him? He forced himself to look at her ankles. She seemed to be in a better mood when he pretended to check her out. He prayed she wasn't setting him up for some sexual harassment claim.

"Could be the guy is sympathetic to the cause he's supporting. If we can make any connection like that to one of these suspects, we could rule out the others."

She nodded thoughtfully. "Or he's too smart to have let on any political interests before this."

"There may not be any obvious ties, but if we do find something, it should be priority to follow up."

"Fine. But no agents. Use the CIs. Cheaper and less dangerous."

For whom? They were also less reliable. You got what you paid for. He stopped before saying that out loud. "The CI pool is pretty slim pickings."

"Figure it out. Get back to me tomorrow." She sat down in her chair and opened a file on her desk, dismissing him.

He gave her a quick salute and left.

Back at his desk, he skimmed the CI folders again. A bunch of untrustworthy deadbeats, addicts, and grifters. How the hell could he run an op with these losers? He slammed the top folder shut and stared at the wall in front of him.

Wall.

The fucking wall.

While he'd been in social media monitoring, they'd moved his desk to the worst location in the room. Before the incident, Deke had one of the best views in the new FBI building, facing a floor-to-ceiling window overlooking the airport, with snow-blanketed Mount Hood in the distance. He glanced over to its new occupant and noticed O'Reilly was on the phone, feet on his desk, yakking away while he flapped his tie, not even appreciating the beauty on a sunny and clear autumn day like this.

Deke turned his attention back to his CI problem. There had to be a better pool of people than this sorry lot.

And he knew just where to find them.

Maybe the months in the basement next to the real cyber team weren't completely wasted after all.

He straightened up, locked the folders in a drawer, and rode the elevator down to the room he'd hoped he'd never see again.

DOWNSTAIRS IN the cyber unit, Deke received cheers, waves, and a softball lobbed at his head. He caught it before it sent him for an emergency dental visit and greeted the team, his former colleagues. This unit handled the serious cyber threats, as an offshoot of the main team in DC, but also the baby unit that covered local social media, where Deke had done time. Some of these guys loved the job—the former hackers and code jockeys who got the meaty projects—while others were here temporarily, in a Bureau purgatory they hoped they'd earn their way out of.

"Never thought we'd see you again, Deke," said Charlie Parsons, another agent who hoped to escape the netherworld. "What you doin' back here? Get kicked down again so soon?"

"What'd you do, Deke? Don't want to make your mistakes when I finally get called back to the grown-up table."

He shook his head. "I actually need something from Cyber this time."

"So now you see things from the other side?" It was Tom Drese, the head of the unit. He'd come out of his office, perhaps to investigate the commotion. This was probably the quietest department in the building; Deke's arrival stirred up an unusual level of activity.

"I wouldn't put it that way." Deke tried to be diplomatic, but Tom knew how Deke and some of the others felt about their assignments.

Tom turned his mouth down into his patented frown that made nearly everyone want to run the other direction.

"Do I need to put in an official request for assistance?" Deke asked.

Tom let out a snort. "Just having some fun with you. What do you need?"

TWENTY MINUTES later he had a new stack of CI prospects. Back at his desk, he pored over their "credentials." They had all been flagged in background checks for local employment. When there was a fingerprint match to a suspect in a crime in another state, the Bureau was handed the information to determine whether there was an open case or warrant on the individual. Usually, there was some error, or the AFIS computer got a little overzealous in its matching protocol with a partial print.

Deke had been assigned to follow up on a batch of these flagged prints six weeks earlier, and now he found a new use for the information.

A few of the individuals—two of the seven were women—matched prints in the system, but the statute of limitations had run out or there was no proof the original print was from a suspect in the case. In one instance, a print found in a hotel room had only a circumstantial connection with the crime.

Nonetheless, Deke tried to match up his own two suspects with the best confidential informant candidates from the flagged background checks. He was always amazed at the level of detail in some of the Bureau dossiers. Imagine that Cheung's file noted his fondness for Japanese food and listed the three restaurants he frequented most. Far from being irrelevant, such information was priceless when trying to get close to someone. Putting an agent or informant undercover at a suspect's favorite bar or restaurant was a perfect way to keep an eye on him in an unobtrusive way.

One of the guys in the loser file—prospective CIs—was a cook. Ideal match if he convinced the guy to switch jobs. Another CI had janitorial experience—another handy skill to get hired into almost any useful situation.

That result had been too easy; Maksim Petrov proved to be much more difficult to pair with a CI prospect.

The more Deke read about Petrov, the more the man intrigued him. He wasn't about to jump to any conclusions, but Petrov was in a class above the rest of the men in the Portland drug scene. He'd only been arrested once—the traffic violation Serah had alluded to—and nothing they had on him had stuck. Neither the local PD or DEA could muster proof of anything else, and they kicked him free.

Deke leaned back in his chair and flipped through the folder like it was a tabloid magazine. Petrov was known to hang out at a male strip club on the other side of town, Club Kiwi. He had never been seen to hook up with anyone there, but he'd also been followed to a local sex club, Dungeon 69.

Deke knew all about the Kiwi, though if anyone at work asked, he'd never been. He hadn't stepped inside the place for years. Dungeon 69 wasn't even on his radar.

But that didn't matter, because Deke knew exactly who he could send in to get more juice on Petrov.

CHAPTER 3

THE FOLLOWING afternoon he glanced into the interview room through the small window in the door. The guy who'd been brought in—Ryan Griffiths—had his back to Deke. He'd been in the room less than ten minutes, but his shoulders already had the forward hunch that meant he was getting worried, probably wondering whether or not he should have come in to "help with an inquiry."

Deke flipped open the file with the basic information he'd collected earlier. Not much, but intriguing. It would be the basis of an interesting interview. He watched as the guy tapped his fingertips on the tabletop as if he were playing an invisible piano.

Griffiths was quite a looker. Not just hot in his own right, he matched the kind of men Petrov had been seen with recently. Deke kept that in the back of his mind as he evaluated the information in Ryan Griffiths' file. If Deke played this right and got his way, tempting Petrov with Ryan Griffiths would be like giving candy to a baby.

The usual technique would be to sweat the guy for a while.

Deke figured another twenty minutes would do it. He went into the observation room, sat, and checked his quarry out through the one-way glass.

Griffiths was wearing a pale green polo shirt that hugged his upper body in all the right places. Glancing under the table, Deke noticed he was wearing shorts. He'd get a better look soon, but for now, he would enjoy the view.

Oh yeah, Deke wouldn't mind some of this candy himself. He unhooked from the case for a minute and imagined how Ryan Griffiths would look naked, spread out on the interrogation-room table. Deke's cock thickened, and his pants felt far too tight. Well, it never hurt to look. He'd heard plenty of comments from his colleagues when they had hot women in the room. What would Serah say if she knew how attracted Deke was to Ryan Griffiths?

The thought that it would end her constant flirtation made him chuckle.

In Interrogation, Ryan glanced around the room, eyes widening. His heart rate had probably accelerated. *Good.* He was really worried now. And he well should be. Deke had a folder full of trouble. Ryan couldn't have cleaned up his act that much, could he?

He'd find out soon enough.

He was just about to head into Interrogation when Serah entered the observation room.

"How long's he been in there?"

"Ten, fifteen minutes."

"Leave him another fifteen. Let him sweat a little. Not ready."

Ready. Oh yes, but for what? "You don't want him pissing himself, do you?"

So much was riding on this case for him. He didn't want to fuck it up. Griffiths had come in voluntarily, and if they treated him like a criminal, they might lose his cooperation.

"Fine. Put your comm in and make sure you listen, or I'll be in there so fast you won't even see me move."

"Yes, ma'am." He gave her a salute and headed into Interrogation.

RYAN GRIFFITHS spun around in his chair when Deke opened the door. He had that Bambi-in-the-headlights look. Big brown doe eyes and his mouth in a perfect O-shape that had Deke thinking about anything but asking questions. He tore his gaze away from the plump lips and looked at a spot just past Ryan's shoulder.

"I'm Special Agent Deke Kane." It had been a while since he was able to introduce himself that way, and he hoped this wouldn't be the last time he said those words. "Thanks for coming in today. Sorry to keep you waiting."

Ryan fluttered his eyelashes and licked his bottom lip. "Ryan Griffiths." He reached out to shake Deke's hand.

The gesture threw Deke off guard. People didn't shake his hand in Interrogation, but Ryan Griffiths wasn't typical of the people who passed through this room. Deke grasped Ryan's hand, warmth and electricity surging between them. Had Ryan felt it too? Deke felt the urge to hold on but broke the contact—a fraction of a second later than he should have.

Ryan Griffiths was like a loaded weapon staring at him. He was even more gorgeous close up. This was going to be a long interview if Deke couldn't get his shit together.

"You gonna stare at the guy all day or question him?" Serah's voice boomed directly into his brain.

Deke sat down across from Ryan. "We were hoping you might have some information that could help with an investigation."

"I wondered what took so long for someone to follow up on my report." Ryan had calmed down, but now Deke felt the tension increasing.

If he thought he was going to have the upper hand with Ryan Griffiths, he'd been wrong. Deke glanced toward the mirror, wondering if Serah knew what Griffiths was talking about.

"Why don't you tell me what you've got."

"I'm not sure if it means anything. I don't want to waste anyone's time."

"Don't worry about that just yet."

Ryan shifted his weight. "Is this confidential? I mean, who's going to hear what I tell you?"

No one unless you actually tell me something. "Just Bureau agents. Why?"

"I, uh… just don't want this to get back to me. I knew I should have just given an anonymous tip." He tapped the table with his fingertips as he spoke.

"We'll make sure that doesn't happen."

Ryan glanced toward the one-way mirror, narrowing his eyes. Then he turned his gaze full on Deke. "Okay."

Deke stared into Ryan's eyes, wishing he didn't notice the little gold glints. He waited.

"It's about Maksim Petrov."

Deke marshaled all of his acting skills not to let his surprise show. He wasn't sure he'd been successful.

"Good call on this guy, Deke," Serah whispered. Deke tuned her out.

"Go on."

"I overheard him on the phone one night at the Kiwi—Club Kiwi. He was speaking Russian, and I heard him use a word that sounded like guns."

"You speak Russian?" This surprised Deke.

"A little. My mother's Russian, and I picked up some, though I never studied it or anything."

Ryan didn't continue, perhaps expecting another question. Deke wished he hadn't said anything to disrupt Ryan's flow. He waited.

"Well, he was talking to one of his colleagues, or whatever they call them. Ivan something. He used to come in sometimes too, but he doesn't like guys. Anyway, Petrov was asking him something about money. It wasn't the usual sort of thing he talks about on the phone." Ryan let out an audible breath and sat back against his chair. He seemed to be done.

"What were you doing at the Kiwi?" Deke already knew the answer, but it would get Ryan talking again.

"I used to work there." Ryan looked at the table as he spoke and started tapping the surface again.

Why did the question make him uncomfortable?

"Did he mention drugs? Ever see him talking to anyone who you know is involved with drugs?"

Ryan shook his head.

"You hear him talking business a lot, Ryan?"

"Once in a while."

"So when was this?"

"Few weeks ago." He licked his bottom lip again. "I didn't want him to know I heard anything."

"Does he know you understand Russian, or that you overheard this conversation?"

Ryan shrugged.

"Anything since then?" Deke would have liked more. It was flimsy, but it was something.

"No. I don't work there anymore. I quit. Got a new job."

"Another club?" Deke couldn't help wondering what Ryan looked like dancing at the Kiwi. He tried to wash the images out of his mind.

"No. Something else." He glanced over Deke's shoulder. "Somewhere completely different."

Deke knew this, too. He'd seen the background check for the new job.

"Thanks for coming in. We'll check into this. Can we contact you again if we have some other questions?"

"I guess." Ryan turned his gold-flecked eyes on Deke. "Okay."

Deke stood, and Ryan leapt out of his chair, knocking it back with a scraping noise. He practically ran for the door. He wouldn't get far. It was locked, which Ryan discovered two seconds later.

"I'll get that." Deke opened the door for Ryan. Another agent was standing outside the door. "Agent Jones will escort you out." That wasn't the man's name, but it was a good, all-purpose name. "Jones" would watch Ryan's body language as they walked out to see if he'd been lying. People tended to discount or ignore someone with a common name like Jones, so Ryan would be less on his guard.

"Okay." Ryan glanced at Deke, and their gazes met for one electrical millisecond before Jones herded him toward the exit. Deke watched him walk away for a moment, admiring the rear view, until Serah came up beside him.

"My office." She turned and left Deke staring toward the elevator, but Ryan Griffiths had already left.

UPSTAIRS IN Serah's office, Deke shifted his weight in the left chair. Maybe she wouldn't be in his face so much at this angle. Why hadn't he thought of this sooner?

"What's your take on this guy?" She raised the outer edge of one eyebrow a few millimeters. She'd already formed an opinion. Was she testing him, or did she want his opinion?

"It's an awfully big coincidence that he comes in with information on exactly the guy we're looking to spy on. But I can't see what his angle is."

Serah tapped at her keyboard. "Aha. He called a couple of weeks ago to the local hotline with some information, and no one ever followed up. Why didn't you catch that contact?"

Deke blinked. He hadn't been looking at FBI contact with the guy. Big mistake. "I'll take another look through that database."

"Good idea. Now, back to Griffiths' information."

"He doesn't have much, just that one conversation. It's not a lead as is."

"If he heard one conversation, you know he heard more. You could have gotten a lot more out of him. I can see you're out of practice."

Deke pursed his lips. She was right. Why hadn't he pushed for more?

When Serah kept staring at him, he scanned his brain for something to offer. "The Russian-language skill is a plus. I hadn't expected that. We could use it. We *should* use it."

"I agree, Deke. Check the guy out. Find an angle to persuade him to cooperate."

Deke recalled the way Ryan Griffiths licked his lower lip when he got nervous. There were plenty of angles Deke could imagine. Not necessarily the same ones Serah would.

"You got an idea?" Her voice startled him.

"What?"

"You're smiling. Thought you came up with something." She peered at him through narrowed eyes. "See what you can find out and let's discuss first thing tomorrow."

"Tomorrow…?"

"He looked a little too nervous for a guy volunteering information. Don't let him run. I want him back in here tomorrow. Where's he working?"

"He left Club Kiwi, and now he's working at some grocery store. One of those organic places." Around here that was almost a given.

"He quit stripping to work at a grocery store?" She pursed her lips. "Interesting. There's a lot more to this guy than meets the eye."

Deke nodded. He didn't trust himself to respond to that comment.

"I want you to get started on the ISR&R."

The FBI's Initial Suitability Report & Recommendation for prospective CIs had nearly twenty categories to research, and Deke hadn't wanted to spend the time on the damn thing until he knew Ryan had something useful. Serah was really pushing hard for this guy if she expected Deke to get the paperwork started.

"Good idea," he said instead of groaning at the prospect of all the information he'd have to track down.

She got off the desk and settled in her chair. When she started tapping on her keyboard this time, Deke knew he'd been dismissed.

He had to make sure they signed Ryan Griffiths up as a CI.

CHAPTER 4

RYAN GRIFFITHS sat at the rickety table in his apartment sipping the first cup of coffee of the day. Seven a.m. Only thirty minutes before he had to leave for work. He wasn't accustomed to early morning hours. Used to be he was just getting to bed—to sleep, to be more accurate—at seven in the morning.

His life had turned almost completely around in the past month. The new job paid far less, but he could make do. He was worth more than the money he earned, which he reminded himself every day. Someday he might believe it without having to tell himself.

He put the empty coffee cup in the sink and grabbed his keys and cell phone. He checked for texts, but he hadn't gotten any during the night. That was another thing he was adjusting to. When he'd quit stripping at the Kiwi, he'd given up most of his old friends and hadn't yet made any new ones. Another goal to start working toward. Maybe ask someone from work to hang out for coffee or a film—the kind of things normal people did with their friends, instead of inviting them to three-ways for extra cash.

He wasn't used to spending every night alone in bed, either. Before, he'd had some choice who he spent time with, but there had been plenty of men he'd rather forget, no matter how much they'd paid. Now that he wasn't making money with his body, he found himself missing the odd intimacy he'd had with his tricks.

Nope. Alone was better than spending time with some stranger you'd just gotten off. Another thing he reminded himself every night he spent on his own. He could choose who he fucked now. It was a luxury he'd never really known. Not for years.

Too bad the only guy he'd met lately who fell into the "want" rather than the "supposed-to-fuck" category was that FBI agent who'd interviewed him the previous day.

What kind of name was Deke Kane anyway? It sounded like he should be riding a horse across the open range, not riding a desk in Portland.

Agent Hot Cowboy hadn't asked many questions. Ryan—thanks to his close friend Gina Alman—had worked up the courage to call the FBI with information on Maksim Petrov. When no one followed up, he figured they hadn't been interested. Maybe they already knew all about him and didn't trust a former stripper like Ryan. Had they checked into his background and written him off?

Or maybe they realized he'd made up the story he'd told when he called the hotline, tying Petrov to a rent boy who'd gone missing. But they'd finally called him back in for a face-to-face, and this time Ryan had something real he didn't think they could ignore: the gun conversation he'd overheard. But he'd fucked up again. Of course the FBI would be suspicious of someone volunteering information like that. What had he been thinking?

Maybe it was for the best. Ryan didn't want to tangle with Maksim Petrov in any way, shape, or form, even via the FBI. People who went against him ended up dead. Even people who weren't involved with him could get hurt.

He'd never forget that night three years earlier when he and his best friend, Rocco, had been partying with a trick in the Tidal Wave Inn. Ryan had left to get some more booze, and when he'd gotten back, he'd seen a figure with a shaved head leaving the room. Inside, Ryan had found Rocco dead and the trick bleeding out, both with their throats sliced open.

He'd called 911 and run like hell, hoping no one had seen him going in or out of the room. He'd stayed away from the Tidal Wave after that, and the cops had never caught the killer. Ryan had never seen him before or since—until his last week at Club Kiwi, when he saw the shaved-head killer shaking hands with Maksim Petrov and sitting down with him for a drink.

There had to be a connection between Petrov and Rocco's murder.

Ryan had hoped the FBI would start looking into Petrov's associates.

He should have told Agent Cowboy the real story about Rocco and the shaved-head guy. Would Kane believe him if Ryan called and asked to come in again?

Ryan didn't want to get involved, but he couldn't just leave it like this.

Time to get to work. He could decide what to do after he talked to Gina. She was on a later shift at the store, and he hoped she'd hurry up in the shower so he wouldn't be late to work. One more glance at his watch. He didn't have time. He'd have to catch up with her at break time.

He was three steps from the front door when his cell phone rang.

"Ryan Griffiths? This is Deke Kane, FBI. I need for you to come back in this morning…."

AT FIVE minutes to nine, Deke stared through the one-way glass at Ryan Griffiths. Serah sat with him in Observation.

"You've got everything you need to get him on board, Deke. Don't fuck it up."

He nodded.

"Or else you may end up on the Facebook team for good."

He shook his head. He hadn't expected the "or else," but now he knew what was riding on the outcome of this interview, this operation. It was make-it-or-break-it for him.

It didn't even surprise him anymore that Serah defined success this way, rather than as locking Petrov up or stopping the flow of money to the arms dealer, whoever was funding him. How many lives would be saved if they shut the transfer down? Serah Cartier—and likely her boss—was all about the stick and not the carrot.

Why did he think anything had changed since he'd gone on leave?

He stood up and reached for the door.

"Don't forget the comm."

Without missing a beat, he pulled the little earwig from his pocket and popped it into his ear with an exaggerated motion. He could hear Serah cursing into his ear as he opened the door to Interrogation.

Ryan Griffiths turned around as Deke came into the room through the door almost directly behind him. Ryan's eyes were wide, inquisitive, but Deke thought Ryan might also be giving him a more appraising glance.

"Thanks for coming back, Mr. Griffiths."

Ryan locked his gaze onto Deke's, probably searching for an explanation of why he was here. He didn't speak.

"So you're working at Farmer Jake's?" Deke glanced at the store's name embroidered on Ryan's shirt, just over his left nipple. He tried not to notice the nipple; in the chilly room, it was somewhat inevitable. *Concentrate.* "How's that going?"

"Yeah…. Fine, I suppose. I'm not sure why the FBI cares, though." Ryan seemed to find some comfort in his logic, and he stepped back from the edge of panic.

"We do and we don't." What Deke really wanted to know was why a pretty stripper—and undoubtedly a rent boy—would give that up and work at an organic produce store. To be fair, in Portland just about everything was organic. "Let me back up a little. We thought your information about Petrov was interesting. It's also a little too vague. Have you got anything else on him? Something concrete we can use. Names of any of his associates, anyone else talking about weapons? Anyone moving money for him?"

Ryan shook his head. His smooth brow told Deke he was lying. He had information he hadn't mentioned yet, probably holding out for something—money. That was a good thing.

"Hurry the fuck along here," Serah roared into his ear.

"We've got an opportunity for you, Ryan."

"I don't like the way that sounds." This time Ryan didn't make eye contact. He was looking through the one-way mirror again, eyes narrowed.

"I think you know more than you've let on. You're looking for either money or protection. I can offer both."

"I don't need money bad enough to get on the wrong side of Maksim Petrov. And I don't exactly trust your protection. Sorry. I can't help you with the weapons. The only thing I know about him isn't related to drugs or guns. I'm not sure how I can help you."

So he did know something.

"Just cut to the chase, Kane. Ask him directly. *Now.*"

Deke could see Ryan tapping the fingers of one hand on the surface of the table, faster and faster.

"We'd like you to consider going back to Club Kiwi, get closer to Petrov so you can—"

"Consider?" Serah practically roared. Deke thought Ryan probably heard her—through the hole she'd just blown into his brain.

"—get close to him, listen in on his sensitive discussions and pass the—"

Ryan held up a hand. "I'm sorry, I can't go back there. I'm done with that life. Tell me any other way I can help, and I'll consider it. But don't send me back there."

Deke could see Ryan's fear bubbling to the surface now. He wasn't afraid of Petrov; it was something else. But what?

"Now, Deke." Serah used her low, threatening tones.

"I'm not sure you really have a choice, Ryan." Deke hated this part.

"Yeah, I do." Ryan moved to stand up. Deke held up a palm, and Ryan glared at him for a moment, then sat down again, eyes defiant.

"You do know Farmer Jake's did a background check on you before they hired you, and there was something... unusual with the results."

"Unusual?" Ryan swallowed loudly enough to echo in the small room.

"You got flagged for follow-up." Deke flipped open the folder dramatically, watching Ryan's face, gauging his reaction.

"But they hired me. It must have been okay...." He leaned forward, gaze seeking the contents of the folder. The table was just wide enough that the suspect couldn't easily see the papers in the folder.

Deke flipped through a few documents, then closed the folder again.

"Sure, you're cleared to work in a grocery store...." Deke left the thought hanging. Sometimes suspects just blurted out what Deke was looking for. Not that Ryan Griffiths was a suspect at this moment in time, even if he was beginning to act like one. Then Ryan folded one hand over the other and sat back in the chair, trying to look calm.

"On top of the arrests for solicitation—"

"Those charges were dropped."

"I'll bet they were," Serah remarked.

"Your fingerprints were found at the scene of a double homicide." Deke saw Ryan flinch. "You a regular at the Tidal Wave? Classy place, isn't it?"

Ryan blinked a few times and got a pinched look around his mouth. His eyes radiated pain, not fear. Deke stood, now directly across the table from Ryan, and measured him up again, wondering about that unexpected reaction.

"Kane, you're in my fucking line of sight!"

He shifted a few feet to his left, not taking his eyes off Griffiths.

"Am I under arrest or something? No one read me my rights."

"No, Ryan, you're not under arrest." He paused. Ryan's expression relaxed when Deke used his first name and the soothing tone. "Not yet."

"Hang on!" Ryan Griffiths stood up.

He had much nicer legs than Deke expected. The shorts accentuated all his assets south of the border, the way the tight polo shirt had his torso. Deke swallowed and stared when he should have been threatening Griffiths.

"Jesus fucking Christ," Serah squawked in his head. "You're gay!"

Fuck. He rubbed his ear until the comm popped out, and he put it in his pocket. He threw her a warning glance and turned his attention back to pretty Ryan Griffiths. She could shout herself hoarse in the observation room because he now had her comment on record, and she was in a far more vulnerable situation at this moment.

"Calm down, Ryan. Have a seat." He paused as Ryan settled back into the chair, gaze wary. "We're not holding you for anything. I told you, we called you in because we need your help. You help us and we give you a clean slate on the connection to those murders."

"Please don't do this." Ryan's voice was scarcely more than a whisper. "Don't make me go back to the Kiwi."

"You're that afraid of Petrov? I told you, we'll make sure you're safe."

Ryan shook his head. His hands were shaking, too, as he played his invisible piano. "Not Petrov. I don't want to—"

Serah came in through the door in a red-and-blue blur. She hadn't been kidding about how fast she could move. Ryan whipped his head around, startled.

"Look Griffiths, don't even think about saying no. We've got the goods on you from the beginning. Every alias, every stop, every little charge you weaseled your way out of... *however* you managed to do that." She grabbed the file Deke had abandoned on the table. "Born Jason Ryan Powers in Buffalo Grove, Illinois. Later you were known as...." She listed two aliases Deke's research had uncovered.

Ryan looked like a dog that had been kicked. He glanced up at Deke for a moment, and Deke's chest ached to see him cornered by Serah.

"You run again, we'll find you again." She twisted the knife in Ryan's chest with the threat.

"What can I help the FBI with?" Ryan stared up at Deke, then Serah, then shut his mouth. Now he realized what the FBI knew. That they knew everything. The pieces were falling into place, and Deke had barely had to say anything.

"I wonder what Jason's mama would think if she saw all the *trouble* her boy's gotten into since the last time she saw him?" Serah added, clearly satisfied with the twinge of regret Deke saw flash over Ryan's face. "Looks like the bodies three years ago aren't the only crime scene you've been at. I have a file here from Texas—" Serah's face lit up with triumph as she fluttered a page at Ryan. "Deke, why don't you share those details with Ryan." She gave Deke a pointed glance and headed for the door. She'd be going back to Observation, leaving him to seal the deal. She couldn't just have left him with the good cop role, to be nice to Ryan and commiserate with him over Serah's threats. She wanted him to rip the heart out of Ryan. In her view fear was a better motivator. It worked on Deke just as well. He kind of hated her guts right then.

But that could wait. First he had to tear poor Ryan to shreds.

"I don't suppose you recall an evening you spent in a cheap motel on the outskirts of Dallas with one Gerald R. Higgins of upstate New York, about eight years ago, would you?"

"Not particularly," Ryan said, clearly aiming for nonchalant again.

"I guess all those old guys and cheap motels sort of blend together for a guy like you, don't they?" Deke threw in a cruel sneer and watched the effect as Ryan began to unravel. "Well, this particular night and this particular guy might stand out in your memory because this is what he looked like when you left." Deke slipped a photo out of the file folder and slid it in front of Ryan on the table.

Ryan gasped and stared at the image: the head and shoulders of a man in his mid- to late fifties, balding, slightly overweight, and very dead. The black and white photo played up bruises on his neck in the shape of hands that had pressed tightly—obviously tightly enough to strangle the man.

"He's dead?"

"Yeah. He was dead when you left the room, and he's still dead. Probably looks just the same after all that embalming stuff they use, but he's at least six feet under, and his kids and grandkids go and put flowers on his grave every year. Thanks to you."

"I didn't kill him," Ryan said, though he didn't sound particularly convincing. He sounded scared, which was exactly where Deke needed him. "How can you pin this on me?"

"There's security camera footage from the motel. It's a bit fuzzy, but it looks enough like you to get you extradited at the bare minimum. And some partial fingerprints in the room that are a probable match to yours. I haven't even started on the DNA evidence yet. Do you want me to keep going?"

Ryan shook his head and turned an unpleasant shade of green. Deke grabbed a trashcan from the corner of the room and shoved it at Ryan.

"If you're gonna puke, do it in there. I don't want to have to smell it for the rest of the day while we go over everything in your file."

"I called 911 before I left. But I didn't kill him," Ryan mumbled again. He glanced up to see whether Deke would respond, clearly expecting the worst.

"They all say that." Deke backed away from Ryan and leaned against the wall opposite, flipping through the papers in the folder, every so often turning his eyes on Ryan, who looked like he might cry. *Perfect.*

The thing was Deke knew Ryan hadn't killed that guy. The guy was dead, sure, but from a heart attack, most likely brought on by some very rough sex with Ryan and an extra dose of little blue pills. Those were undoubtedly Ryan's handprints on Higgins' neck, but even the man's wife admitted he was into erotic strangulation. It wasn't Ryan's fault the guy had a faulty ticker. Autopsy report showed he had died almost instantly, and even if Ryan had called 911 sooner, the man would have been dead before they finished taking down the address of the motel.

The wife hadn't been too keen on indulging her husband's particular sexual fantasies and had admitted she suspected he'd been frequenting hookers for that reason, but she'd been shocked when the local investigators told her that her husband had been with a *man* in that hotel room on the night he expired. Deke's take on the subsequent interview with the wife led him to believe that old Gerald R. Higgins was probably lucky he'd died from the heart attack and not his wife's wrath at the discovery he'd been fucking pretty young men like Ryan Griffiths.

As for Ryan, he was simply in the wrong place at the wrong time and must have freaked out rather than sticking around. The autopsy also revealed additional bruising on the chest that was typical when CPR was administered. Ryan *had* tried to save the guy but must have cut and run when it was clear Higgins was dead. There was some evidence of drug use in the room—and in the victim's blood work—that probably had a lot to do with Ryan's reluctance to stick around and explain things to the authorities. There was also the dead man's missing wallet that needed an explanation, but Deke decided not to press the point. Ryan wasn't a Boy Scout or anything; he'd clearly broken the law, but none of it was enough for him to be in serious trouble.

But of course, Ryan wouldn't know any of that. He didn't need to. All Serah wanted him to know was that it looked like he'd killed this guy and that Deke was going to be nice and not extradite him to Texas for trial. If Ryan cooperated.

"We're here to play a little game," Deke said. "You know that show where crazy housewives dress up and try to win prizes?" Ryan looked bored and avoided meeting Deke's gaze. "Well, today you're the housewife, and I'm the guy with all the prizes behind the secret doors. Are you ready to play?"

"You're offering me a deal?"

"That might be behind one of the doors. A ticket back to Texas might be behind another one. We just haven't gotten that far yet. It all depends on you."

"Back to *Texas*?"

"Oh, sorry. I meant back to a secure federal facility back in Texas," Deke clarified, watching the faint look of hope fall from Ryan's face with mixed feelings. "The kind of place where they'd probably be thrilled with how pretty you are at both ends. I'm sure you'd have lots of admirers down there. They'd be fighting over you and auctioning your sweet little ass the minute you step off that Department of Corrections bus."

Ryan stopped playing the invisible piano and stared at Deke. "Fine. What do you want from me?"

The guy seemed tougher on the outside than he really was, Deke realized. Serah had found it easy to swing him and force—let's call that *encourage*—him to make a deal. Ryan didn't want to upset poor sweet Mama Powers back in Illinois, and Serah had played that knowledge—and Deke's own fear of repercussions—for all it was worth.

Deke walked back around the table to face Ryan, staring down at him while looming from his great height before getting right up into Ryan's face. Usually, he got a little thrill from the reaction when he violated a suspect's personal space. But not today. Not with Ryan Griffiths. Face only inches away from Ryan's, Deke could see a sprinkling of freckles on Ryan's nose and cheeks, and he realized entirely too late the magnetic intensity of Ryan's chestnut brown eyes. They bored directly into Deke's soul, and he straightened quickly—he hoped it didn't look like a retreat—out of the range of their power.

Suddenly, elation turned sour in Deke's stomach. He thought about his own mother, thought about how and why Ryan had disappeared in the first place. Had it been to *protect* someone and not simply to escape prosecution? That was the case for a lot of people who hadn't done anything seriously wrong, just illegal enough to get caught and fucked over by the so-called justice system. The system was nowhere near as fair or just as the majority of Americans hoped it was—or as the founders of the system had intended. But then again, it was his job to uphold the law. No matter how poorly the system worked, he was part of it. And right now, he had to use that flawed system to his advantage in order to track down and catch someone who threatened the safety of an uncountable number of people—perhaps the security of the entire country.

Ryan was just a means to that end.

Deke cleared his throat as menacingly as possible and steeled himself, forcing himself to believe in the nobility and necessity of his cause and reminding himself that Ryan Griffiths/Powers wasn't quaking in his boots because he'd been helping old ladies cross the street.

"So, are you arresting me, or just practicing your soliloquy skills?" Ryan asked coolly. He had spunk and Deke liked that.

"I'm not arresting you... yet." Deke's tone warned that it was entirely possible.

But that had been the last of Ryan's will to resist. He looked defeated now. His shoulders sagged and he'd gone pale. This wasn't how Deke wanted to play it, but Serah insisted the threat of prison—especially in Texas—put the fear of far worse than God into Ryan.

Deke prayed he'd never end up in prison—as a gay Fed he'd be in for the worst treatment imaginable. And the guys in prison had twenty-three hours a day stuck in their cells to get pretty fucking imaginative. Deke hoped he didn't shudder visibly at the thought.

"So, what do you want from me?" Ryan asked.

"Aren't you eager?" Deke mocked.

"Just get to the point. I'm here, a captive audience for you; there's no need to pull the Dirty Harry routine on me."

So he still had a little spunk left over.

DEKE NEEDED a break after the high-pressure sales pitch and retreated to the men's room to splash cold water on his face until the waves of nausea passed. If he didn't need a win on this operation so badly, he would have stood up to Serah and told her it was the wrong approach for Ryan. Deke preferred to use carrots rather than sticks to motivate people.

But he already had one foot out the Bureau door, and Serah was the one with the office and the power. The system was fucked up. Or it really was time for Deke to leave the FBI.

Deke got Ryan to sign a preliminary CI agreement; then he let the guy get to work at Farmer Jake's and explain he needed to cut his hours for the next couple of weeks. He would be required to come in the following afternoon to consult with a public defender, have a psych eval, and sign the paperwork. It was as far as Deke could go with him today.

Now he had to face Serah. He wasn't sure which was worse: her realizing he was gay or her annoyance that she'd had to force Deke to lean on Ryan Griffiths.

"What the fuck is wrong with you, Deke?"

"What specifically do you mean?" He hoped she'd say the wrong thing so he could sue her ass or, at the very least, get her moved out of this division. He'd rather have practically any other supervisor.

"Why'd you go soft on that guy, Deke? Forgive the unfortunate turn of phrase." She quirked one corner of her mouth. "Look, I don't care who you fuck. But you can't let that get in the way of an interrogation. Treat them all the same."

"I didn't ease up on him because I was into him. I don't think it was the right way to play him. He's afraid of something, and he was going to tell me what. Now I'll have to work much harder to get him to trust me. He didn't kill Higgins, and I don't think he had anything to do with the Tidal Wave stabbings either."

"Of course not. But you can't let him know that. It's leverage. Use his fear."

"He's willing to help, but he doesn't want to go back to Club Kiwi. I wish I could figure out why. It's not Petrov that frightens him."

"You're not the shrink. She still has to approve his participation and she'll let us know if it matters. But if it's not connected to our case, ignore it. Just make sure to seal the deal when he comes back tomorrow."

RYAN ARRIVED for work at Farmer Jake's three hours late.

"Got it sorted out, Griffiths?" Paul Bloom, the store manager, asked as Ryan clocked in.

"Not exactly. Can I talk to you about it?"

"Sure. Come by my office around two thirty. You want to make up the hours you lost this morning?"

"Yes. I can stay tonight."

"Fine. Come by later and we can talk."

"Thanks." Ryan put on an apron and wrapped the long strings around his waist before tying them. He didn't look forward to the discussion with Paul. It was still preferable to dealing with the FBI, Club Kiwi, and Maksim Petrov, though. His stomach churned.

"Everything okay?" Gina asked when he hit the sales floor in produce with a crate of blueberries to merchandize. "You were gone when I got out of the shower, but Paul said you'd be late. And you didn't answer my calls or texts."

He shrugged.

"You know you can tell me anything."

"I know." He stacked the last container of fruit and turned toward the back room to get something else. Gina followed along, even though she hadn't finished restocking the grapefruit display.

"Ryan, what is it?"

"Not here. Later, on break."

"Okay." She put a hand on Ryan's arm and squeezed.

He picked up her hand and kissed it. Just then, Paul Bloom came by, holding his ubiquitous clipboard. He glanced sideways at Ryan before giving Gina's chest his full attention. She buttoned up the last button on her polo shirt and kept her gaze on Ryan until Bloom passed.

"Subtle, isn't he?" Ryan asked. "I've got a spare shirt in my locker. Men's large." It would be loose on Gina's curves, and she would be more comfortable.

"Thanks." She went into the locker room while Ryan tackled the next pile of merchandise to put out on the sales floor. She knew his locker combo; they'd had few secrets during the four years they'd been friends, and now roommates, since they'd both left their previous profession. He hated knowing he had to keep some now.

But not everything. He still needed her advice.

THEY MET up during break time, hanging out in the parking lot. Gina puffed at a cigarette.

"What's with the smokes?"

"I heard Bloom saying how much he hates smokers. Figured it couldn't hurt."

"Sorry he's being a prick." Ryan paused. "I wish we'd had other options."

"Oh, don't be. I'm grateful to you for bringing me along. I can even put up with Paul Bloom. He's harmless compared to the clients we used to spend time with."

"I hoped this would be a completely fresh start, get us both away from the clubs…."

"Ryan, what's going on?"

"I had to go back to the FBI this morning. That's why I was late. They want me to be an informant—on Petrov."

"So they took your bait? Do you actually know anything? I mean besides seeing the bald guy."

He shook his head. "I didn't even mention him. Not yet. They want me to go back to the Kiwi and get close to Petrov, find out something to connect him with drugs. Now they—" He lowered his voice, and she moved closer. "They think he's involved with arms dealers. I just made that up, but either they completely believed it, or he really is."

She stared at him but didn't say anything for a few moments while she took a last puff on the cigarette before grinding it out with her heel. "Shit, Ryan. You're not considering going back."

"Yeah. I don't have a choice."

"You do. You're out of there now."

"I can't let Rocco's killer get away with it. Petrov must have ordered it, but they think he's into something bigger, more dangerous than drugs or a dead hustler."

"That's enough for you to risk your own life? Come on, you know Rocco wouldn't want that for you. Two dead guys aren't better than one. Don't be stupid."

"It's not the only reason. They found out about Higgins, and they're threatening me with it."

"The guy who died back in Texas? How'd they find out?"

"Fingerprints. Gregory did a background check—or had Bloom do one—and my prints matched some from the crime scene."

"But they hired you...."

"Maybe Gregory didn't care. He owns the place; he can hire whoever he wants."

"So you're gonna do it?"

"Yes."

Gina pulled another cigarette from the pack. Her hands shook as she tried to light it, so Ryan took the lighter and did the job for her. She took a few fierce puffs and looked him in the eye.

"You can't do it, Ry."

"I can. I *want* to. Want to nail Petrov. For Rocco, for the drugs, for whatever shit they think he's involved in. I never did the right thing before. Always took the easy way out, thought about myself first. I can't make a real break to a clean life if I don't start taking some responsibility."

Gina puffed like she was getting oxygen with each hit. "You have done the right thing. Getting me this job, getting me away from...." She put her arms around Ryan and held him tight.

He felt tears trickle down the back of his neck. "Don't worry. This guy Deke Kane is going to be watching out for me. I'll be safe. And it's just going to be a couple of nights a week, not full-time. I'm going to keep working here. Just have to arrange it with Bloom."

"What kind of a name is Deke?"

Ryan let out a chuckle. "Same question I had."

"This is going to fuck you up again."

"No. This time, I think it's going to have the opposite effect."

CHAPTER 5

JUST AFTER two thirty, Ryan knocked on Paul Bloom's office door.

"Come in."

Paul sat behind the desk and motioned for Ryan to enter and sit in one of the chairs across from him.

"What's up, Griffiths?" Bloom asked.

"I've got something I need to take care of in the evenings for the next week or two." At least he hoped the FBI thing wouldn't last longer than that. "I was wondering if I could stick to days, get out by six or seven?"

"What kind of thing?"

"It's personal."

"Fine. Thanks for letting me know. I'll see what I can do. You've only been here a few weeks, so schedule requests go in order of seniority. I can't promise there will be many hours after the other staff are scheduled."

Ryan nodded. He had expected this answer. It never hurt to try. "Okay. Thanks." He stood to go.

"Griffiths, you may get special treatment from Mr. Antony because you brought Gina along. She may be polishing his wood to get the cream of the shifts and the easy jobs around here, but that's not going to protect you for long. One fuckup and you will be out. Even Mr. Antony won't let you keep getting away with anything you want."

"This is the first time—"

"Are you kidding? With your criminal record, you're lucky he let you stay. Didn't want to upset Gina, but I suspect you've outlived your charmed existence by now. So watch your back."

"Got it," Ryan said and left. He stood outside for a moment to gather his thoughts. Paul Bloom was not the sharpest crayon in the box. He'd gotten everything turned around regarding Ryan and Gina—and Gregory

Antony. But Ryan needed to keep his nose clean anyway. He couldn't risk Paul Bloom getting wind of the truth.

And he'd have to thank Gregory for overriding the background check results.

RYAN HEADED into the back room to clock out just before nine. Bloom had let him make up the lost hours from the morning shift, or he would have left by five. He was about to swipe his badge on the time clock when he noticed Gregory's office door ajar at the end of the hall. Now would be a good time to thank him.

Better clock out first. He'd learned early on that nothing ever happened on the clock. He swiped his badge and headed down the hall.

He rapped softly on the door. "Mr. Antony? Gregory?"

"Ryan? Come in."

Ryan stepped in and found Gregory sitting on the couch at the other end of the office, reading a stack of documents. Ryan shut the door behind him and made his way toward the man he'd never be able to properly repay, no matter what.

"Everything okay, Ryan?"

Ryan nodded. He stopped in front of the desk. Gregory was in his late fifties. He owned five Farmer Jake's, as well as a chain of high-end men's clothing stores. He'd been Ryan's client at Club Kiwi. After the first few times, they'd talked at least as much as they'd fucked.

Gregory had seen more to Ryan than a nice body and a repertoire of useful sexual skills. He'd promised Ryan a good job at one of his stores if he could prove his value by starting at the bottom. He'd graciously made a spot for Gina too.

"Yes, Mr. Antony."

"You can still call me Gregory." He grinned. "Have a seat."

Ryan sat down on the couch about a foot away from Gregory. "I wanted to thank you again for helping me—and Gina—out with the jobs here."

"You're welcome. But I only gave you the jobs. It's up to you to get the most out of the opportunity—on your own."

"Paul told me about the background check. That sounded like a favor. *He* thinks it's a favor."

"Don't worry about Paul Bloom."

Ryan nodded and slid closer to Gregory, then put his hand on Gregory's thigh.

Gregory put his stack of papers down, and Ryan slid his hand to stroke Gregory's cock through his pants.

"Don't," Gregory said softly. "You shouldn't do that."

"I want to. We can go somewhere else." Ryan put his cheek against Gregory's chest.

Gregory took hold of Ryan's wrist and pulled it away. "No. This isn't your job anymore. All I expect from you is your job duties. Your body is no longer a form of currency. That's what you're leaving behind."

"Don't you like this?" Ryan put his hand back. He felt Gregory's cock thicken. "You can't fool me."

"Of course I like it. It's just not appropriate."

"Why can't we have a date? A real date. No money."

"Because now I'm your boss. It's illegal in a different way." Gregory pulled Ryan's hand off his cock and held it for a few moments, then stroked Ryan's hair, still holding him to his chest. There was nothing sexual about the touch; it was pure comfort. Ryan didn't want him to stop.

"Are you seeing someone else now?" Ryan heard his voice quaver and crackle. "What's wrong with me?"

"Nothing. Nothing's wrong. You need to stop judging your value by how many people want to sleep with you."

He'd been going to the classes. They hadn't done much good. Not yet. This was the hardest lesson to learn.

But he'd have to forget it again to do what Agent Cowboy wanted from him. Was there any way to get the kind of information Deke wanted without falling back into the familiar, safe patterns?

"But you want to sleep with me, right?" Ryan grinned at Gregory.

"Yes, of course I do." He ruffled Ryan's hair.

"Do you think I could get a couple of shifts back at the Kiwi, just waiting tables? No dancing. Just the legit stuff?"

"Ryan, we had an agreement. You go back there and you'll lose this job and my support to help you make a new start. You're not going to get another chance to get out of there. Not one this easy."

"No college?"

"Not from me. You get through the program, and I'll cover your tuition."

Ryan nodded. Of everything Gregory had offered him, help with expenses, a real job, and the counseling for former sex workers, the lure of college was the one that made Ryan take him up on the deal. He'd had to drop out his sophomore year at Northwestern, and he'd given up on the chance to earn a degree.

But for once, Ryan wished Gregory didn't care so much about him and his damn future. Ryan was grateful for the support, but he'd promised to help Agent Cowboy. Was nailing Petrov worth losing Gregory's help? Deke hadn't told Ryan everything, but he suspected it was about far more than drugs. They needed him badly, or they wouldn't have made those threats.

He just had to take the risk, for something bigger, whatever it was. For Rocco.

Ryan wrapped his arm around Gregory's waist, and they sat together, embracing, for a few minutes. The closeness meant everything to Ryan, even if it didn't go further.

"Mr. Antony." Paul Bloom's voice made Ryan glance up.

Gregory sat up and let go of Ryan, but he didn't push him away.

"Oh-uh, sorry." Bloom started backing toward the door, not taking his gaze off Ryan. Then the door shut.

"He thinks you're fucking Gina." Ryan chucked. "Or he did."

"I suspect he'll be too afraid to bother either of you now."

"So, let's give him something to talk about." Ryan cocked his head, and Gregory pushed him away gently.

"Sure, as long as you get your therapist's permission. In *writing*."

Ryan frowned. She'd probably agree to that before she'd condone what he was signing up for with Petrov at Club Kiwi.

Chapter 6

The next morning, Ryan sat with Dr. Lin, the FBI shrink who needed to sign off on his mental fitness for the CI ISR&R. Had to make sure he wouldn't crack under pressure or hurt himself.

She asked the usual questions about drug and alcohol use, previous mental illness, and therapy.

"I'm seeing someone now—in a group for former sex workers. Does that count?"

She made a note in the folder, then turned her gaze back on him. He didn't say anything. The intensity of her stare increased and Ryan felt the need to say something, anything.

Deke sat in front of Serah's desk as the Bureau headshrinker came in with Ryan Griffiths' folder. She settled in the chair next to Deke.

"What's the verdict, Doc?"

"I'm not convinced he should be doing this."

"And why not?" Serah folded her arms over her chest, just under her breasts. The result made them spill out of her blouse even more abundantly. She knew Deke was gay at this point. Was the gesture for the doctor's sake? Deke would never figure Serah out.

"He's far too susceptible to manipulation and influence. He's used to doing what pleases someone else. He will put himself in danger if asked. Plus, he's in a program for recovering sex workers—sex addicts. This assignment will derail whatever limited progress he's made."

"You're not approving him? This is a national security risk. We're not just trying to take down a pimp or drug dealer."

"Do you have anyone else?" The doc rubbed her palm up and down one thigh. Was she nervous, or was it some response to Serah?

"No. He's also got special language skills. This case is dead in the water if you rule him out."

"Agent Cartier, there's a reason these initial authorizations allow up to four months to authorize the use of the CI. The process isn't designed to be rushed. It's not good for the case, or for the informant."

"Thank you, Doctor. When you're my boss, I'll keep your comments about the program in mind. Until then, I just need your approval in the narrow scope in which you are authorized to give an opinion. Yes or no on Griffiths?"

"Fine. I'll sign off on him. But I want extra support measures, and I'd like to be able to see him every week or two. Can you arrange that?"

"Sure." Serah grinned. "Absolutely. You'll need to meet him offsite to avoid blowing his cover once he's back in the club."

"I can handle that."

Serah held out her hand, long, thin fingers stretching out toward Dr. Lin.

The doc opened the folder, signed a form, and handed it to Serah. "He's all yours now." She stood and headed for the door.

Serah followed her, hand on one of Lin's shoulders, and stopped for a few words spoken so softly Deke couldn't hear what they said. Then the doc left. Deke wasn't precisely sure what had just happened, but he knew the doc had been played perfectly by Serah.

Serah sat back down in her chair. "You got the surveillance tech ready?"

"N—" Deke hadn't finished the word before he got up and left to make sure the job had been done.

How the hell did Serah do that?

The only conclusion was she had to be a witch.

CHAPTER 7

DEKE SCRAMBLED to finish the rest of the paperwork to get Ryan Griffiths signed up as a CI. The doc had been right. Usually, this process took a month or two. Why was Serah rushing things? Petrov hadn't been spooked, and as far as Deke knew, he didn't appear to be working on a specific deal.

Unless the discussion Ryan overheard was part of a new deal, and given that it was a month earlier, the deal could be going down any day.

They needed Ryan back at Club Kiwi fast.

But it would be too risky—and they might not collect enough hard evidence—unless the surveillance was ready. That meant more paperwork. Serah had saddled him with it; then all she had to do was sign her name and take credit for whatever it uncovered.

"YOU CAN'T do it, Ry. You can't give this up. Not even to get Petrov. Don't risk everything with Gregory."

"I can't walk away this time. It's not just about me. It's more important than that. I need to—"

"Don't forget we're a package deal. If Gregory cuts you off, he cuts me off too. Isn't that what he said?" Her hands shook as she fidgeted with her hair.

Ryan realized how close to the edge she still was. She was clean right now, but any little stress could send her back for a fix. He wouldn't let that happen if he could help it. She wasn't asking out of a selfish desire not to lose this apartment. Her life probably depended on his decision too.

"Okay, Gina. I'll figure out some way to do both. Some way Gregory won't have to know anything."

"Thank you, Ry." She put her arms around him and squeezed tight, then let out a few huge sobs that shook her whole body.

"Shh, shh, Gee. It's going to be fine. We'll be fine." He stroked her hair and let her tears soak his shirt.

How could he meet his obligations to everyone? Gina, Deke, Gregory, Rocco.

Who could he ignore?

His own future was last on a very long list.

THE NEXT evening Ryan met Deke at a Kentucky Fried Chicken on the other side of town. Normally, he'd never be caught dead in a fast-food joint, but at least he could be certain no one would recognize either one of them or pay any attention to their discussion.

Ryan never ate this crap. He stared down at the chicken dinner Deke had ordered for him and lost most of his appetite. He'd gotten surprisingly fond of healthy food in the few weeks he'd been at Farmer Jake's.

Deke picked up a drumstick but didn't start eating. "So, Griffiths, we're working on the surveillance equipment. We'll be putting bugs and a camera or two in your apartment." He punctuated his words with jabs from the drumstick. "You'll get a call from the cable company to rewire something tomorrow."

"What about my roommate?"

"You have a roommate?" He swirled the drumstick like he was drawing a question mark in midair.

"Yeah."

"That's not going to work. We'll find another place for him."

Ryan wondered how good an agent this Deke guy could be. Wasn't he watching Ryan? Didn't he know about Gina already? "Her. And Gina can't stay on her own. She needs me around."

Deke blinked a couple of times, then put the drumstick down. He wiped his fingers slowly on a napkin before he looked at Ryan again. "Is there a vacant apartment in your building?"

"There might be. There's always a 'For Rent' sign on the lawn, but maybe the manager is just too lazy to take it down."

"I'll call when we're done here. We can move her—Gina—into there. She'll be close enough for you, but she won't get in the way. We need a place Petrov can visit you—privately. It has to look lived-in, or he'll sense a setup."

Ryan nodded. Sure. He got it. He was supposed to bring Petrov home for sex, and Gina would ruin the mood. It might also be dangerous, and Ryan didn't want Gina getting hurt.

"Okay. I'll let her know."

"Did you tell her about this?"

"Just the basics. She tried to talk me out of it. Still trying, in fact."

Deke looked into Ryan's eyes. The gaze almost hurt. Did Deke see what he was looking for there? "And?"

"And I'm still doing it."

Deke nodded. Ryan sensed a measure of respect in his gaze.

"There's just one thing…."

"You mean 'one more' don't you?" Deke's voice held a surprising playful note.

"I can't go back to Club Kiwi. That's not gonna work."

Deke slammed his fist on the table, making the two paper boxes of greasy chicken jump. "That's not negotiable. That's the main point of contact. He won't question your presence there."

"That can't be the only club he goes to. Most of those guys have a few places they alternate between when their favorite dancers are working. But you probably knew that." Ryan took a chance, adding a flirty raised eyebrow on that last sentence. He liked the way Agent Cowboy started at the comment.

"I-I don't know much about those kind of places."

"You're missing out. Are you going to be following me around there?"

Deke looked rattled. Ryan had been 99 percent sure the guy was gay, and it was time to find out for certain.

"There will be a team, not just me." Deke's gaze slid along Ryan's upper body.

Ryan nodded. Yup, Agent Cowboy couldn't quite hide that he was looking forward to watching Ryan dance. Well, well. But there would be plenty of time to tease the uptight agent.

Deke pulled a tablet from his breast pocket and accessed some information. "Okay, the last three weeks of surveillance show him visiting Club Kiwi, Petrograd, and Dungeon 69."

"Petrograd's upscale. Wealthy Russians. It's a dinner club with—"

"An underground casino. Yeah, we know about it."

"I could go in there as a dealer, or even a waiter." Ryan wondered why he hadn't thought of it first. Nice and safe and no sex.

"Not an option." Deke paused. "He won't let his guard down around other Russians. What he's into, he won't be chatting about openly. We need him to think no one is listening. Club Kiwi is perfect."

"Are you expecting him to talk about his deals there?"

"Why not? He already has, and you overheard."

Ryan bit his lower lip. He'd forgotten that particular lie, just part of the web of lies he was spinning all over again. He was out of practice already. Until now he hadn't appreciated how freeing telling the truth had actually been for those few short weeks.

"Well, like I said, it was just the once. He might not slip up again."

"True. But we want him to meet you and keep going back—for you."

"And I'm supposedly such a great lay it will loosen his tongue? He wasn't my—uh, client before."

Deke pressed his lips together until they formed a narrow white line. "That's not what I meant. We want him to get attached to you and hopefully bring you to business discussions or be relaxed enough he won't censor his phone calls when you're with him out of the club. That sort of thing."

"Why can't he fall for a busboy at Petrograd? I can be a great busboy." Ryan already knew the answer, but it was worth a shot.

"Is he the kind of guy who would? Even the hottest busboy in the place?"

Ryan let himself enjoy the unexpected compliment for a moment. "You're right. He's not that egalitarian. He wouldn't be caught dead in front of his associates with a busboy." He nodded. "He wants a dancer, someone like that. Someone to show off to his friends."

"That's what we need. If you don't want to go to Club Kiwi, then it's going to have to be Dungeon 69. Whatever that is." Deke picked up his drink and sipped.

"That happens to be the gay bondage club."

Deke spurted Coke all over his extra-crispy drumstick and biscuit. "Bondage?" He coughed, and his voice was all twisted and tight.

Ryan leaned back in the booth and watched Deke's expression morph from emotion to emotion. In any other situation, it would be funny. But Ryan had to remember he was about to do something dangerous— more dangerous than anything before.

And this danger had nothing to do with whips or ropes.

CHAPTER 8

IT TOOK a week for Deke and Serah to get the necessary approval for surveillance in Dungeon 69 and to have fake repair teams install cameras in the bar area of the club and in Ryan's apartment.

The FBI rented the vacant apartment down the hall from Ryan and moved Gina in.

And Ryan went to his grocery store job as usual.

Bloom had scheduled him on days, as requested. Clearly, he didn't want to make waves with Gregory after he'd seen Ryan in his office—and his lap.

Ryan was nervous Thursday morning as he reported to the store. Gregory had asked to see him after lunch. He didn't need any drama today because he had an interview that evening at Dungeon 69 for a job serving drinks in the bar. It was the only opening, and Ryan had to take anything he could get.

He and Gina had lunch in the break room. "You don't know what he wants?"

Ryan shook his head. "I hope he hasn't seen what's going on at the apartment." He kept his voice low. No one paid them any attention. The other employees were used to them whispering under their breath. They were so close no one had made much effort to befriend them.

"Well, good luck, Ry."

Ryan got up, took a deep breath, then headed for Gregory's office.

"Sit down, Ryan." Gregory waved him to a chair in front of the desk.

This would be a formal talk. Usually, Gregory met him on the couch. Maybe Ryan's unwelcome overture the previous week had caused the switch.

"Ryan, I'm hearing a few comments about you from the other employees."

Oh, fuck. What had he done? "Comments?"

Gregory smiled. "Ryan, this is a grocery store. People bring their kids in here, and they shop with their partners or spouses. We sell food and things for your kitchen. Everyday items like that."

"I know. I'm still learning all the merchandise, but—"

"This isn't about merchandise." He paused. "You need to tone it down a little. You're here to put food on shelves and help people find the granola or organic coconut oil."

"I've been doing that."

"You have, but some people think you're trying to sell more than our products."

"What?"

"Comments have been made… that you're a little too friendly with some of the male customers."

"Too friendly?" Ryan blinked. What did that mean?

"It's making people uncomfortable. Can you just tone it down a little?"

"Tone it down? Stop being helpful to customers?"

Gregory let out a sigh and leaned back in his chair. "You don't see it, do you?"

"No." Ryan's heart felt heavy, empty. "No."

"The way you smile, how your eyes light up when you're talking to someone. The way you lick your bottom lip." Gregory let out a sensual groan. "When you're talking to men. If you could turn that on when you're helping the female customers, we'd probably sell more of whatever you tell them to buy."

"I didn't notice I was doing anything like that." Ryan started tapping his fingers on the armrest.

"I can see. I didn't think this was the right place for you. It was the easiest, if not the best fit."

Ryan stood up. "Please don't fire me. Or if you do, please let Gina keep her job. Please."

"Sit down. No one's getting fired. I think you're a better fit for the menswear boutique. Gina can stay here if she wants. She's doing well." Ryan's stomach settled down as Gregory continued. "But I want you to try the other position. It's more suited to you. And enough of the customers are gay that if you do come on to them, they'll just buy a more expensive suit to make you happy, or spend more time trying things on." He smiled. "The straight guys usually have the female staff help them. It's a self-selection thing."

Ryan could picture himself selling expensive clothing to rich guys. Just clothing. It would be a nice change. "Where's the store?"

"Half a mile from here. I'll take you over there now and pick out some clothes for you."

"Clothes?"

"You'll need to look the part. I'll have the tailor fit you, and you can have a few days off until that's ready to go. How does that sound?"

He couldn't remember a job where he actually needed to put *on* clothing. It sure as hell could be worse. "Sounds great."

CHAPTER 9

AFTER GREGORY introduced Ryan to the staff, then selected a thousand dollars' worth of suits, ties, and dressy shirts for Ryan, he left the menswear store. Ryan hopped onto his motorbike and rode home to get ready for his Dungeon 69 interview.

Gina was waiting for him in the apartment—Deke said she didn't have to start sleeping in the new place until Ryan began working at the club, assuming he got the job.

"How on earth is Dungeon 69 better than Club Kiwi? You know what kind of place it is."

"I don't have a choice. Gregory would see me at the Kiwi. Besides, I should be fine. I'm not what most of the patrons are looking for. They bring their own play partners, or they find one of the guests or members, not the staff. I'm only trying for a bar job. And I'm only trying to attract one specific person. Relax."

"You don't look too relaxed yourself."

Ryan noticed his hands were shaking as he flipped through the clothes in his closet, waiting on Gina's advice.

She had her arms crossed over her chest. Every time Ryan stopped on an item of clothing, she shook her head or made a disparaging noise.

"Then what the fuck *can* I wear? You've said no to everything."

"Just go for simple. Black tee and leather jacket. Tight jeans, but not too tight. Don't put on any other leather stuff or you'll make them think you belong in another job."

"Good point."

He slipped on a tight T-shirt, stepped into a clean pair of the smallest briefs he had, and slid on the tightest jeans he could still walk in— regardless of what Gina said. She sneered at his choice, then grabbed a well-worn black leather jacket from the front closet and helped him into it.

She whistled as he checked his image out in the full-length mirror in the hall.

"You look good."

He nodded. His throat was tight, and he felt it cracking when he tried to speak. "Th-thanks." The room felt warm and his head spun a little. He sat down on the couch to clear his thoughts.

"You look like you're gonna puke, Ry. What's wrong?"

"Nothing. I'll be fine. Just some water, please?"

A few sips of cool water helped his parched throat but did nothing for his gut or his spinning head.

Gina shook her head but didn't stop him when he left.

The club was nearby, and he rode his bike there. He parked and brought his helmet inside.

It was dim inside the club, and it took a few moments for his eyes to adjust as he approached the desk in the entry hall.

"Hi. Are you a member?" A leather guy with a thick mustache greeted him with an appraising glance. He wore jeans, and a black leather vest hung open over his furry chest. The gaze intensified, clearly undressing Ryan, and from the smile, Daddy Bear liked what he saw. "You been here before?"

Ryan shook his head and started to open his mouth.

"You can have a day membership for ten dollars, and that gets you in the bar and public play area." Daddy Bear jabbed a thumb presumably in the direction of the public sections of the club.

"Actually, I'm looking for Luke. Here 'bout a job. Name's Ryan." Deke had told him to use his real name.

Daddy Bear nodded. "I'm Luther, Luke's brother. We own the place. I'll take you back."

"Thanks." Ryan followed Luther into the bar. There was some heavy metal throbbing away in the background, loud enough for atmosphere, but not too loud for conversation.

The place was done in dark reds and grays. A dozen small tables filled the center area and six more exclusive booths lined one wall. Along the back wall were several doors. "Those are the nonmember playrooms," Luther said. "They can hire a sub or play with anyone they meet here. We have a one-drink policy. More than that and you can't play. No exceptions. The members' area is downstairs. We have the typical specialty playrooms. You wouldn't be working there, so I'll spare you the details."

Ryan nodded as he took in the eight or ten men seated at the bar and tables. All of them turned to look at him, and a tingle of excitement went through him. He'd missed being the center of attention.

A man who could have been Luther's twin was pouring beer behind the bar. But the resemblance stopped at the face. In a crisp white shirt and slim leather pants, Luke was a much more elegant and restrained version. He nodded when he saw Luther and Ryan come in and served the beer to the guy sitting at the bar.

The customer had light brown hair, tastefully slicked back, and wore a white T-shirt and a crackly brown leather jacket Ryan would have gone down on a whole football team to acquire. The guy was hot, in a dark, broody way that Ryan usually hated but was reevaluating. Working here was going to be much more tempting—dangerous—than he'd expected. Ryan had to look twice at the guy to realize it was Agent Cowboy. Deke had looked through him, not acknowledging him.

"Want a drink, Ryan?" Luke asked.

"Just a beer's good."

"Bartender's running late, so I'm holding the fort till he changes." Luke pulled Ryan a draft, and the bartender arrived before the glass was full. Luke nodded a greeting, then said to Ryan, "Let's go over to one of the booths."

When they were settled, Luke sipped a bottle of Pellegrino. "Didn't you used to dance at Club Kiwi?"

"Yeah."

"You're good. Why do you want to work here serving drinks? You'd make way more staying where you are."

"Not at Kiwi anymore. I had some trouble with a stalker. Kind of want to lay low for a while. Stay off the stage."

"It's really a waste, y'know?"

Ryan felt Luke's gaze peeling off his jacket and T-shirt. He'd been away from that treatment for a while, and at first it felt uncomfortable, but the more Luke stared, the more Ryan liked knowing he was staring.

"I wouldn't mind getting to know my way around here. I know there are a lot of opportunities...." Ryan let the sentence slide away.

"Sure. You could clean up once you learn how things work. You could do demonstrations, or sub for hire. The sky's the limit on that. You subbed before?"

Ryan shook his head. He knew only the basics of BDSM. Hadn't needed to know more than enough to please the clients.

"We can find a good Dom to train you. Give it a month and you'll be in high demand, especially if you take to it. Lots of guys don't realize they really are subs and find it's something they actually need, once they get a taste. And if not, you'll still be a hit if you look as good out of those clothes as you look in them."

Luke's gaze was still appreciative, not leering—at least in comparison to what he'd experienced dancing at the Kiwi. It was part of the hiring process—and the job. Ryan would be expected to disrobe at some point soon.

"Job's pretty simple. Serve drinks here in the bar. It's basically open to the public. Guys can get a day membership for ten bucks. They can play with each other, with members, or with the subs for hire—that would be you." He paused and sipped his fizzy water. "You can decide how you want to play, and you can say no to anyone. There are no restraints allowed in the public playrooms." He motioned to four doors along the back of the bar area. "It's safer for the subs that way. You can get out if you need to."

Ryan hadn't really thought much about having to play with other guys. Deke had focused on Petrov, but Ryan wasn't going to have as much choice in the matter as he'd hoped. How many guys could he turn away before they'd fire him?

"After you get some training, members may want to hire you for the other side. No drinking over there, lots more rules, and all the Doms have to be approved by me or Luther. They will pay quite a lot to play with a well-trained sub, especially one as pretty as you. Some Doms are looking for regular subs, or full-time subs, but that's probably putting the cart before the horse. You still interested?"

"Yes." The job description was completely irrelevant, but he realized he didn't sound enthusiastic. "Yeah, it sounds like fun."

"Got any questions?"

Ryan asked for some details about the rules and safety protocols, which seemed to please Luke.

"Then there's just one last thing, Ryan…."

Ryan nodded and leaned back in the booth as he took a swig of beer. He spotted Deke watching him out of the corner of his eye. Now Ryan felt self-conscious.

"Hey, Lu!" Luke called to his brother, and Luther came over to the booth. "You seen Ryan dance at the Kiwi?"

"Don't think so."

"Would you show Luther?" Luke grinned. "You know he needs to see."

Ryan grinned as well, but it was harder than he expected. He saw the raw hunger in Luther's gaze. This was the club's owner. How would the clientele look at him? This was just the interview. It would only get worse. Could Ryan handle this?

"Sure thing." He cocked his head and went over to the bar. He swung himself up with a move he'd learned in gymnastics back in high school, a million years ago.

Every eye in the place was on him. He focused on the music and not on the hungry looks and soon his hips were moving with the beat.

DEKE HAD been shocked when Ryan hoisted himself onto the bar three feet away and started dancing. Was he crazy? Was he trying to blow Deke's cover?

But as soon as Ryan slithered out of his leather jacket, Deke realized this little performance was not for him; Ryan was showing off for the owners.

Ryan moved back and forth on the bar, swinging his hips and stopping to touch each man within reach. He tugged one guy's ear, slipped a finger under another's collar, and fluffed Deke's hair playfully when he passed. The brief contact had Deke's pulse soaring, and he felt electricity jolt through his body, leaving his nipples tingling. Ryan had moved on to the next guy.

Everyone in the place converged on the bar, wanting to get a closer look at Ryan. At the end opposite Deke, he shed his boots and socks. By the time he got to Deke again, he'd peeled off his T-shirt, displaying plump pink nipples. He pinched one, then encouraged a spectator to pinch the other till they were both dark and hard.

Just like Deke. His cock had swelled, and it throbbed with each movement of Ryan's hips. The cash was already out, and guys were stuffing bills into Ryan's jeans, down the waistband.

Ryan unbuckled his belt and let someone slide it out of the loops, grinding his hips hypnotically as more cash got stuffed into his pants. He strutted around before coming back to stand in front of Deke. Ryan popped open the top button on his jeans, and Deke couldn't help staring at his crotch. He glanced upward, noticing the moist sheen of sweat on Ryan's chest and abs. He wondered how the hard, budded nipples would taste.

Shit, if he kept this up, he'd come in his pants.

Ryan popped another button and motioned to Deke to do the next one. Against his better judgment—which he had apparently left in the car—Deke popped the rest of Ryan's buttons. Ryan made a well-practiced move that caused the jeans to slip right down his slim hips.

Now Deke was completely riveted. Ryan's cock was hard, the smooth crown of it pushing above the waistband of his tiny, pink silk bikini briefs. Deke hadn't seen that many strippers, but none had ever been this hard while dancing.

The room exploded in shouts and whistles, and guys were cramming money down there, getting in a good grope as they did so. Deke bit his own lower lip and shifted in his seat to keep himself from coming as he watched.

Ryan stopped dancing and was reaching for his jeans when a beefy guy reached up and grabbed Ryan's dick through his briefs. Another guy reached for him, and Deke saw a look of fear flash over Ryan's features, wiping away his sexy grin.

In a moment, Luther was there, pushing the men away. "You know the rules here. No touching without permission. Show the man some respect." Luther practically scooped Ryan off the bar, onto his shoulder, and through a door.

Luke collected Ryan's clothes and followed, first shouting to the bartender, "Gary, get another monitor in here, please."

Even then it took the men a few minutes to calm down, and Deke was no exception. He hadn't pawed at Ryan, but he'd been caught up in the raw sexual power and the electric atmosphere. This had been an impromptu performance, but what could Ryan do to a roomful of horny men when he was prepared, with the right music and costume and choreography?

Deke realized it was probably better not to see that. He'd never get another wink of sleep. If he didn't need to stick around until Ryan finished his interview, he'd head right home and jerk off till he sprained his fucking wrist.

How the hell would he get through this case? He stared into his beer.

On the other hand, luring Maksim Petrov with Ryan would be like shooting fish in a barrel.

LUKE AND Luther had offered Ryan the job as soon as the office door had closed. They waited until he was dressed to discuss the details and pay.

Ryan's first requirement: no dancing.

Luther said, "You're gold dust, dude. We could use you once a week to bring in more clients. You'd clean up."

Luke held up a hand. "Those aren't the clients we want. You saw those guys out there. Dancing changes the whole atmosphere." He glanced at Ryan. "Not that I didn't enjoy it, but…."

Luther shrugged.

Ryan was glad Luke seemed to be more in control. Luke's primary concern was the club and the employees, not how much money they could bring in.

"I'm done dancing. That was just a one-off thing. I'll do anything else you want. Wear anything—or nothing. Just don't ask me to dance."

"Okay, okay." They offered him a good hourly rate plus tips. And they'd need a week or so to find him a Dom to start his training.

Ryan hoped he wouldn't need to be there that long, but he went along as if that was something he'd wanted his entire life. They bought it and asked him to start on Friday night.

It had been easy. Too easy. Too easy to get right back into that world. He'd loved dancing. Loved teasing the audience, loved driving them crazy. He hadn't ever realized that the sexual tension could flow both ways. What had he been thinking when he'd practically pushed his cock into Deke's face? The guy had surprised him by unbuttoning his jeans. Even more of a surprise: that minimal contact and the electricity flowing between them had Ryan hard as a rock.

He never got hard dancing, unless he rubbed himself to get extra tips. Getting hard was for the suckers in the audience—the ones who would stuff a week's pay against his cock and buy him drinks while he sat in their laps, or gave him even more for a blowjob or a real fuck.

But Agent Cowboy had thrown Ryan off his game; he'd lost control and the rest of the audience had seen it, even if they didn't understand it. Ryan was supposed to be the one who manipulated other men. So how had Agent Cowboy been able to push all of Ryan's sexual buttons?

He couldn't wait to find out.

CHAPTER 10

DEKE SAT in the bar and tried to cool off after Ryan left.

One of the other men sat on the stool next to him. He wore black leather shorts and no shirt. He had big nipples like Ryan, but this guy's were pierced. The rings had glittery crystal beads on them that glinted in the dim light.

"Jesus, that was something else." He met Deke's gaze for a second before his eyes homed in on the bulge in Deke's crotch. "Want to play?"

Deke sized up the guy. He was slim, in his midtwenties, and one of Deke's types. Deke wasn't into kink, and frankly, he didn't know what the guy expected. Was he a Dom or a sub? Deke couldn't tell.

"We don't need to do a scene. I'd just love to get you off."

Deke licked his lips and opened his mouth.

Then his phone dinged. Reflex made him glance at the screen. A text from Serah reminded him he was on duty. He could sit here drinking or watching Ryan Griffiths strip, but the Bureau probably wouldn't sanction on-the-clock blowjobs that weren't necessary for the case.

Deke shook his head, genuinely disappointed.

"I'm Phoenix. I work here on the weekends, but tonight I'm off duty, so to speak. Maybe another time." He got up and walked around to the other side of the horseshoe-shaped bar, where he settled next to another guy.

Deke watched them exchange a few words; then Phoenix followed the other man to a private room off the back wall of the bar. He let out a sigh. Missed opportunity. At least Phoenix hadn't just gone for the next guy at the bar. And he had approached Deke first.

Little comfort when his jeans were still too tight and he couldn't shake the memory of Ryan's performance from his brain.

Then he remembered the text from Serah.

Update?

Deke texted back: *he's hired.*

One more item crossed off the list to get this operation moving.

DEKE NURSED his beer for another twenty minutes. Ryan didn't come back through the bar, so he must have left via another exit. He'd follow up on that later. Luther came back to help the other bartender when the place started getting crowded around eight. Deke had stayed another hour, getting a feel for the place, the way the clients interacted, and choosing the best spots to put in surveillance equipment.

He'd be spending a lot of time here going forward, so he had to make sure he didn't stand out. This was his third time here, and he hadn't hooked up with anyone. That alone probably drew notice. He wasn't acting like the typical customer.

He glanced at his watch: nine o'clock.

Off duty.

He glanced around at the other customers. He really had quite a choice here, from inked and pierced leather guys, to bears of all shapes and sizes, to a wholesome-looking college-age guy. There were a handful of men who looked like they'd just come from office jobs, not playing any role at all.

It was one of these who caught Deke's attention. The guy was in an expensive suit, silk tie loosened slightly at his neck. He had salt-and-pepper hair cut close to his head, and he looked like he'd slipped out of a Bentley. The man came over to Deke.

"I'm Roy." He had his head bowed, not making any eye contact with Deke.

Deke didn't give his name. "Want a drink, Roy?"

"No, sir." Roy shook his head. Deke noticed his hands were manicured, the nails cut square and even. He had nice hands. Soft hands. "What would *you* like, sir?"

"Just a blowjob. You?"

"A spanking, sir."

Fair trade, Deke thought, and he and Roy went into one of the private rooms.

Roy took off all of his clothes, laying each piece carefully over the back of one of the chairs. Deke sat on the couch and watched but didn't undress. Roy had a nice body, fit, with hair on his lower legs and a dark cloud of curls around his more-than-adequate dick. He was half-hard when he stepped forward and stood in front of Deke.

Deke didn't know much about BDSM, but he knew Roy was waiting for some instructions or encouragement.

"Unbutton my shirt." He bit off the "please" he normally would have added. Roy nodded and dropped to his knees, then reached out for the top button. He worked his way down, fingertips moving deftly, brushing against Deke's chest.

Roy was getting harder as he worked, and so was Deke.

"May I play with your nipples, sir?"

"Undo my pants first."

"Yes, sir." Roy went for the belt buckle, then the button at the waistband. He glanced longingly at the bulge and smiled as he worked.

Deke wanted him to hurry up, but he liked the way Roy touched him. It had been a while since he'd been with Timothy, and he'd been pretty worked up since Ryan had danced. The memory of Ryan's body, his confidence and pure sexuality, bumped Deke's arousal another few notches. He lifted his hips so Roy could pull his jeans down toward his thighs.

Roy made a satisfying groan when he got Deke's erection out of his shorts. He played with him for a moment then leaned forward to lick at Deke's nipples, grip firm on his cock. Deke groaned and gave himself up to the sensations, feeling a twinge of guilt as he imagined Ryan's hands and mouth on him.

Once Roy slipped his lips around Deke's cock, time stood still. The guy was good, knew just when to suck and how hard. He played with Deke's balls and ass and made the kind of noises that turned Deke on. Even without touching himself, Roy was hard, and his cock jutted out from his body. Deke felt a little guilty lying back and letting the guy pleasure him. But that's what they'd agreed.

Orgasm snuck up on Deke, and he wasn't prepared when it hit hard. He had a hand on Roy's head and fucked up hard into his mouth. Roy took it, moaning, then swallowed everything down with a smile.

Deke fought the urge to thank Roy.

Roy looked down.

Deke took a few minutes to recover, rubbing Roy's hair. He didn't really know what he was expected to say.

"Come here and lie across my lap."

Roy smiled and nodded, not meeting Deke's gaze. He stood and grabbed a towel from a pile stacked to one side of the couch, then spread the towel over Deke's lap and lay down. His cock dug into Deke's leg, and his abs rubbed against Deke's half-erect cock. It felt good.

Roy posed so his ass was in easy striking distance of Deke's hand.

"How many strokes do you normally get?" Deke asked, not having a clue.

"Thirty, sir. That should do it."

"You count for me."

"Yes, sir."

Deke raised his hand and brought it down with a slap on one cheek.

"One." Roy sounded pleased, so Deke gave him one on the other cheek.

"Two."

Two pink handprints appeared. Deke smoothed a hand over the firm curves of Roy's ass. He felt Roy's cock stiffen. Two more strokes and more rubbing had Roy making soft little groans.

Deke continued spanking, varying the intensity until he could tell from Roy's groans what he liked. They were on number nine when Roy sucked in his breath and shuddered. He held on to Deke as he came, shooting against the towel; then he went limp and lay like a rag doll across Deke's lap.

Deke stroked his back and his reddened ass as Roy's breathing returned to normal. Then Roy straightened up.

"That's a record, sir. No one's got me off in less than twelve. Thank you."

Deke grinned at the compliment.

Roy got up and started dressing. Deke felt some guilt at the large red marks on the guy's smooth, pale ass, but Roy seemed pleased as punch with the results.

Deke cleaned himself, tucked everything where it belonged, and stood to buckle his belt.

"I'd like to play again, sir," Roy said.

"Daniel." Deke rarely used his given name, but it seemed the safest one to use here. "Me too."

As Deke started his car and began to make his way home, he decided he'd actually meant it. If he had to spend much time around that club—and around scantily clad Ryan Griffiths—Deke was going to need some physical release. The sexual intensity of the place permeated everything, even when Ryan wasn't there, and Deke found how easy it would be to fall under its spell.

This could turn out to be the best—or the worst—case he'd been assigned.

At minimum, it would be memorable.

He just had to make sure he remembered he was there to stop a drug dealer funneling cash to terrorists, not to rack up orgasms with attractive, willing men.

He'd have to make sure Serah never stepped into this club, or he'd be off the case quicker than Ryan Griffiths could shimmy out of skintight jeans.

CHAPTER 11

RYAN TOOK a roundabout route home. He wanted to clear his head before he saw Gina. He hadn't quite processed things himself. Ryan pulled up outside their building and straddled his bike as he looked up at the lights on in their apartment. He pulled off his helmet and waited for a few moments in relative peace and quiet before he had to face Gina. What would he tell her?

He steeled himself for the inevitable conflict and headed inside. Gina glanced up from a book she'd been reading as he walked through the door.

"Well?" Gina crossed her arms over her chest, and hostile vibes emanated from her.

"Well, what?"

"You gonna start working at the Dungeon?" She practically spat the words at him.

"They offered me the job. I can start right away."

"Doing what?"

"Serving drinks in the bar." He wouldn't mention the rest of the possible job duties as a paid submissive. She wouldn't approve.

"No dancing?"

"No dancing. I made that crystal clear."

She inhaled and stared at him, gaze boring deep into his eyes.

He hoped he looked more confident than he felt, and that she wouldn't see the turmoil he needed to resolve. But she knew him as well as he knew himself, knew his needs and weaknesses.

If Luke and Luther kept at him to dance, he'd cave. He was good at dancing. He loved it. There was nothing like walking onto that stage knowing nearly every guy in the place wanted him. Or walking off knowing most of them were willing to pay plenty for it. He'd made good money on the dancing at Club Kiwi and lots more for private dances or anything from a hand job to a four-way. That had been his limit.

How the hell had he thought he could work in a fucking grocery store after that? Helping someone find the kale never earned quite the appreciation of a good striptease. No tip and certainly no orgasm.

"You're gonna get yourself killed. I can just feel it. Please don't do this. I'm begging you. Don't get caught up again."

"Gina, don't."

"Two weeks. If you last that long. Two weeks, then I'm telling Gregory what you're up to. Even if he fires my ass or worse. I can't watch this."

"Watch what? I've been back two minutes."

"Ten seconds was enough to see the look on your face. The way you move. The high you get from performing. It's your drug, and you're already hooked again."

He reached for her, but she stormed out of the apartment and into the hall. He heard her clomping to her new apartment. Ryan raced after her, but before he caught up she slammed the door so hard he felt his teeth rattle from ten feet away.

She was right about the high, but he'd show her he wasn't hooked. He could get out after he'd helped Deke and the FBI. Until then it was all just an act.

But the job at Dungeon 69 offered something else he hadn't known he'd wanted. Once Luther explained the duties of a sub-for-hire, Ryan found he really wanted the job, above and beyond any obligation to Deke and the FBI.

Gregory had moved him to the menswear shop. That offered a real opportunity to leave the life behind forever, to get clean and finish college, and he'd never dream of giving that up for a server job at Dungeon 69.

Would he?

CHAPTER 12

FOUR DAYS later Deke was at the bar in Dungeon 69.

Ryan had been working for two nights, but Deke hadn't been in yet. He couldn't afford to wear out his welcome or blow his cover by staring at everyone and not playing like the other customers. That experience with Roy had been a one-time thing. It had to be. Deke couldn't keep getting off like that while on duty for so many reasons.

Deke also knew he couldn't stand too much of watching Ryan work. Tonight he wore a collar made of red chain links and skimpy black latex shorts. Thankfully, another server had waited on Deke.

It was ten thirty, and Petrov had arrived back in town the night before. They were betting he'd come in here tonight. They'd bet correctly because at five till eleven, Petrov arrived.

Petrov was medium height, about forty-five, with a neatly trimmed goatee of salt-and-pepper, still mostly pepper. His chin-length hair had more silver streaks in the glossy medium brown and a severe widow's peak. He had sharp Slavic cheekbones, and had Deke met him almost anywhere else, he would have found the man attractive. Even walking across the bar, Petrov had a commanding presence, and other customers greeted him warmly, but respectfully.

He had brought along two of his known lieutenants—recognizable from Petrov's dossier—who hadn't gone out of town with him, according to surveillance reports. This was good. Maybe they'd be talking business. Luther seated them at a booth with a "Reserved" marker on the table.

It was the only reserved table in the place, and Petrov's favorite, thanks to information Ryan had gleaned from the staff. Deke had seated himself within ear- and eyeshot of the spot.

The bad news was that another server headed off for the table. He was slimmer and a couple of inches shorter than Ryan, with silky, dark blond hair that reflected the low lights. He wore the club's red chain collar and black latex shorts with a sailor front—a panel with two parallel zippers that allowed for easy access. At the moment he had it half-zipped so the resulting flap revealed a pale, feathery treasure trail, but tantalizingly hid its final destination.

Petrov greeted the server with a kiss and a swipe across the front of his shorts. The boy rubbed himself against Petrov's hand.

"Nice to see you again, sir."

"I missed you, Dakota."

The other men in the booth with Petrov spoke to each other while Dakota sat in Petrov's lap and let the man fondle him.

"There's a new boy here, I see."

"Yes, sir. He started a few days ago. Name's Rio."

Petrov peered across the room to where Ryan was serving a table with two uptight-looking guys who tried to pretend they weren't staring at his body.

"Tell him to bring our drinks. The usual."

"Yes, sir." Dakota's smile faltered as he replied, but he made a show of grinding against Petrov as he got up.

The men spoke in Russian, and Deke hoped they were talking business. They'd bugged the booth, and Serah had arranged a Russian translator for Deke's team.

A few minutes later, Ryan brought a tray containing a bottle of whiskey, three glasses, and a small bucket to the table.

"Good evening, sirs." Ryan set the tray down with a shake of his hips. It got the attention of Petrov and his two companions.

"New boy, what is your name?"

"Rio."

"You look familiar. Where else you worked?"

"Club Kiwi, sir."

"Ah yes. The dancer." Petrov nodded to his friends and said something in Russian. "You play here?"

"Yes, sir. I'm starting my training with Master Luke."

"Luke, eh?"

Petrov watched as Ryan prepared each customer's drink as requested. As he served, he put a red band on the man's wrist. Deke had an identical band on his, representing the one-drink limit in the public bar. Any more and you couldn't play. Strict club rule.

"Anything else, sir?"

"Turn around."

Ryan did, back to Petrov. He briefly met Deke's gaze but quickly looked away.

"Bend over."

Ryan bent, and this time studiously avoided looking at Deke.

Petrov slid his hand along Ryan's ass, covered in the shiny black latex. He used both hands, sizing up each cheek and giving it a squeeze. Then he yanked the back of the shorts off. Deke hadn't realized they were cutaways. Petrov tossed the piece of latex on the table and gave Ryan's naked ass more attention. He whispered something Deke couldn't hear.

Then Ryan straightened up. He reached for the latex piece, but Petrov shot out a hand to stop him.

"Leave it here."

"Yes, sir." Ryan nodded and headed back to the bar.

Deke couldn't help staring at the way Ryan's naked ass looked, bobbing as he strode. When Ryan turned, Deke got another surprise. The thin latex couldn't hide Ryan's hard-on. What had Petrov said or done?

Deke was curious, and a little turned on too. He just wasn't sure why.

DEKE WATCHED Petrov—and Ryan—for another hour, politely declining overtures from two men who knelt down by his chair. If he hadn't been working, he'd be having the time of his life. Both men were decent looking, clean, and eager. Just what Deke needed after things had gone south with Timothy. It wasn't the sex, or the convenience of an anonymous hookup. It was the self-esteem boost from having total strangers wanting to give themselves up to him; Roy's interest hadn't been an anomaly.

After they finished their drinks, Petrov's lieutenants left, and he went over to the bar, bringing the back of Ryan's shorts with him. Deke couldn't hear the conversation with the bartender, but when it was over, Petrov went into one of the rooms along the back wall.

This was not working out as he'd expected. Petrov hadn't touched Ryan after that initial ass-fondling, but he'd groped a few of the other servers who had stopped by his table to say hello. He was clearly the big fish in this pond. But Ryan was the hottest guy here. Other customers were all over him. Why hadn't Petrov gone for him?

Then Ryan went up to the bar and had a short conversation with the bartender. He put his tray down and headed for the back. Deke still couldn't help the way his cock responded to Ryan's ass in the cutaway shorts.

Ryan knocked on the door of the room Petrov had entered, then let himself in.

Game on!

But why did it make Deke's gut ache?

HALF AN hour later, Petrov left the room alone and headed for the door.

Five minutes after that, Ryan left the room. He went up to the bar to retrieve his tray. Deke noticed Ryan's ass was bright red, and he moved slowly. As he worked his way to the tables he served, Deke noticed many of the customers rubbing Ryan's ass or cupping it. Another customer went into a back room with him. What was going on in there now? It wasn't Deke's concern. Ryan had the freedom to refuse to do anything. It was up to him if he chose to go into the room with anyone he wished.

Deke's role here was over, now that Petrov had gone. He made sure he was gone before Ryan came out.

RYAN LEFT his bike at the club and took a taxi home. His ass was on fire, and at least he could sit somewhat comfortably in the cab. He hadn't bothered to change or shower, just slipped a long jacket over the latex shorts. He was physically drained but still on edge. He slid his key into the lock and relaxed as he entered his apartment. The TV was on low in the living room. Gina. He needed her right now, though he wasn't sure what he'd say about the evening.

"Hey, Gee—" Ryan began, until he realized it wasn't Gina in his living room.

"Well?" Agent fucking Cowboy was sprawled on his couch, feet on the coffee table, drinking a Perrier he must have gotten from the refrigerator. Like he owned the place.

"What the…?"

"I let myself in." Deke dangled a key from a key ring and then stuffed the keys into his jacket pocket—the same gorgeous leather jacket he'd worn the other night. "Tell me about Petrov."

Ryan took three deep breaths, but he still wanted to knock Deke's head off. "Nothing to tell. He didn't say anything about his business, drugs, money, nothing."

"What happened in the room?"

"It's not relevant."

"You're supposed to be getting close to this guy so he spends time with you on a regular basis, hopefully outside of that club. So, if what happened in there is relevant to your future relationship with Petrov, you better tell me or Serah's gonna have them wire your ass."

Why had Ryan thought this guy might be nice? He was such a lousy judge of men. So far, the only man he could trust was Gregory. And Ryan was repaying that trust with lies. But Deke made it sound like Serah was the one demanding details, not him. Was it too late to get out of this stupid CI deal?

"Turn around, Ryan."

"No."

"Please." Deke's tone softened, betraying a hint of concern. "Let me see what he did."

Ryan had let plenty of customers check out his ass, but Deke's request was surprisingly unwelcome, perhaps because it had sounded caring and sincere. But he turned and pulled the back of the shorts away.

Deke's fingertips grazed the surface of his skin, setting it on fire anew. He flinched.

"You're not okay."

Ryan nodded. "I'm fine." He bit off the words.

"Petrov hurt you?"

"Yes, it hurt. It's a fucking S and M club. People go there to give or receive some degree of pain."

"I'm sorry." He sounded like he meant it. Deke got up and went into the kitchen. Ryan heard him getting ice from the freezer. He came back with a towel stuffed with ice. "Lie down."

"No. I don't need this." Ryan pushed Deke's hands away. "Don't need your help. Just tell me what you want to know."

Deke pressed the towel against Ryan's bare ass. He held it for a few seconds, and Ryan didn't pull away as the soothing cold seeped through the towel. Every ten seconds or so, Deke moved the towel to another spot. It felt good. Deke held on to Ryan's upper arm with his other hand. The firm pressure of his grip felt good too.

Deke continued with the icing for at least five minutes. Ryan lost track of time.

"That's too cold now." Ryan took the towel from Deke and sat on the couch. He shifted his weight to stay off the still-smarting portion of skin. "What do you want to know?"

"What happened and what did he say?"

"He wanted to spank me. I let him."

"That's it? No sex, no blowjobs? No fucking?"

"Just spanking." Ryan didn't want to go into details about the spanking.

"You think he's gonna want to go further next time?"

"I don't know if there's going to be a next time."

"Why not?"

"He… he… uh, he didn't get off from it."

Deke raised his eyebrows.

Ryan continued. "He was hard, but he didn't come. Is that the level of detail you wanted?"

Deke chewed his lower lip.

"He wasn't really into me. I can't exactly say what it was, but he didn't say he'd ask for me again the way the other customers did."

Deke's gaze bored into Ryan's. Didn't he believe Ryan? Did he want to know more? Well, Ryan wouldn't give in to his prurient curiosity. How could he explain how good Petrov's hand felt coming down on his ass? He didn't know how the man did it, but he found just the right spot every time, each slap and stroke pushing Ryan closer to the edge, the pain blooming into exquisite warmth that traveled directly to his core. He couldn't tell Deke that he'd begged for more when Petrov had stopped and that he'd come like a high-school kid losing his virginity at the barest sensation.

Petrov had sounded pleased with Ryan's reactions and called him pretty names in Russian, but Ryan hadn't been allowed to please Petrov. He knew not all Doms wanted that from a sub.

But Ryan could never admit to Deke how much he'd wanted to please Petrov, or that he hoped he'd be invited to play again.

"So you don't think he's going to ask for you again?"

"I'm not really his type. He wanted to try me out, and we didn't click." Ryan hated how much that hurt. He'd never failed to get a guy interested in him before. He'd never wanted a guy this much. Ryan was the one in control with the tricks. Everything had been on his terms, until now. He'd never been with a guy like Petrov. Ryan couldn't get him out of his brain. After only one session.

"We've seen who he leaves with—that Dakota kid. You're Petrov's type. Coloring, build." Deke looked Ryan up and down for a brief moment, cheeks coloring slightly as he realized what he was doing.

"He likes piercings." Ryan shrugged one shoulder. "I don't have any."

"Piercings?"

Ryan brushed his nipple with his fingertips and nodded.

Deke swallowed audibly. Ryan did it again, but he wasn't in any mood to tease the uptight Fed. Too bad Petrov didn't respond the way Deke did. Ryan fought the urge to see if Deke was hard. It didn't take much with some guys.

"A piercing," Ryan said, looking down at the nipple pinched between his fingers. "I should get one." Would that spark Petrov's interest?

CHAPTER 13

THE FOLLOWING afternoon Deke drove Ryan to a tattoo shop across town. He felt wrong about this, but Ryan insisted. The place was clean and well-lit by the floor-to-ceiling windows. It looked more like a hair salon than the dark, seedy tattoo place of Deke's imagination.

"Hey, Victor!" Ryan shook hands with a dark-haired guy wearing a white tank top. His shoulders were covered in beautifully drawn and shaded tats in vivid colors, like a human comic book.

"Ryan. Never expected to see you here."

"I changed my mind. And you're the best."

"Who's your friend? Looks like a fucking cop."

"Dan's fine. He's been trying to talk me out of this."

"Can't you just get a temporary piercing, like a temporary tat?" Deke asked.

"You can't draw a hole on something, dude." Victor shook his head and grinned at Ryan. "And you can't fake how it feels."

"Let's do this."

They went into a cubicle in the back that reminded Deke of a dentist's office. It was that clean. There was a table and a chair, both of which had adjustable angles.

Ryan pulled his shirt off and sat in the chair.

Victor sat down. "Before we do anything, let's talk about the procedure and aftercare." He explained in more detail than Deke wanted to hear, then asked, "Which one?"

"Left."

"Okay." Victor moved the chair to the other side, and Deke watched him examine Ryan's nipple first visually; then he pinched it and tugged at it. It was like watching foreplay. Deke wondered why he suddenly was getting off on watching stuff like this.

"You have good nips for this. Big enough to hold the bar and still look good." He wiped disinfectant on the nipple, now even bigger and harder, then drew a couple of dots on it with a felt-tip pen. "Let me put on some topical anesthetic, or do you want to feel some pain while I do this?"

Deke replied before Ryan. "Numb it all. No pain." He hated that Ryan was doing this, and he couldn't stand and watch him endure pain, even if Ryan thought he wanted to.

Victor glanced at Ryan, who shrugged. "Numb it. I think it's going to hurt Dan more than it hurts me."

Victor sprayed something on Ryan's chest, and Deke's stomach twisted again as Victor got the tools ready. They looked like instruments of torture. Deke imagined pain shooting from his own nipples to the base of his spine and hoped he didn't visibly react.

"You just want the nip today? How about something a little more exciting to go along with that? How 'bout a PA?"

Ryan glanced at Deke.

"What's a PA?"

"Show him," Ryan said.

Victor pulled his dick out of his shorts to show Deke. Deke blinked a couple of times, caught off guard. He stared at the thick ring through the head of Victor's cock. Just looking at it made Deke's dick hurt.

"Are you serious?" Deke asked, voice rising.

"Just the nipple today, Vic." Ryan winked at Deke. "Dan, you don't have to stay. Wait outside."

Deke shook his head. He was the reason Ryan was here; he had to see the result of his pressure to attract Petrov.

The procedure took less than a minute. Deke watched the needle pierce Ryan's flesh, and then Victor slipped the metal bar in quickly. Ryan gritted his teeth but held up better than Deke would have.

"What do you think?" Ryan asked, thrusting his new piercing at Deke.

"Uh, nice." It did look nice. Deke recalled the guy in Dungeon 69 with the sparkly crystals hanging off his piercings. How would Ryan look with jewelry hanging from his nipple?

Victor went over the aftercare instructions again, and Ryan didn't bother putting his shirt back on when they left.

AFTER DEKE dropped Ryan off at his apartment, he went back to the Bureau to give Serah an update.

"So far, looks like you've got nothing for two weeks of work." She tapped her pointy-toed shoe slowly, accusingly, at him as she sat on the edge of her desk. "Did you at least get laid yet?"

Deke blinked at her, wondering whether that had been a rhetorical question. Or did she know about his little session with Roy?

"No," he said in the most insulted tone he could muster.

"Too bad. You're a little tightly wound. I thought you'd want to sample the goods we're trying to sell Petrov."

This conversation was leading both of them toward some sensitivity training or sexual harassment write-ups—or both—so Deke let the topic drop.

"It's not as simple as we thought."

She waited.

"The surveillance is in place, and Ryan's made first contact, but Petrov didn't bite the first time. Ryan says he's not Petrov's type. Guy's into piercings, so Ryan got one."

"What kind?" Serah raised an eyebrow and leaned forward. She must have realized she'd crossed a line because she sat up again. "Never mind. That was good thinking. Good job."

"I don't want credit for that. I don't like where this whole thing is going."

"But it's going. We need results on this. We need to know what Petrov was doing in Albuquerque, and we need to find a way to stop him. Your little secret weapon is the only chance we've had at a CI in his organization for a long time. No one's been willing since that last one— until Ryan."

This was news to Deke. He'd read through the whole file but hadn't seen anything about other CIs. "What last one?"

"The guy they found strangled in the trunk of Wallace Turner's car."

Turner had been Petrov's biggest rival until Turner had also been found dead. "You can tie Petrov to it?"

Serah shrugged. "No evidence, just circumstantial. Wasn't that in the jacket?"

"No."

"That's funny." Serah smirked. "Anyway, you keep matchmaking between our two kinky lovebirds and try not to rack up too much overtime at the sex club. I need to show Ward some progress within a week. He's getting pressure from Washington. They're willing to expand your OIA list on this one. Just let me know what you need."

The OIA list was a free pass for an informant to engage in what the Bureau called "ordinarily illegal activities." Deke could get authorization for Ryan to sell drugs, offer sex for money, or engage in a variety of other misdemeanors or felonies if it would get the dope on Petrov. No one had the James Bond license to kill, but sometimes the definition of self-defense got interpreted surprisingly broadly.

This one was important, and everything was riding on Ryan's shoulders—or ass, as the operation seemed to be headed that way.

TWO DAYS after Ryan got his piercing, the "Reserved" sign was laid out on Petrov's favorite table. He'd texted Deke and gone about his shift as usual. The piercing stung a little, and he had to be careful dressing and in the shower, but he didn't regret getting it done. He was looking forward to seeing how it would feel when someone else played with it. He hadn't told Gina about the piercing yet. Or the spanking.

Just before eleven, Petrov came in. Tonight he was alone. He wore an open-necked shirt of red silk, and dark pants. His beard looked freshly trimmed, and he smiled and greeted everyone as he followed the host to the table.

Deke wasn't here yet. Ryan hoped he wouldn't show up. It was hard to work with his prudish gaze following Ryan's every move. Deke didn't look at him the way other men did. They let their desire show, as if it would sway Ryan in their direction. Deke held his in, but it was there below the surface. He was fighting a war with himself over that desire, and it would either spring to the surface, or Deke would fuck himself up even more trying to pretend he didn't feel it.

Ryan moved past Petrov's table on his way to the bar, but Petrov barely noticed him. It was harder than he'd expected to get the guy interested in him, but not impossible. He had plenty of experience, but thankfully, it had been a couple of years since he'd needed to rely on that skill for his survival.

Now Ryan had let the FBI put him right back where he'd never wanted to be again. Back where he'd promised Gina and Gregory—and himself—that he'd never return. He'd wanted to help get Rocco's killer and stop whatever else the FBI thought Petrov was into. And he hated himself even more for getting into the kind of trouble that had made him easy pickings for the Feds. Still, he'd rather be here, trying to stop drug dealers, than in prison—or dead—and he certainly didn't want to cause any more pain for his mother than he already had. Deke might not make good on that threat, but Ryan suspected there was someone higher up in the FBI who wouldn't balk at pushing on all of Ryan's weak spots, someone like his ruthless boss, Serah Cartier.

He gathered his wits and went to work.

Dakota was waiting on Petrov's table again tonight, so Ryan had to come up with a way to get his attention without angering Dakota. The guy had been the top dog here, and Ryan's arrival had shaken things up. In less than a week, Ryan had picked up some of Dakota's favorite clients, even without playing.

But not Petrov. Ryan had planned carefully how to get his attention tonight, and he walked in Petrov's general direction, first grabbing a plastic cup from the bar and filling it partway with ice cubes. He winked at the bartender, Gary, as he did so; it never hurt to get him on Ryan's side too. So what if he misunderstood Ryan? There was time enough later for sorting that out. But he needed the ice.

He stopped a couple of feet away from Petrov's table and leaned against the wall, one hand supporting his tray, and he scooped an ice cube from the cup, making enough noise to catch Petrov's attention. With his right hand, Ryan applied the ice cube to his still-painful left nipple, easing the very real swelling. He swore under his breath. Petrov heard and turned around. Ryan didn't try to catch his eye but rubbed the ice on his nipple in the most arousing way he could.

"Looks painful," Petrov said casually after watching for at least a minute.

"Hurts worse than I expected, sir," Ryan said, letting his eyes travel over Petrov while Petrov was obviously doing the same to him.

Petrov waved Ryan over, and he brought the tray and presented himself to Petrov, the way Luke had taught him to. Petrov took the tray away from him and set it on the table.

"When did you have it done?" Petrov sounded genuinely interested.

"A few days ago, sir." Ryan added a low groan at the end of the sentence. "Monday."

"Monday?" Petrov had a thoughtful look on his face.

Ryan hoped he'd realize it was the day after he'd been in here and had the short session with Ryan. "Let me take a look," Petrov offered.

"You a doctor, sir?"

"Something like that. But I've had a lot of experience with these," Petrov replied, and Ryan nodded. "Come closer so I can see better." Petrov shifted so he was sitting at the end of the booth. He held his hands out, and Ryan stepped closer, standing between his knees.

Petrov moved the candle from the center of the table toward the edge so he could see more clearly. His gaze traveled from the nipple down Ryan's torso, staring at the shorts that were barely there. The intensity of his stare nearly melted them right off. Ryan grinned. He'd chosen the right pair.

Petrov had one hand on Ryan's back and the fingers of the other gently brushed Ryan's chest a couple of inches below his left nipple. He smelled like citrus and sunshine, so light and breezy for a man who supposedly did many dark things. Petrov leaned in close to examine the swelling around the piercing. His fingers settled onto Ryan's flesh, the touch soft and intimate.

Ryan could feel Petrov's breath on his nipple. He felt his cock swelling too. Could Petrov see it through the shorts?

"I didn't realize it would hurt so much," Ryan said. "I wanted to do both, but…."

Petrov looked up, their gazes meeting.

"Looks like it's healing okay. You shouldn't have any pain after a few more days. Why did you do it?" Petrov smiled as he asked.

Ryan lowered his head. "I got it for someone who… well, I hoped someone would notice me," Ryan said, his voice soft, forcing Petrov to lean in more closely to hear him. Then he locked gazes with Petrov for a split second. Enough to get the message across. He was available, and he was willing to do a lot to please a lover. Precisely the kind of thing that would appeal to Petrov.

"I'd say you must be excelling at your sub training." Petrov turned his mouth up at one corner. "I have an oil that should help with the pain.... It's at my home, if you're interested. Or are you enjoying the pain?" Petrov's voice got low and gravelly.

Ryan glanced away then back again, and whispered, "This isn't the kind of pain I like."

Petrov nodded. "What time do you get off work?"

Ryan reached out to take hold of Petrov's arm, rotating it so he could see the time on his watch. He let his other hand casually brush against Petrov's crotch as he did so, prolonging the physical contact, reeling him in.

"In about an hour."

"I can wait," Petrov said, and Ryan smiled with just enough heat to make sure Petrov stuck around.

"It feels better already," Ryan said, giving him another sly, promising smile and turning away slightly. Petrov let his hand travel down Ryan's back and ass, and Ryan watched the hand slip off his hip as he picked up his tray and walked back over to the bar.

That was when he glanced toward the far corner of the room and spotted Agent Kane sitting, sipping at a club soda with a twist, studiously not looking at him. Ryan wasn't sure why that upset him. Deke had treated him nicely when they'd been alone, and Ryan wanted Deke to notice him here. He had half a mind to flip him the bird across the room, but he knew Petrov was probably still watching, and he couldn't risk it.

Was Deke getting off on Ryan trying to peddle his ass like this? He couldn't decide whether he wanted the last hour of his shift to go quickly or slowly, knowing that in a little more than an hour, he'd probably have to let Petrov fuck him and pretend he liked it enough to get the guy to fall for him. Maybe he wouldn't have to pretend.

Now, across the room from Petrov, Ryan had some perspective. But next to the man, with his fingers on Ryan's body, it was a lot more difficult to think straight. He had to remember this was just another role, and he was the one manipulating Petrov, not the other way around. And the sooner he could get what they needed from him, the sooner Ryan could get out again.

When he'd moved to Portland, hustling had been a game. He'd had steady clients and could pick and choose—much better than the situation in LA. Now the fun was over, and it was deadly serious. Lives really were at stake—possibly his own if he fucked up and ended up accused of murder. It took all the sport out of it. The FBI said he could keep any money Petrov gave him, though at the moment, he'd pay any amount not to be here, doing this, again. Ryan sighed—loudly enough for the bartender to hear.

"Well, look at you and that cute little ass of yours. Got a bite from the biggest fish after just a few nights on the job," Gary joked.

Ryan could tell there was a hint of jealousy in the comment, a hope that Ryan wouldn't end up leaving with a customer after work and might want to have some fun with him.

"I'm not counting my chickens just yet. He barely noticed me the other night." Ryan let loose with a dimpled smile that lit up Gary's face with hope. "The big fish might not stick around if someone else gets there first."

"He's still got his eye on you." Gary subtly pointed toward Petrov with his chin. "You'll have to deal with Dakota, though, and he's practically breathing fire."

Ryan flashed a shy grin, as if Petrov's attention and Dakota's response surprised him. "Uh-oh."

"Can you take this drink to the guy at the end of the bar? Daniel, I think his name is." Gary handed Ryan a drink, and he put it on the tray.

When Ryan got close to Deke, the agent's expression was worth whatever Petrov might do to him later. He practically saw steam coming out of Deke's ears as he set the drink down.

DEKE NEARLY fell off his stool as Ryan approached. The shorts he had on tonight were made of some translucent plastic that left almost nothing to the imagination. They were like wearing a thicker, fitted version of a Ziploc bag. The zipper obscured some of his cock, but what Deke could see made him eager to see the rest. It was apparent that Ryan's balls were shaved, but he had a shallow fringe of dark hair at the base of his cock. As he approached Deke, he shimmied his hips in a way that made his cock and ball sac dance around in the shorts.

Deke couldn't catch his breath. He nearly choked on his own tongue when Ryan put his drink down and walked away. The rear view showed several parallel lines of red marks across Ryan's ass and thighs. He'd had a play session with someone before Deke had arrived. The raised welts looked painful, and he noticed some of the other customers slid their hands along Ryan's legs and ass to feel them before slipping their hands inside his shorts to leave tips. He had quite a bulge of money on one hip. Deke wondered how much Ryan could make in a night here, knowing it was probably nothing to what he'd earned stripping at the other place, given the reaction to his short, spontaneous routine the previous week.

Deke picked up his drink and took a long sip, wishing it was alcohol. He needed to steady his nerves. It was then he noticed something written on the napkin Ryan had left.

Going home with P.

DEKE GLANCED at Ryan again, but it wasn't safe to catch his eye. Only one way to do this. He signaled the bartender.

"I want to play with the dark-haired one. What's his name?"

"Rio. I can give you twenty minutes, then he's off duty, and he's got a late booking."

"Twenty minutes. Fine."

"Which room?" Gary handed him a menu. Inside he found photos of the rooms in the bar area and the equipment in each one: mostly floggers, small whips, riding crops, and canes, but one had a wide selection of dildos and another had a suspension mechanism. "If you want to use the cross or any bondage, you'll need to book those on the other side, and that's a minimum of ninety minutes—full members only. Here's Rio's limit list. I'll need your signature that you understand and agree."

Deke didn't want to look at the list. It might give him too many ideas. And he didn't want to imagine what other men might do to Ryan in one of the little rooms. He just signed it without reading.

"The little room at the end will be fine."

"The fee." Gary slid a credit card slip made out for $100 toward him.

Deke slid the Bureau Visa over and figured he'd find a way to explain the charge later. Next time he'd bring cash.

"That covers the room and the sub's fee. You can leave a tip if you like. That's cash only."

"Thanks." Deke went directly to the room. He didn't want to see Ryan's reaction when Gary sent him in here.

Five minutes later there was a knock on the door. Then Ryan opened it and came in. He was still wearing those shorts, and up close in the bright lights, Deke got more than an eyeful.

"You wanted to play, sir?" Ryan asked.

Deke stared at him. The piercing glinted in the lights, the nipple still swollen and red. The other nipple was peaked and hard in the chilly room.

"If you're going to his place, you should take another camera. Place it in any room we couldn't get one in yet."

"Okay."

Deke handed Ryan the camera; it was small enough to drop into his shoe. Good thing, since there was no way he could hide it in the see-through shorts. "You remember how they work?"

"Yes, you told me five times."

"Fine."

"Sit down." Ryan nodded toward the bench.

"Why?"

"You have to do something. I can't go back out there without a few new marks or people will get suspicious."

Deke glanced around at the whips and riding crops. "I don't know how to use any of this stuff."

"Then just spank me. Leave some good handprints." Ryan peeled the plastic shorts down and Deke stared, trying to pull himself together. Ryan put a towel over his lap and lay down, completely naked, across Deke.

The red welts on Ryan's ass and thighs caught Deke's gaze. He ran his fingertips across them, feeling the warmth of the skin where Ryan had been caned or hit with the crop. Ryan squirmed on his lap.

"Sorry," Deke whispered. A moment later he realized he hadn't hurt Ryan. Instead, Ryan's cock hardened against Deke's thigh. Deke's cock responded. Ryan could probably feel it against his stomach, and Deke froze for a moment. Then he looked down at Ryan's perfectly shaped ass and the welts and raised his hand and brought it down on one cheek with a loud slap.

Ryan's hips jerked. Deke watched the spot turn pale pink. He put an identical mark on the other cheek, then rubbed the spots like he'd learned. Curious after his session with Roy, Deke had looked up how to give a proper spanking, just in case he had to administer another. He'd never expected it would be Ryan, naked and squirming, ass-up on Deke's lap.

Two more strokes and Ryan let out a pleasurable sigh that had Deke hard as stone under him. A few more strokes and Ryan was pressing his hips against Deke. He went for the spots that made Ryan react the most. Then Deke found he didn't want to stop. He kept going, feeling Ryan tremble and moan beneath him until he finally shuddered and came on the towel.

Deke rubbed Ryan's ass for a few moments. The welts made lines across his handprints, and he liked the way the raised flesh felt under his fingers. He wondered how they'd get past this moment, but Ryan straightened up, face flushed, cock still jutting from his body. Deke tried to look away but ended up catching Ryan's gaze.

They stared at each other for a moment, sharing something neither would say out loud.

Deke watched Ryan pull his shorts back on, come smearing across the front as his half-hard cock distorted the plastic. Ryan zipped up and turned toward the door. The plastic shorts displayed Deke's handiwork. At least between that and the obvious fact Ryan had gotten off in here, Deke wouldn't have any trouble keeping his cover in the bar.

After Ryan shut the door, Deke pulled himself together. He gulped air and pulled the towel off his lap. Had he really needed to talk to Ryan tonight? Yes, but not in here, like this. But he *had* come in here with Ryan. Deke needed to clear his head and think about the case, not about why it felt so damn good spanking Ryan and even better when he got Ryan off.

He wasn't prepared to consider how or why he'd come in his pants about two seconds after Ryan did.

CHAPTER 14

RYAN WAS heading toward the back to clean up after the session with Deke when Petrov called him over. He tried to calm his pulse and breathing, but Deke had gotten him so worked up he'd lost all semblance of control over his body and brain. It hadn't felt that damn good with any of the other clients—even Petrov, who actually knew how to give a good spanking.

"I arranged for you to leave now. Before anyone else gets their hands on you." Petrov raked his gaze over Ryan's body, taking in the telltale signs of his recent orgasm. "Next time I'll have to book your last hour myself. Make sure you have plenty of energy left for me."

"Yes, sir." The mention of "next time" encouraged Ryan. "I wasn't sure if you wanted to play tonight."

"I didn't know either, but now I want to play with you. If you do."

"Yes, of course I do. Let me change…."

"No. I like how you look. A lot." He stared at Ryan's cock. "Turn around."

Ryan did, and Petrov skimmed his hand along the welts on the backs of his thighs. "Nice work. Your skin is perfect for caning." He didn't take his hand off Ryan's thigh and increased the pressure. "Beautiful."

He spun Ryan around, eyes widening when he saw Ryan's growing erection. "Nice young cock. Very nice." He put his palm over it, and Ryan felt the heat of his hand through the plastic. His knees went weak, and he found himself getting hard again. Why did he respond like this to Petrov? "Yes, you have much more play in you tonight. Get your things and meet me at the door."

"Yes, sir." Ryan headed for the staff locker room, knowing dozens of eyes were on him. For the first time in a very long while, he felt self-conscious as the other men saw his hard-on and the smears of come on his shorts from his session with Deke. And they all knew he was leaving with Petrov. Dakota stared daggers at him.

Ryan had fucked plenty of men for money, in all sorts of scenes and situations, but at this moment all he could think was that he hoped Agent Cowboy didn't see him leave with Maksim Petrov.

PETROV HAD a car and driver waiting for him at the curb. The driver held the door open as Ryan in his see-through shorts slid gingerly into the backseat, followed by Petrov. The ride was short, and he sat on Petrov's lap the whole time, letting him rub his back and neck. Petrov never even touched Ryan's cock, but he was hard and throbbing by the time they got to Petrov's penthouse in a high-rise building in the Pearl District.

Ryan got a quick tour when they first arrived. The suite was the entire top floor, and every room had floor-to-ceiling windows, affording a 360-degree view of the city, and in the morning there would be beautiful vistas of the sea on one side and Mount Hood on the other.

"Have a seat." Petrov motioned to the couch in what could be a living room or a den. "I'll get some drinks."

He came back with bottled water and made sure Ryan drank at least half a bottle. "Stay hydrated. It's very important."

Ryan nodded and kept sipping.

"I promised you the oil for your nipple," Petrov said after a companionable silence. "It's in my dungeon. Shall I bring it here, or would you like a look?"

Ryan liked the way Petrov offered him a choice. The man appeared to offer no immediate danger or threat. He seemed to genuinely want to play. Of course Ryan didn't know much about what Petrov liked yet. Dakota wouldn't tell him, and no one else at the club that night had played with him.

"I'd like to see it."

"First, we should discuss the rules."

Ryan nodded.

"I have a copy of your limits list from the club. Is there anything additional I should know? Anything you particularly want or don't want?" He handed a copy of the paper to Ryan.

Ryan glanced at it. His activities for the club were pretty limited, given his lack of training. Luke had only permitted him to receive spankings, light caning, and flogging with certain toys. And so Ryan wouldn't have to do too much with the clients, he'd limited sex to hand jobs if he or the client didn't get off from play. Now Ryan took the pen Petrov offered and marked "Yes" to nearly every other thing on the list, and wrote "no limits" in the section for sexual activities. He licked his bottom lip and handed the list back to Petrov, who looked at it without commenting. He signed the paper and put it back on the table.

"Let's go to the playroom."

Ryan followed Petrov to a room at the back of the suite. It was through a locked door, but Petrov didn't lock it once they were inside.

It was dim, but Petrov switched on the lights, illuminating a well-equipped room with several tables, a Saint Andrew's cross in the shape of an X with places to restrain hands and feet, a suspension machine, and two walls lined with an array of toys from single tails and crops to dildos, wands, and items Ryan had never seen or used before.

"For tonight, we will not be very formal. Feel free to speak as you wish, ask questions, make any noises. You have permission to ask for something you would like. I can refuse, but I want to hear your thoughts and desires."

"Yes, sir."

"You do not need to address me as 'sir,' unless you enjoy that."

While he looked around, Petrov opened a small cabinet and took out a clear bottle. "Here's the oil." He handed it to Ryan.

"Thank you. Would you put it on for me?"

Petrov grinned. "My pleasure. Why don't you have a seat here?" He motioned to a chair similar to a dentist's chair.

Ryan lay on the reclined chair. Petrov moved to his feet. "Let's make you more comfortable." He began to unlace one shoe.

"That's okay. I'll do it."

"Nonsense. You're supposed to be the sub, remember?" Petrov pulled the shoe off and set it on the floor, then went for the other shoe.

Ryan tried to get there first, but Petrov gently pushed him back down. He pulled the other shoe off and tossed it under the chair. Ryan could see it fall over, and the bug Deke had given him rolled right across the floor. There was no way to retrieve it without drawing attention to the item, and Petrov would know what it was. That would be dangerous.

He hoped it worked and that Deke or someone else was listening, just to make sure he was okay, because it suddenly dawned on him how much fucking danger he might actually be in.

"Just relax, Rio." Petrov sat at the edge of the chair. "You know what the most important thing is for a sub?"

Ryan shook his head.

"Trust. You should trust the Dom to take care of you. I know you are new. I can tell from your limits card just how new. You have very few Nos. Astonishing."

Ryan wished he'd put down a few more Nos. He had been worried he wouldn't get the job if too many things were off-limits. Stupid!

"Astonishing and foolish. You have no training in most of the play techniques, and a poorly trained or unscrupulous Dom could easily take advantage of you." He smiled and suddenly looked so kind. "But do not worry. We always start easy. I want you to relax and trust." He eased Ryan back down to the chair and stroked his cheek. "See, it is safe. I can see you are getting tense. Wide eyes are pretty, but look, we lost your even prettier hard-on. Let me fix it, okay?"

Ryan nodded, slowly inhaling. He wasn't restrained. He could get up and leave, even shoeless. The doors weren't locked. He was fine.

Petrov squeezed a few drops of oil on Ryan's new piercing. It was cool. "Just tea tree oil, vitamin E, and essential oil of lavender. Antibacterial and helps avoid any scarring. Nice and soothing." He gently swirled the oil around the nipple, avoiding the tender part. He massaged the oil into Ryan's aureole, fingers firm and skillful. He had a gentle touch, but somehow, he connected with the most sensitive nerve endings, and Ryan felt a hot-cold, pleasant sensation tingling through his nipple. Petrov dripped oil on the other nipple.

"Cannot let him feel unloved." He massaged around the nipple, never quite touching the nub. The sensation was arousing, yet infuriating. Ryan's nipples screamed for attention, for pressure, for friction. But Petrov never gave in.

The shorts were unbearably tight now. Ryan's cock had swollen to full erection from the nipple play. He was panting and bucking his hips.

"Not yet, pretty one. I'm not ready for that yet."

"Take off my shorts, please, sir." Maybe the "sir" would help this time.

"Not yet. Have patience." Petrov put some more oil on his hands and proceeded to massage Ryan's shoulders and neck until he relaxed under the pleasure of the touch from Petrov's strong hands. He closed his eyes and sank into the warmth, floating on a cloud of pure pleasure. He was still hard, but the ache had blended with the other sensations, and he was in a state of completely heightened sensual awareness.

He felt Petrov's fingers circling his nipples again, right where they'd started. Then he pinched the unpierced right nipple, not too much pressure, then a tug. Harder. He alternated pinching and tugging and twisting until Ryan lost awareness of everything except the sensations zinging up and down the nerves connected to his right nipple.

Then without warning, he felt wetness and warmth on his left nipple, a little pressure, and a gentle tug on the bar from Petrov's tongue. It started a chain reaction that ricocheted through his body, and when the tugging increased, he lost complete control and came, the waves of orgasm shaking his entire body. He felt hot splashes across his abs, and he spurted and shuddered for what seemed like hours.

"I'M NOT sure why the reception keeps going out."

"Just fucking fix it already. My CI might be in danger up there." Deke narrowed his eyes at the tech guy, who was adjusting settings on the surveillance tech in Petrov's apartment. They were in the van unit parked half a block away.

"The penthouse is on the twenty-first floor. We have to take that distance into account. I'll need to power up the bug and transmitter and hope it doesn't cause any audible feedback in the suspect's premises." He adjusted something.

"That's a possibility?" Deke didn't want that either. If Petrov thought Ryan had brought in the bugs....

"A remote one." The tech guy fiddled with something else, and the audio came in even though the image was still a blur.

There were no words, just sounds. Little gasps and agonized groans. Deke recognized Ryan.

"Get the picture. I need to know what he's doing to my CI. Petrov's into some rough shit...."

Then the image came in sharply. Ryan, eyes closed, with Petrov pinching a nipple. They watched Petrov bend down and put his mouth over the piercing.

Then Ryan came, semen splashing against the plastic shorts like a fountain.

They both stared as Ryan's body kept shuddering.

"That's rough," the tech guy said. Then he stared at Deke. "Where do I get me one of those piercings?"

Deke wondered if he'd underestimated the value of piercings but rubbed a nipple at the memory of the needle sliding in and out. The main point was that Ryan hadn't been in any danger. Quite the opposite.

"Thanks. You can split now. I've got it under control."

The tech guy was still staring at Ryan lying there incapacitated by pleasure. "Fuck. Fuck."

He took the words out of Deke's mouth.

CHAPTER 15

DEKE DECIDED to sleep in the surveillance van. The small couch was uncomfortable, and he would toss and turn the rest of the night, but he didn't want to go home either. At least he would never get deeply enough asleep in the van to dream. That was the point, really. At home he'd have the nightmare.

Instead, his brain replayed the images of Ryan with Petrov. He saw Ryan coming over and over, on some mental infinite loop. Finally, Deke drifted off and woke with a start to discover he'd come in his sleep. How long since that had happened? His heart raced, and he couldn't catch his breath. He was covered in sweat, and his mouth was dry as dirt.

He almost preferred the nightmare. Almost.

THE NEXT morning at ten, Deke sat in the KFC waiting for Ryan, but he didn't show. By eleven, Deke took a chance on making open contact, only because he had to make sure Ryan was okay.

Deke drove past Gregory Antony's menswear boutique and saw Ryan inside. He looked fine, but Deke needed to talk to him. He entered the store, and a red-haired woman greeted him.

"How can I help you today, sir?" She had a nice smile. "I'm Julianne."

"The other guy was helping me last time," Deke lied, motioning toward Ryan.

Ryan came up. "Hello, sir. Glad you came back." He quirked one corner of his mouth until his dimple came out. "Did you decide on something yet?"

"Why don't you show me something new?"

"For work?"

Deke nodded. He was wearing one of his older suits, a bit worn around the edges and somewhat out of style. He actually could use a new one.

Ryan showed him three nice suits, all above his price range, but probably everything in this shop was. Ryan helped him into one of the jackets and stood behind him while they both looked in the mirror.

Deke could see the girl watching them at first, but when Ryan smoothed the jacket across Deke's shoulders, making plenty of contact, the girl grinned and looked away.

"You missed our date this morning." Deke spoke at barely more than a whisper, but in case Julianne overheard, she would think his visit was personal.

"What date?"

"The newspaper signal. Did you forget the code?"

"Let's see how the pants look." Ryan spoke in his normal voice. He grabbed the trousers and led Deke into a large dressing room.

"I'm not trying these on for real."

"Another guy just walked in. If I'm not helping you, I have to go back outside. I can't afford to lose this job."

"Fine." Deke shut the door—with Ryan on the other side—and changed. The pants looked good, but they might be a bit too short.

"Let's see those." Ryan shook his head right away and sent Deke back into the dressing room.

Deke slipped into the next pair and came out of the room.

Ryan had a finger on his chin as he watched Deke. He made a little spinning gesture with one hand, and Deke turned around.

"Now the shoe's on the other foot," Ryan said with a grin. He looked Deke up and down and back up again. "But very nice. I could look at you in that suit all day."

Deke inhaled. This guy must have been very successful as a rent boy, just based on the way he flirted and made Deke think he was telling the truth. "It's nice. You think it looks good on me?"

Ryan nodded. "I can get you a discount." He named the price.

Deke nodded. "Yeah, okay." It was a good price for the suit.

"Get changed and I'll ring it up." Ryan stood in the doorway of the dressing room, not making any movement to leave. "Fair play, right?"

Deke shrugged and slipped out of the trousers, self-conscious in his clingy boxer briefs. His cock threatened to jump and be noticed every time Ryan smiled. Was he flirting just to sell a suit, or was he teasing Deke for another reason?

Deke managed to dress under Ryan's scrutiny without springing a boner, but just barely. He followed Ryan to the desk and waited for him to write up the purchase.

"You'll need alterations, sir." Ryan pulled a tape measure out of his pocket with the kind of grin the doctor flashes right before he tells you to cough.

Ryan had Deke step up to a small platform, where he took the appropriate measurements of his arms, chest, neck, and waist. Then he dropped to his knees to measure Deke's inseam. It felt more like he was taking inventory of Deke's family jewels, but Ryan was certainly enjoying himself.

Deke paid for the suit and slipped a note to Ryan as they shook hands.

FOUR HOURS later, Deke sat in a Starbucks around the corner from the KFC.

He stared at Ryan as he sat down with a tall drink topped with a mound of whipped cream and drizzled with caramel and chocolate.

Ryan looked at Deke's short coffee, then back at his own confection. "Hey, I'll burn it off."

Deke couldn't help grinning. "I hope so. Your wardrobe at the Dungeon doesn't hide much." He paused for a second before adding, "I mean, extra weight." He felt his face on fire. "Shit. You know what I mean."

Ryan's gaze bore into Deke's, but he was grinning too. "You've noticed."

Deke shifted his cup around on the table, avoided Ryan's probing eyes. Why did the guy have to be such a fucking tease all the time? Back to business.

"I shouldn't have had to risk going into the menswear shop this morning." Deke narrowed his eyes, hoping it would get Ryan to be serious.

"That suit looked great on you. Really. Once it's altered...."

Deke shook his head, remembering Ryan's measurement technique. "You know, I've had hand jobs with less contact than that."

Ryan grinned. "I aim to please." He poked a finger into the whipped cream and licked it off, keeping his gaze locked on Deke's the whole time.

Deke tried not to squirm in his seat, but the heat level was rising. "What would really please me...." He left the sentence hanging. Two could play this game.

"What?" Ryan's eyes widened, and his mouth made a perfect kiss shape when he pronounced the "wh."

For a split second, Deke considered telling Ryan, but he counted to three and calmed his nerves and hormones. He just couldn't win here. He gave up. "For you to remember the fucking meeting code."

"Code? Remind me."

"With the newspaper. If the front page is ripped, you meet me at the KFC. If the second page is ripped, we meet here, 10:00 a.m."

Ryan nodded and licked at the whipped cream with his pretty pink tongue. "Gina swiped my paper this morning. Sorry."

"I'll get her a subscription. No more excuses." Deke sipped coffee. "What's the status with Petrov?"

"I went to his place last night. You know that."

Deke nodded. He knew everything, but Ryan didn't know where the surveillance equipment was located. This was partially a test to see how much Ryan would tell him. He had to make sure he could trust Ryan when they didn't have cameras and mics.

"I fucked up with the camera thing. He took my shoes off—I wasn't expecting that."

Ryan's admission pleased Deke. "And?"

"I was able to pick it up later, but I didn't have a chance to stash it anywhere. I'm sorry."

"We'll try again another time. What happened there?"

Ryan took a long drink of his coffee. "He gave me some cream for the…." He brushed his fingers across his left nipple. "It's a good thing I got the piercing. He definitely liked it."

Deke raised his eyebrows.

Ryan sipped coffee again, then looked down at the table. "And he rubbed it in for me."

"That's it?"

"And he got me off. Is that what you want to hear?" Ryan glared at Deke, eyes flashing dark. Then he looked away again.

"What else?"

"Jesus, what's it matter? He didn't fuck me if that's what you're getting at."

"It's not, but why not?" Was that why Ryan was suddenly so touchy about the subject? Because he'd failed at seducing Petrov? Deke wished he didn't find that so pleasing. Ryan was here for the operation, and he was absolutely off-limits to Deke, no matter how much spanking or flirting went on between them as part of their covers.

"He says it's too early in my training for that. Wants me to learn more first."

"So he wants you back?"

"Yes, he wants me back." Ryan turned the glare up another notch.

"Good. Keep doing what he wants."

Ryan glanced at his coffee; the whipped cream was starting to melt away. He wrinkled his upper lip and pushed the drink away. Then he got up and left without saying a word.

Deke watched him storm out.

CHAPTER 16

PETROV DIDN'T show up at Dungeon 69 that night.

The following night, Ryan was off from the club, and Petrov hadn't reserved a table. Deke went to the van to monitor Petrov. He watched Petrov scramble eggs for dinner while drinking wine and listening to opera—*Boris Godunov* if Deke's memory served. He'd heard Timothy play it for years, and they saw it performed in Seattle once. He made one phone call to a cell phone Deke would look up later. The conversation was short:

"Hello?"

"Ten tonight." Petrov hung up before he got a reply.

Deke's curiosity was piqued. He hoped this would be business. He couldn't see everything Petrov did since they hadn't put cameras in every room, but it was enough. He could do without watching the guy shower or piss. Chances were, nothing relevant to the case would happen in the bathroom.

At five to ten, Petrov's buzzer sounded, and he let his guest into the building. Deke made a note requesting a camera in the elevator, to see the comings and goings.

A few minutes later, Petrov's doorbell rang, and he went to the door and opened it. In walked Dakota, the Dungeon 69 waiter/sub who seemed most put out by Ryan's appearance. He was wearing jeans and a long-sleeved shirt. It was more clothing than Deke had seen him in before.

He knelt down in front of Petrov in the hallway, gaze on the floor.

"You're late." Petrov narrowed his eyes as he spoke, and his tone was hard.

"Yes, sir. I'm sorry, sir. The—"

"Don't make excuses."

The on-screen clock read 10:01. Deke considered that on time.

"No, sir." Dakota's shoulders hunched for a second, and then he straightened up again, still on his knees.

"You know what that means." Petrov turned away and left the room. Dakota slowly got up and followed him.

Deke switched camera views until he found them again in the dungeon room where Petrov had taken Ryan the night before.

Petrov sat in an armchair in the middle of the room, and Dakota stood, back straight, in front of him, not quite at attention but alert and waiting.

"Get undressed while I decide how to punish your tardiness."

"Yes, sir." Dakota proceeded to remove his boots and socks, which he set under a table near Petrov's chair. Then off came the pants and his shirt. He moved slowly and gracefully, showing himself off as he peeled away his clothing. Petrov grinned and nodded, making soft groaning sounds. Dakota had a nice body, a little on the thin side, but he didn't even come close to Ryan's moves. Deke thought Petrov might have a heart attack if he saw Ryan do a proper strip job.

The memory made Deke smile. It got him hard too. He had to stop thinking about Ryan.

Dakota stood wearing only his underwear, pale blue microbriefs. Petrov reached out and pulled the front down. Dakota's cock flopped forward. He wasn't hard, and Petrov seemed annoyed. He yanked the briefs off, and Dakota nearly lost his balance until they tore. Petrov tossed them away and got up, leaving Dakota standing there, visibly trembling.

Petrov sat down on a bench with a paddle he'd pulled off the wall. "You have fifteen strokes, boy."

"Fifteen?" His voice wavered as he gazed at the paddle Petrov brandished. But he meekly draped himself over Petrov's lap.

One corner of Petrov's mouth quirked, perhaps in response to Dakota's fear; then to Deke's surprise, he put the paddle aside and spanked Dakota with an open palm. Even though Deke could hear each slap echoing through the room, he sensed the boy's relief. After the fifteenth stroke, Petrov shoved Dakota off his lap, and the boy stood at attention again while Petrov inspected the state of his erection. He was only half-hard, but it seemed to please Petrov.

"You play with someone else tonight?"

"Yes, sir."

"Ah. Did you come for him?"

"Yes, sir."

"So you don't need to come again tonight."

"Oh, please, sir."

"I decide later. Not without my permission."

"Yes, sir." Dakota's voice broke as he replied.

Petrov put some cuffs on him and attached his wrists to a hook hanging from the ceiling, forcing Dakota to stand on his toes, arms stretched over his head.

Petrov retrieved the paddle and moved up close to him. He smoothed its face along Dakota's ass. Deke couldn't see very well and zoomed in. He watched as Petrov slid the paddle between Dakota's legs, pushing his thighs apart, putting him further off balance. The boy swung around, and now Deke could see he was fully hard, his cock bobbing back and forth as he tried to steady himself. His cock was already bright red, but not very big. It had one of those piercings like the tattoo guy. Petrov really was into piercings.

Petrov bounced Dakota's balls against the paddle, then quickly pulled it back and slapped it hard against one upper thigh. The sound scared Deke. It was much louder than a hand on a firm ass. Three, four, five more strokes, and Petrov muttered under his breath and put the paddle on a table.

Next he picked up a small whip, which Deke now knew was called a single tail. Petrov flicked the whip so it made a cracking sound. He stepped back and began flicking the whip along Dakota's back. Over and over he flicked, and soon, even in the dim light, Deke could see the boy's back blooming bright red, with a few raised welts here and there. Dakota moved slowly back and forth into each stroke.

When Petrov snapped at one shoulder, Dakota twisted so he was now facing Petrov and the camera. He was still hard, and Petrov flicked the whip across Dakota's chest and abs, and occasionally against his cock. When he started flinching, Petrov went to his back and ass again.

The man kept flicking, not even breaking a sweat. He got into a good rhythm; then he'd switch it up, which was when Dakota would squirm. Every now and then, the boy would groan or gasp.

The sounds were exactly the same ones Roy had made when Deke spanked him. They weren't pain, they were pleasure. Ryan had made the same sounds under Deke's hand, and he remembered how good it felt to hear them, to feel Ryan's body tremble and shudder as he grunted. Even better, Deke recalled the catch in Ryan's throat and the gasp just as orgasm overtook him and he came with Deke's hand still hard against his ass.

Deke could have come thinking about it. He was hard again. Was it the sounds Dakota made? The boy's groans dug deep into Deke's core.

"Please, sir? Please?"

Petrov stopped the flicking.

"Please? Sir, oh, pleeeeeeeese?"

Please what? Deke wondered. Petrov had stopped whipping Dakota.

"Not yet. I told you, you don't come tonight."

Dakota let out a pitiful sob. "Wouldn't that please you, sir?"

"No." Petrov unclipped Dakota's wrists and the boy tumbled onto his knees. "Very good. You can stay there. I come first."

"Yes, sir." Dakota steadied himself and went for Petrov's belt, then undid his pants. He sucked down Petrov's cock like he hadn't eaten for a month.

Petrov pushed him off. "You suck so you can get off. That does not please me. Do it slow. Make it last thirty minutes. Then maybe I let you come."

Dakota nodded and started again. He played with Petrov's cock, which was thick and slightly curved. It was surprisingly huge. It wasn't circumcised or pierced.

A noise outside the van made Deke jump. He thought it might be a homeless guy, or worse, one of the techs coming in to check the equipment. How could he explain why he was sitting here watching the suspect face-fuck another guy? Well, Deke did need to keep an eye on Petrov, for Ryan's safety. He had to know what Ryan was in for if he managed to become Petrov's favorite. This might even help him achieve that if Deke could tell him what the mark liked.

Petrov got bored with Dakota's blowjob long before the thirty minutes was up, carried the boy to the bench, and set him on hands and knees. Then Petrov put on a condom and, with no warning, thrust his cock deep into Dakota. He fucked the guy like a piston until Dakota started moaning "please" with each stroke.

How long could he last? Deke knew he should stop watching, but he really wanted to see if Dakota was going to get his orgasm. He found himself urging Petrov on, just to get Dakota his happy ending.

Petrov let out an ironically anticlimactic little grunt and pulled out. Then he made Dakota stand up straight and tall. "Now."

And damned if Dakota didn't shoot his load on command before he collapsed into an incoherent pile on the floor.

DEKE WENT home thinking about what he'd watched. He'd learned more about BDSM in the past two weeks than he'd ever wanted to, but it fascinated him. He already felt the allure, the power of it. He'd only had two very mild experiences, yet he found himself thinking about how good he'd felt in the little room with Roy and then Ryan.

Petrov was a skilled Dom, and he knew how to get what he wanted from his subs, while giving them what they wanted. But Deke realized what he'd seen wasn't very extreme. He couldn't stop thinking about sassy Ryan Griffiths kneeling for Petrov and following his every command. How could he watch that?

The thought haunted him until he fell asleep.

He woke up naked and sweaty a couple of hours later, heart pounding, unable to catch his breath.

This time it wasn't the dead children that had frightened him awake.

He'd dreamed he'd watched Ryan in Petrov's playroom. Petrov invited Deke to come in and spank Ryan till he was good and hard; then Petrov used the crop and cane on Ryan until he had painful raised welts striping his body. Then there were two Petrovs. One made Ryan suck his cock long and slow while the other fucked Ryan from behind.

Deke was handcuffed to the ceiling, and every way he turned he saw the same thing. He couldn't escape the images of both Petrovs having Ryan at the same time.

The memory of the dream churned in Deke's gut, and he ran into the bathroom to throw up.

TWO DAYS later Deke sat in Serah's office. She hadn't been there when he arrived for their 10:00 a.m. appointment, but the door was open, so he sat down to wait.

She arrived fifteen minutes late, looking like she'd run a 10K in record time. Her usually glossy blonde hair frizzed around her face, and she was out of breath.

"Glad you made yourself at home." Her tone was neutral, but Deke suspected she was annoyed.

He waited for her to finish fiddling with the folders she'd brought with her.

Without looking up she said, "Status report on Petrov? How's the romance progressing with the rent boy?"

Deke's brain flashed to Ryan on his lap as Deke spanked him, then to the way Ryan had his hands all over Deke at the suit shop. "Romance?"

"Yeah. Has Petrov fucked him yet?"

"No."

"Get this show on the road, Deke. Get the boy to wiggle his ass and use his stripper magic." She fluttered her fingers as if throwing fairy dust.

"The stuff Petrov's into—his kind of BDSM—isn't just about sex. It's about power, control."

Serah looked up from the folders and leaned forward slightly. "Go on."

"Petrov wants to control—dominate—Ryan. And apparently they don't rush these things."

"How do I justify this operation, Kane? I can't say we're footing the bill for a drug dealer with terrorist ties to get his rocks off with a former hooker unless we have some results. Show me some *results*."

"Petrov arranged to take over Ryan's sub training."

"Sub? Like submarine? Is that a euphemism for someone's dick? I'm not into all this gay sex shit, but I sure as hell hope so."

Deke shifted in his seat. He didn't want to be having this discussion. "No. It's a BDSM thing. But it means Petrov's going to be spending a lot of time with Ryan, and Ryan should be gaining Petrov's trust too."

"Great. Why didn't you lead with that?" Serah smiled for the first time since she sat down.

With her mood improving, Deke hesitated before he spoke again. "I'm kind of worried, though, Serah."

"Worried about what?"

"About Ryan. Petrov's into whips and… and pain. I think Ryan's in potential danger."

"He agreed to this. It was his idea to work at that club instead of the other one."

"Even so, I can't support this. I think now Petrov likes him, we can try—"

"Deke, this operation is making progress, moving forward, finally. Petrov is starting a relationship with the CI that can only get us more access as it progresses. We aren't going to change anything until we hit a wall."

"It's a big risk."

"It's an even bigger risk if we don't stop Petrov. We have to find out where he's moving his money. We have to get enough proof to stop him. I understand your concern for this CI. That's admirable, but he agreed to this role."

Deke opened his mouth, but Serah held up her hand.

"You're a good agent. You have great instincts. I know what happened on the Morales case hit you hard, made you question your judgment. You're just giving in to your own doubts. The only way to get over that is to stop listening to that little voice that keeps trying to sabotage you." She paused. "I have faith in your abilities. I want to keep you on my team, but the only way is if we get results on this operation. We follow the original plan until we have a concrete reason to change tactics."

Deke nodded. He'd never heard Serah express her support for him so vehemently. It raised his spirits, but it didn't quell his concerns. "Serah, thank you. But I—"

"The brass—starting but not ending with Ward—have made it crystal clear. You don't have room for any fuckups on this one. I can't support you if you do. Got it?"

He nodded again. If Ward's superiors were watching his performance now, Deke wouldn't survive anything going wrong, much less a fuckup of even modest proportions.

"Now get out of here and see if you can run down any leads from the surveillance on Petrov and his buddies."

Deke left Serah's office and made his way to his own desk in a daze. He returned to a stack of paper three inches high: printouts of the surveillance transcripts. He'd asked for hard copies since reading on a computer gave him a headache.

With a fresh refill of only slightly burnt coffee, Deke started on the first stack of transcripts. It was tough reading. A computer program transcribed the audio, and it had trouble with foreign accents and slang. Just trying to figure out how to interpret some of the phrases was headache inducing. The conversations in Russian hadn't been translated, and neither of the regular translators was available this week. Even Serah didn't have enough pull to get her boss to prioritize their reports.

So much for the Bureau backing him 100 percent.

Maybe Ryan could look at these and find something useful for Deke to follow up. The plan brightened Deke's mood. He'd power through these and choose the best way to make contact with Ryan later.

Petrov wasn't planning to be at the Dungeon tonight, according to Ryan, and it was too risky for Deke to show up too. He didn't want to be obtrusive and risk the rest of the staff getting too curious about his not-so-random appearances.

That was only part of it. Deke didn't want to put Ryan off his game if he thought he was being watched.

Deke started on the first transcript, fighting to concentrate on the words.

Not going to Dungeon 69 tonight meant he didn't have to watch Ryan flirting or playing with the other clients—the ones he didn't need to please, except as part of his cover.

And not going meant Deke wouldn't have to keep himself from finding a reason to get Ryan into the little booth again.

He blinked as the words on the page blurred into incoherence and his breath got shallow. He shifted in his chair as his cock started filling at the image of Ryan's naked ass perched across his lap.

DEKE WAS on the fourth transcript when his cell phone buzzed. It was just after six, and he'd barely noticed the time.

"Kane."

"Babe, dinner's almost ready. I hope you're on the way?"

"Timothy?" Deke racked his brain for the context of this call.

"Don't tell me you forgot about dinner. You're spending so much time on this new assignment, I know you're not eating well. We planned this last week." Timothy huffed on the other end. "I should have called to confirm. Should I eat without you?"

"No. I'm leaving the office in five. Sorry, just caught up in this case."

"You can tell me all about it over dinner."

Deke locked the transcripts and his notes in his desk and headed home. He only vaguely remembered Timothy calling to arrange dinner, one of their prearranged "dates" while they were having some downtime in their relationship. Really, it was a way for Timothy to gauge if Deke had recovered enough from his PTSD to be capable of resuming a normal relationship.

Timothy still had a key to Deke's—the apartment they'd once shared. It had a great kitchen, so it made sense for him to cook dinner here. It would have made more sense for Deke to move out, but Timothy was the one who'd said he needed a change.

Deke opened the door to aromas of roasting chicken, garlic, and a medley of fresh herbs. Soft jazz played in the background, and the table was set with the nice dishes Timothy's mother had given them two Christmases ago. Timothy had gone all out. He came out of the kitchen as Deke locked the door and gave him a hug and a peck on the lips. Then he moved in for a real kiss, catching Deke off guard. Timothy tasted like lemon and peppermint. The kiss was unexpected, and Deke dropped his messenger bag.

"Now that's the kind of reaction I like," Timothy said with a grin. He helped Deke out of his jacket, reminding him of the way Ryan had touched him at the suit shop under the guise of helping him into the jacket.

"Why are you in such a good mood tonight?" Deke asked as Timothy led him to the couch and handed him a glass of wine.

"Sounds like your operation is going well. I'm glad you landed this high-profile case. It's a good sign everything is getting back to normal."

Deke sipped the wine. It was white. Deke didn't know one white wine from another, but Timothy was really into wine. "This is fantastic. What is it?"

"Sauvignon blanc. I knew it was one of your favorites."

Deke smiled, wondering how he'd gotten that impression. And why did it feel like Deke had walked into a Stepford scene? They'd split up, even though neither had officially declared a breakup. They'd had these little dinners every few weeks, but it felt like they were simply weaning themselves away from each other, until tonight.

"Dinner's ready, but I can leave it warming…."

Deke noticed Timothy had brought his overnight bag, another regular feature of these dinners. It saved both of them from having to deal with the hassle of finding bed partners. The bedroom had been the one place they'd never had any trouble.

Except for Deke's nightmares.

But neither had any complaints about the pre-bedtime activities.

"I'm actually starving," Deke said. He hadn't expected the look of disappointment on Timothy's face.

"Sure. Have a seat and I'll bring everything out."

"I'll help."

"No. It's fine."

Deke sat at the table, sipping wine and feeling like a dick for not wanting to fuck Timothy before dinner.

Timothy served, and they made small talk as they ate.

"Tell me what's going on with you?" Timothy asked as he pushed his plate away. He'd nearly finished his food.

Deke stared at his own half-eaten meal. "This case is starting to make some progress, but I'm not counting my chickens yet."

"Which chickens?"

When Deke didn't respond, Timothy stared at him until he broke down. "Serah said I could be back permanently. Maybe even back on track."

"On track? You mean back in line for a promotion?"

Deke wished he had learned to play chess. He should have seen this coming. "She didn't say that."

Timothy took a sip of wine with no trace of emotion on his face. Had he really gotten over it? Deke's disaster on the Morales case hadn't just resulted in a major Bureau publicity clusterfuck and derailed his mental health, it had fucked up the promotion he was slated for, which would have sent him to Quantico to serve on a high-profile task force. Timothy had tentatively accepted a job offer at a law firm there. It had been a common topic of argument for the first month after the incident. But now he let the topic drop.

"How's your work going?" Deke asked, then wished he hadn't. Timothy's career progression had hit a roadblock, and he needed to move to a more prestigious law firm for greater upward potential.

"They offered me a partnership again." He left unsaid that he was expected to accept or move on. "They offered me a spot on the team defending Romulo. I passed." Romulo had been running a child sex-trafficking ring in Portland. Deke had done some preliminary work on that case until taking the lead on Morales. He should have stayed put.

"Did they really think you'd bite?"

"The signals are getting progressively less subtle. But there's an opening at the U.S. Attorney's office. I'm going for that."

"That's great. You'd be perfect there, Timothy." Deke found something he could be genuinely pleased at and held up his glass for a toast.

"It's not like I have the job yet."

"To new opportunities, then." They clinked glasses and sipped. For a few minutes, it almost felt like they were a real couple again. Or had too much happened? Deke frowned.

"What's wrong, Dan?" Timothy didn't care for nicknames. He thought using Deke's real name was more intimate than the nickname everyone else used.

"Nothing."

"Don't lie. Something's wrong, and I get the impression my being here is making it worse." He stood up and reached for the plates.

Deke reached for Timothy's wrist. "No. You're not. I'm just really preoccupied. I know you don't want to hear about my work."

Timothy sat back down. "Tell me. Really. I do want to hear. I'm over any and all animosity I have about your job. I do care about you, though."

"This case I'm working on. I've got a CI in what could be a dangerous situation. He's getting close to the suspect, and Serah's pressuring me to leave him in."

"Does he know about the danger?"

"Yes, but that's not the point."

"I understand. But if he knows, he has a chance to protect himself, right?"

Deke nodded. "I suppose."

"Does he want to get out?"

"I haven't asked him."

"You're worried, but he isn't?" Timothy was taking this more seriously than Deke expected. It must be the lawyer in him, getting at the problem from every angle. It wasn't a bad strategy.

"Yes."

"You could tell him what you're worried about, and see if he agrees. If so, then you can formulate a solution."

"Good idea. You always were good at helping me find the right thing to do." Deke sighed.

"I can see you're tense. Let me give you a massage. It'll help you relax."

Deke smiled and nodded. That sounded perfect right about now. If he could relax, he might get in the mood for Timothy's other agenda that night.

They clasped hands and went into the bedroom they'd shared for four years. They moved easily into each other's arms. They kissed, slow, familiar, comfortable kisses as they slid out of their clothes and into bed.

"Roll over," Timothy said and reached into the drawer for the massage oil. He squeezed some into his hand and spread it across his palms, then started in on Deke's shoulders.

"Mmmm," Deke moaned. He'd missed this. He needed this right now.

Timothy gave him a decent back massage, then rolled Deke onto his back and straddled his hips. He leaned forward and they kissed again, while he slid his oiled hands down Deke's chest, pinching his nipples and then reaching for his cock.

Nothing happened.

"Sorry, I'm not good company tonight—in any capacity."

Timothy shook his head. "It's okay. I was being a little pushy about this. I'm sorry."

He lay down next to Deke, and they wrapped their arms around each other.

"Did you meet someone else, Dan?" Timothy whispered, mouth an inch away from Deke's.

"Not exactly."

"Tell me." Timothy ran his finger along Deke's arm. "Really."

Deke exhaled. They had always been honest with each other. Even though they'd separated, there was still affection, even if the love might have stretched too thin. Timothy meant it when he asked.

"It's not so much meeting someone as finding myself in a new situation that's confusing."

"What kind of situation?"

"This case I'm working. The suspect is into BDSM. I've never been curious—you know—but now I have gotten involved to a degree."

"What does that mean?"

"I'm spending time at one of the gay bondage clubs, and to keep my cover, I had to play a little bit."

Timothy nodded, raising his eyebrows. "What kind of play?"

"Spanking."

"You let someone spank you?"

Anyone else would have laughed or joked, but Timothy didn't make Deke feel uncomfortable or embarrassed. "No, I spanked a couple of guys. I kind of liked it. And that's what's confusing me."

"Nothing wrong with that."

"Isn't there?"

"Why should there be?"

"I felt wrong liking it. I know they wanted it, and I hit them hard."

"Did they like it?"

"They both got off on it."

Timothy's eyebrows went up again. "From spanking? Nothing else?"

"I didn't even touch their dicks. It surprised me. And the second time, making that guy come from smacking his ass a few times got me off too." Deke felt his face heat up.

"Would you like to spank me?"

"No!" Deke recoiled at the suggestion.

"Okay. But why did that upset you so much?"

Deke looked into Timothy's eyes. It had been a genuine question, not a dig. "When you touched me, I didn't react. What if now I need to do something more extreme just to get excited? I'm scared of that."

Timothy reached out and pulled Deke's head to his chest, stroking his hair and neck.

Deke needed all his willpower not to cry. He was so fucking confused and disgusted with himself. He hated how he responded to watching Petrov play with his subs.

"It's okay, Dan. There's nothing wrong with trying things out. That's normal."

"I don't feel normal."

"Look at it this way: lots of people do these things. If it were wrong, it would be illegal by now."

"That doesn't help much."

"I'm here if you want to talk. No judging."

"Thanks."

They stayed up late talking about sex and love and their past and future. Deke fell asleep still wrapped in Timothy's arms.

In the morning they made love before the sun rose, slow and sweet, like when they'd first fallen in love.

When Deke kissed Timothy good-bye, he knew that was the very last time they would be lovers. But they could remain dear friends for the rest of their lives.

CHAPTER 17

THE NEXT night, Deke went to Dungeon 69. He wanted to arrange for Ryan to look over the Russian transcripts. He went early, before Petrov usually showed up, but there was no reserved sign on the usual table.

Ryan was wearing chocolate-brown leather shorts that looked good with his tanned skin.

Deke ordered a Perrier with lemon from Dakota, who had on tight white latex shorts. Deke could see the outline of his cock piercing when he presented himself after serving the drink. Tonight he had chains dangling from his nipple piercings.

"Would you like to play tonight, sir? There are some new single tails in. You might enjoy trying them out." He left a play slip and menu on the table when Deke dismissed him.

Deke flipped the menu open like a normal customer. He noted that Dakota had put his limits sheet in there. He didn't actually have many limits from what Deke could see. Rio's list was in there too, and he didn't offer single-tail play. Ryan had explained Luke's rules for brand-new subs. So Dakota's mention of the single tails must be his sales pitch. Clearly, he was feeling the effect of the clients preferring to play with Rio.

Deke almost felt guilty requesting a light flogging session with Rio. But he needed to talk to Ryan, and this was the easiest way. Dakota spotted him filling the slip out and came over and kneeled.

"Yes, sir?"

Deke handed him the menu and slip. Gary came over with the paperwork, and Deke went into the last room to wait for Ryan.

"Yes, sir." Ryan stood in front of him at attention. "How can I please you?" He didn't even crack a smile.

"You're getting awfully good at that. Enjoying yourself?"

"Yes, sir."

"You don't have to give me the full treatment, Ryan."

Ryan sat on Deke's lap. "Aren't you going to flog me?"

"You do deserve it for such bad behavior, but I won't." Deke shook his head. "That's not what I want from you."

"Maybe I'd like it."

"That's exactly why I won't." Only one of the reasons, and Deke wouldn't let Ryan know the other: how much *Deke* would enjoy it.

"You are already learning how to be a Dom, you know?" Ryan stood up but didn't back out of Deke's personal space.

He smelled like leather and musky arousal, and his plump, perky nipples were inches from Deke's lips. Deke cleared his throat.

"The Russian translator is overloaded. Could you listen to some of the recordings and let me know if there's anything important?"

Ryan nodded. "Sure. When and where? I hope you don't expect me to go to your office."

Deke was pleased Ryan hadn't said "FBI" or "the Federal building."

"Your new beau may be watching your place already. Can you come to my apartment tonight after work?"

"To listen to your tapes? Is that like showing me your etchings?"

Deke shook his head, seriously reconsidering the wisdom of his plan. But Ryan was right, it was dangerous at this point to bring him to the office. "Here's the address." He put a napkin he'd written the information on into Ryan's hand and stood up.

"But you still have fifteen minutes left. It will look suspicious." Ryan couldn't suppress his flirty grin.

"Boy, you have earned yourself a spanking."

"Oh, goody!"

"Somehow I don't think that's the appropriate response."

"What about this?" Ryan slid the shorts off, giving Deke a close-up view of his erection.

Deke took a deep breath. "Over my knees." Why bother to fight it?

TWO HOURS later, Ryan pulled up outside of Deke's apartment building on his motorbike. He went around to the parking lot in back and buzzed Deke's apartment, then took the stairs up to the second floor.

The apartment was sparsely furnished but clean and mostly tidy. Aromas of Thai food lingered in the kitchen area as Deke brought Ryan in to sit at the dining room table.

"I've got the equipment set up here. The audio clips are on this laptop. Headphones, pads, paper, whatever you need." He seemed a little on edge, moving his hands a lot as he spoke. He'd changed out of the black jeans he'd worn to the club and now had on worn gray sweats and an FBI T-shirt that was probably a size too small. Maybe he had an identity crisis if he didn't wear some FBI gear all the time.

Deke opened the application and loaded the first clip for Ryan.

"You can change the speed on this playback… faster, slower or—" Deke moved the cursor around the control panel, focusing his attention on the equipment as if afraid to look at Ryan.

"Could I get something to drink?" Ryan interrupted.

"Sure. What do you want? I have almost anything, except yak's milk."

"And that's just what I was in the mood for." Ryan cocked his head and peered at Agent Cowboy in his native habitat. "Has anyone ever asked for yak's milk?"

"Actually, yes. My old b—a friend asked for some the first time he came to my place." Deke didn't say more, but Ryan could see he wished he hadn't begun the story. There was plenty of emotion surrounding that story, from a world Ryan didn't belong in. Ryan didn't have any old boyfriend stories. Sharing an old trick anecdote wasn't in the same league.

"A beer would be my second choice."

"Coming right up."

Ryan sat down at the table and watched Deke go into the kitchen and pull a beer out of the fridge. He put it on the counter, then opened a cabinet.

"Hey, I don't need a gl—" Ryan stopped as he watched Deke reach upward, the T-shirt riding up and exposing a strip of flesh between his navel and the top edge of Deke's sweats. The hint of an elastic waistband was visible as the sweats slid lower on his hips. Ryan hoped Deke was going for a glass on the very top shelf. He stared, enjoying the view. Usually, the guys Ryan got to see naked really needed to keep their clothes on. It made a nice change to get an eyeful of a well-built body like Deke's.

Deke got the glass he wanted and poured beer into it, then headed back into the dining room. "Thanks for helping out with this. I know it's not part of your obligations to us. I'll put in a request for payment at the rate we pay the outside translators."

"You don't have to do that."

"It's only fair. It's in the budget. You might as well get what you deserve."

"Another spanking?"

Deke's face colored. He genuinely blushed. Ryan never saw that in his normal world of strippers and sex for money. The guys he had as clients were never ashamed of their needs and desires. Agent Cowboy was a refreshing change in so many ways.

"Well, I probably didn't need to do that today. I'm sorry. It wasn't... respectful."

"It was the most respectful treatment I've gotten. And it's okay to like it. That's what keeps Dungeon 69 in business, remember?"

"It still doesn't feel right."

Ryan looked into Deke's eyes just long enough to take a good read on him. Deke was uncomfortable with his attraction to Ryan, but he was definitely interested. It would be so easy to use a couple of tricks on him and end up in bed. It would be too easy. Ryan could use a good fuck. It had been over a month, and Agent Cowboy pushed all of his hot buttons. But it wouldn't be a good idea. It would be great until it was over, but then Deke's overactive need to be respectful would kick in and make him miserable. Deke would be worse off afterward.

No, best not to tease the gorgeous FBI agent.

Ryan shrugged, put on the headphones, and clicked Play. It was Petrov and another guy talking on the phone about real estate. Ryan started taking notes.

Deke watched him write for a few minutes, then moved over to the couch and picked up a book.

Ryan sped up the playback since it didn't require much concentration. He took notes as he listened. When it was over, he clicked on the next file in the folder. This discussion was about buying some clothing. Ryan glanced over at Deke, still on the couch reading, then focused on the translation again.

He'd been there a little over an hour and was on the fifth tape when the shouting began.

DEKE OPENED his eyes to find himself in bed, head in Ryan's lap. Ryan peered down at him, eyes wide, hands smoothing Deke's hair.

Disoriented, Deke blinked and looked around. Then he realized he was naked. He chanced looking at Ryan again and calmed a little. He didn't see the disgust he'd expected to find in Ryan's eyes. The concern and fear in Ryan's expression and the gentleness of his touch surprised Deke.

"Go back to sleep. It's okay."

Deke sat up. He pulled the sheets over his lap. "Wh—? What—" But he didn't need to ask. He'd had the nightmare. He had that familiar hot-cold clammy feeling, but this time nausea joined in because he'd done it in front of Ryan.

"I wasn't sure what to do. I didn't know if I should wake you up or not."

"Shit. I'm sorry. You can leave. I'm fine now."

"You're still shaking. I can't leave you like this."

"Please, just go." Deke couldn't look Ryan in the eye. He wanted to be alone right now.

"I'll go when you're sleeping soundly."

"I don't need a fucking mother hen." Deke saw Ryan flinch at the volume and the meaning of the words, and he wished he could take them back. Ryan hadn't had a helpful, supportive family. He'd been on the streets—literally or figuratively—since he was about twenty. It was a miracle he had any compassion in him at all. Deke should feel grateful for the concern. "Sorry. I'm sorry. I'm just...."

"Let me get you some water. Try to relax. I'd offer a backrub, but I know you'd take that the wrong way, and it wouldn't do you any good." He left, and Deke felt like more of a shit.

Ryan came back a few minutes later with a glass of water and some paper towels. He took the glass when Deke was done, then sat on the edge of the bed and wiped his brow with the cold compress. It felt really good. Soothing. Ryan's touch was comforting and gentle. Deke felt his heart rate returning to normal and his nerves losing that painful edge that made him hate to go to bed every night.

Deke held on to Ryan's wrist loosely and closed his eyes. The images didn't return. Ryan hummed a song Deke had never heard before, but it helped him calm down. Now he felt safe enough to let go of Ryan's wrist, but he didn't.

He opened his eyes. Ryan was still there at the edge of the bed.

"Deke, are you okay? Do you want to talk about it?" Ryan asked, his voice soft, caring.

It was the first time he'd asked, and it made Deke think the offer was genuine. Despite what Deke had put this guy through, Ryan still wanted to help him. The realization hit Deke like a tidal wave, and the next thing he knew he was sobbing.

It only lasted a minute, and Ryan stroked his hair instead of running for the door.

"Tell me," Ryan said when it was over.

"There was a case I worked on earlier this year...." And Deke told Ryan everything. About the kids, about his part in it, about the nightmares and the desk duty. He didn't mention Timothy or the psych eval or that if Ryan didn't get Petrov's complete and utter trust, Deke would be lucky to get a job checking boarding passes at the airport.

Until now, Deke hadn't told anyone except the Bureau shrink and Timothy. Today, with Ryan, was the first time it felt good to let it all out. He reined in the tears this time, but Ryan still held on.

AFTER TELLING his story, Deke fell asleep almost immediately. Ryan watched Deke sleeping from a chair near the bed. He was tired, but his brain was still on alert. Every time Deke shifted or made a sound, Ryan's heart raced and he reached out toward the bed. He hoped Deke wouldn't start shouting again. The memory of that alone kept Ryan from falling asleep, but the pain in Deke's voice and his despondency over what had happened made Ryan want to stay.

He'd heard and seen people react like that, but they'd mainly been homeless people he'd shared a shelter with, and once a guy Ryan had seen in the ER as he waited to get patched up after a trick had beaten him up. The nurse had told him it was PTSD when he'd asked about the man—a Gulf War veteran.

Deke could be a vet. He'd been through something awful, and his brain wouldn't let go. But he'd calmed down when Ryan sat with him. It was good to help someone, to be needed for something other than as a plaything.

Since he couldn't sleep and he didn't want to leave, Ryan grabbed the laptop and brought it into the bedroom. He could keep an eye on Deke and work on the remaining tapes.

More of the same. One of the men talking real estate with Petrov sounded familiar, but Ryan couldn't place the voice. It was likely a man he'd only heard speaking English, and his ear for Russian wasn't attuned enough to connect the voices.

During a break he decided to do something he should have done sooner. He went onto the Internet and googled Special Agent Daniel Kane. There were dozens, hundreds, of results.

Ryan chewed his lower lip and glanced over at Deke, feeling guilty but wanting to know.

An hour later he knew everything relevant about the Morales investigation and Deke's role in the botched raid that had killed two kids on the outskirts of town. He'd gone from one step away from a coveted promotion to suspension, while his partner, already close to retirement age, left the Bureau.

It wasn't difficult to fit together the pieces, and Ryan now understood almost everything that mattered about Deke: the nightmares, his need for results, and why he lived in a half-furnished apartment with a very big bed.

When the first licks of light brightened the sky, Ryan took the laptop back to the dining room. He could leave before Deke ever knew he'd stayed. He grabbed his jacket and headed for the front door.

"Don't tell me you stayed all night."

Ryan was halfway to the door. He turned around to see Deke standing there, clutching a towel around his waist. His hair stuck up in all directions, but he looked like he'd finally gotten some rest.

"I wanted to finish those recordings."

Deke stared at him for a moment, and Ryan stared back, daring him to question the excuse. They locked gazes, and again something unspoken passed between them.

"Thanks." Deke didn't need to say anything more. Ryan understood.

"The notes are on top of the laptop." Ryan turned toward the door again.

"Want some coffee?"

The unmistakable longing in Deke's voice prompted Ryan to stay, for reasons that had nothing to do with Maksim Petrov. "Love some."

"The machine's automatic. Should be ready by the time I'm out of the shower, if you can wait."

"I can wait."

DEKE HANDED Ryan a mug of steaming coffee. "Sorry I don't have any of that whipped cream shit you like." His hair was wet and he wore a shirt, tie, and trousers, all dressed up for another day behind an FBI desk, a far cry from the sexy bad-boy look he sported at the club, or the wide-eyed, terrified look following the nightmare.

Ryan grinned and took a sip. "How the hell do you make this? It's strong enough to put hair on your balls."

"Oh, that explains it." Deke sat across from Ryan at the table and let out a laugh.

Ryan joined in, and they sat there for a full minute laughing their asses off. Then, just as suddenly, they were both silent again.

"Ryan, I'm sorry about last night." Deke's voice quavered slightly, and he gulped down some more coffee.

"Are you okay? Really okay?"

Deke stared into his coffee for a moment as if expecting to find the answer in the mug. "Yeah. Ninety-nine percent of the time. Especially this morning."

"Probably better than average."

"You think?"

"Unfortunately, I know." Ryan sipped his coffee, wishing he didn't.

AT HIS desk later that morning, Deke read over the notes Ryan had made from the audio clips and compared them to the notes and transcripts from the Bureau translator. The content seemed similar to other conversations, so he could probably trust Ryan's work. He didn't really have any incentive to lie.

Most of it looked like useless real-estate discussions. One thing caught his attention, however: Petrov was planning to go to Vancouver in two weeks, to meet with the whole real-estate investment team, including his mortgage broker, a Realtor, and someone he referred to as "Security."

What would that meeting really be about? Deke hoped Ryan could get Petrov to take him along.

It was only much later that Deke let himself analyze what had happened between them the night before. He'd shown Ryan too much of himself, exposed his weaknesses and vulnerability. How would that affect the investigation? Or the distance he needed to keep from Ryan in order to do his job?

By the end of the day, Deke was exhausted, so he had Agent Campbell go to Dungeon 69 in his place. Campbell had been to the club several times already, sometimes overlapping with Deke's visits. Ryan didn't know about Campbell, by design. It was a way to keep an eye on the CIs without seeming to.

Feeling guilty for not going to the club, Deke brought the Petrov file home and pored over it yet again, looking for a missed angle or lead. He fell asleep on the couch, and when he woke, dawn was just streaking the sky.

He hadn't had the nightmare for the first time in months.

Chapter 18

TWO DAYS later Deke was feeling better than ever. The nightmare hadn't come back, and he missed Ryan. Dwelling on how he'd acted that night was useless. He needed to move forward without feeling any shame or regret over opening up to Ryan. Given how Ryan left himself open and vulnerable every day to help the FBI gather evidence on Petrov, it seemed a fair exchange.

Deke went to Dungeon 69 after work and sat in Ryan's section.

Ryan was serving drinks to a table full of men. He let each man play with his nipple ring for a moment or two, flashing a smile at all of them.

He came up to Deke. "You're next. Let me just place these orders." Then he was gone in a flash.

When he came back, Ryan stepped right up to Deke in the way the subs were trained to stand for the Doms. But Ryan swiveled his hips coyly and smiled at Deke.

Was it his imagination, or was it a brighter smile than the other group received?

Ryan started right up where he'd left off after that spanking on Deke's last visit. "How can I please you tonight, sir?"

Deke had to stop himself from blurting out precisely how. He stared at Ryan, tonight in a pair of tight shorts that perfectly outlined his cock. "A beer. Draft IPA, if you've got it."

"Yes, sir. Would you like to give it a tug?"

Deke couldn't help that his gaze shot to Ryan's cock.

Ryan smiled and pushed his chest out. The nipple ring shone under the lights.

It was part of the cover, Deke told himself as he reached out, brushing his fingertips across Ryan's pec, and took hold of the nipple ring. It was warm.

"Pull it. It doesn't hurt."

Deke tugged. The nipple plumped further. He played with it a little more and realized Ryan was getting hard. He hadn't when the group had touched him.

Ryan gave him another smile and their gazes met, a more intimate look than he'd given the others.

"I'd like a play slip."

"I'll be right back with that." Ryan spun away. Today he had crisscrossed welts on his back and thighs. No telling what the shorts covered up.

Deke shuddered, and his good mood ebbed away.

Ryan served drinks to the large table first, making a show of putting wristbands on each one and earning extra tips; then he returned to Deke's table. He put the beer down, attached a wristband, then slid the play slip over to him and waited, standing at attention. Deke looked at him, shoulders straight, chest out, nipples hard, and the outline of a hard-on visible through the thin fabric of the shorts, waiting for whatever Deke wanted. He could understand the allure of being a Dom.

He filled in the slip, requesting Ryan for half an hour of "various activities," then slid the paper back across the table before picking up his beer.

A few minutes later Luther came over to his table.

"Hi, Daniel, nice to see you here again. You're getting to be a regular."

"I like the atmosphere. Still getting my bearings, though."

"We've got classes, you know. You want to try your hand at some different activities, that's the way to start."

"Thanks. I'll check that out."

"All on the website." Luther looked Deke over. "You wanted a session with Rio tonight?"

"Yeah."

"I'll let you have this one, but he's got a new Dom who doesn't like for him to play with nonmembers anymore. Worried it might set his training back."

Deke sipped his beer, trying to process the information. "But tonight's okay?"

"Yeah. Rio says he liked playing with you the other day. But no marks on him that his new Dom wouldn't like."

"Got it."

"You should think about joining." Luther stood up.

"I will. Thanks." Deke raised his glass to Luther, who headed back through the staff door. Deke left his beer, nearly untouched, and went into the small room at the end.

Five minutes later Ryan entered after a soft knock.

"How would you like me?" he asked.

"Just sit down. I'm here to talk to you."

"No thanks."

"Sit. You make me nervous hovering like that."

"I'll stand."

Something in his tone caught Deke's attention. "It's not part of your training, is it?"

Ryan shook his head.

"Come here. Turn around." Deke had Ryan stand so he could see his back. Up close in the light, he could see the welts were dark ridges. He could see welts along Ryan's ass through the skintight shorts. "Ryan, when did this happen?"

"Last night."

"And you still have marks? Do you need a doctor? Petrov—"

"It wasn't him. It was someone else."

"I'll kill him."

"My hero." The tone was playful.

"Who...?"

"Another Dom. I botched the lesson on purpose. He punished me, and Petrov nearly ripped his arm off. Spent the next hour tending to me. Now Petrov doesn't want anyone else to touch me. It's a good thing."

"Fucking crazy plan. You're supposed to tell me what's going on. Where did this happen? At Petrov's?" Surveillance hadn't reported that Ryan visited Petrov's again.

"Here, on the other side of the club in one of the member-only playrooms. They don't allow you in if you've been drinking."

"You're okay?"

"Yes. And with Petrov training me, I'll be at his place more. That's what you wanted, right?"

"But not at this expense."

"You should find a way to punish me." Ryan grinned.

"I can't exactly spank you now, can I?"

"How about a blowjob?"

"How is that a punishment?"

Ryan shrugged. "It depends how big your dick is." He reached a hand out, and Deke caught it, smiling.

"Do you ever stop?"

"Do you ever relax?"

Deke stared at Ryan. "Sure."

"No, you don't. I don't think you *can*. You're always planning something or analyzing the results of your plan, or worrying about when the plan will work. A blowjob is something you don't have to plan. Something you can just enjoy. Not something you *need* to do, or something you think you're supposed to do. And not for someone else. Just for you."

Ryan knelt down between Deke's knees.

Deke put his hands on Ryan's shoulders, stopping him from moving. "Yes, I can do something just because I want to." He pulled Ryan in close and pressed his mouth to Ryan's.

Ryan let out a little gasp and melted into Deke's arms, opening his mouth.

Deke kept the kiss gentle to start. A first taste so sweet he had to have more. He increased the pressure on Ryan's soft, full lips, which felt even better than Deke had imagined. And his tongue was velvety smooth as Deke's touched and tangled.

The kiss went on for a long time, and when Deke let go, it was a feat of willpower. He was hard as a rock, and when Ryan stepped back, Deke saw he was in the same condition.

"Thank you," Deke whispered, one arm still around Ryan.

"That's all you wanted from me?" Ryan whispered back, voice breaking.

Deke nodded.

Ryan turned and rushed out of the room.

Deke sat on the couch, contemplating his desire. He wanted Ryan in a way he couldn't understand. He didn't just want to fuck the guy; it was something bigger, deeper, more complicated. He wasn't quite sure what he wanted, but it hurt inside to think about him. Hurt worse to think about him with Petrov.

Ryan's words came back to him: "That's what you wanted, right?"

Ryan had given Deke what he wanted, and Deke felt like a monster.

RYAN RUSHED through the staff entrance and into the bathroom, locking the door behind him.

He couldn't hold the tears back any longer and let them out. He sobbed uncontrollably, not even sure why, until he heard a knock at the door.

"Rio, are you okay?"

"Yeah." His voice was shaky. Luther would never believe him. "I'm fine."

"What happened? Do I need to throw that guy out or call the cops?"

"What? No. He didn't do anything. Really."

"Open the door."

Ryan let Luther in.

The big man looked him up and down. "I knew I shouldn't have let you play with him. Petrov will—"

"No, Luther. Please don't tell him. I just came down really hard, and he didn't know what to do. But he didn't hurt me."

"I'll tell him not to come back."

"It's fine. He's a good tipper. Let him stay." He paused, gauging Luther's mood. "Okay, I won't play with him again." Ryan bit his lip. He shouldn't have said that, but it was probably the only way Luther would let Deke in again.

He wouldn't tell about the kiss. Petrov would make sure Deke was banned if he knew.

Luther pulled Ryan to his chest and smoothed a hand across his hair and arm, carefully avoiding the painful welts. "Come to my office."

Luther carefully put Ryan over his shoulder and carried him to the office, where he deposited Ryan on the soft couch. He gave him water and a blanket and held on to him with gentle murmurs and a delicate touch surprising in a man his size.

Ryan felt safe and warm and let himself drift close to sleep.

DEKE WENT home and changed before calling the guys on audio surveillance.

"Norris."

"Evening, Norris. Kane here. Where's Petrov?"

"He's having dinner with a guy at Petrograd, and they're talking about investing in real estate. A snoozer conversation."

"Let me know where he goes when he leaves."

"Sure thing."

Deke hoped Petrov wouldn't go to the Dungeon tonight. Luther had given Deke a warning that he wouldn't be welcome to play with the club's subs unless he became a full member and took some classes. They didn't even want him playing with other customers.

How was he going to explain to Serah why she had to authorize him to expense the membership? He needed to get back in the club. He couldn't leave that up to Campbell alone now. The couple of cameras Ryan had managed to place at Petrov's favorite table weren't enough. They had an audio feed too, but it took time to get someone in there if Ryan got into trouble.

Ryan.

Deke slammed his fist on the kitchen table. What the hell had he been thinking when he kissed Ryan? He blinked to get the images out of his brain. But the taste of him, the feel of him in Deke's arms, and the smell of him didn't go away. Nor could he forget how Ryan kissed back.

It felt so real, so perfect.

Deke reminded himself Ryan was a hustler. No matter how caring he'd been when Deke needed it, Ryan did things to please people with his body, and he was just pleasing Deke at that particular moment.

Get your head on straight!

Deke couldn't afford to get attached to Ryan for about a million different reasons, all of them good. It would cloud his judgment about this operation, potentially put both of them in danger, and it would increase the chances of Petrov figuring out Ryan was a CI plant.

Not to mention Deke would still have to not only put up with, but actually watch, a wide variety of sexual encounters between Petrov and Ryan.

There was little room for personal connection between them, and a physical relationship was grounds for severe discipline. OPR would be on his ass before he finished spelling the acronym.

This operation would function far better if Deke treated Ryan like every other CI. He was hired to do a job, and that was the limit of their interaction.

Or so it had to be from this point forward.

CHAPTER 19

THE NEXT several days went by in a blur for Ryan.

Petrov had him training every evening, sometimes in the club, other times at the dungeon in his penthouse.

He learned how to stand or kneel or display himself to Petrov's standards and whims. If he made a mistake, Petrov didn't punish him. But when Ryan did a good job, he would be rewarded. If he served Petrov dinner properly, he would get a bite or a sip of wine. Other rewards might be a caress or an embrace, or the permission to touch himself or to come.

At first Ryan simply went through the motions. He didn't feel particularly submissive, but he could pretend. If he got the FBI the information they wanted, Petrov would go to jail for the drug dealing, the money laundering, and enough other felonies that even if they couldn't connect him to Rocco's death, Ryan could handle that.

By the third day of training with Petrov, something inside of Ryan shifted. Petrov's expectations of him increased—though still he demanded nothing strictly sexual from Ryan—and it took more concentration and effort for Ryan to perform. Now it became a challenge. He wanted to succeed, to get it right, to please Petrov.

The punishments for failure began. If he made a mistake, Petrov wouldn't speak to him for fifteen minutes. Ryan had to sit on the floor, but Petrov wouldn't pet him or play with his hair. If Petrov used the flogger or paddle on him, he would stop the session just when Ryan was getting into it and craving more stimulation.

So Ryan found himself working hard to please Petrov in the smallest of ways. He wanted to earn rewards, but he wanted to avoid the punishment that came with Petrov ignoring him.

IT WAS three days since Deke had kissed Ryan. Ryan wondered why he hadn't come into the club, but he couldn't ask. He was getting drinks from Gary when Luther came up to the bar.

"Everything smooth out here tonight?" Luther asked Gary. "Need any help?"

"Got it under control," Gary said as he put a draft beer on Ryan's tray. "Just a few regulars. You seen that tall blondish guy lately? Roy's been asking about him. Danny, I think his name was."

Ryan paused before retrieving his tray and drinks.

"I kinda kicked 'im out." Luther glanced down at Ryan, then back to Gary. "He didn't know enough to play here. Told him to sign up for some classes."

"So we've seen the last of him? I'll tell Roy—"

"Actually, he signed up this afternoon. First class is on Saturday. I'll work on matching Roy up with someone suitable until Danny's cleared to play here. Thanks."

Ryan lifted his tray and headed to the table where he served a member named Dragon and two of his friends. They all took their time slipping their tips into the waistband of his shorts, not missing the opportunity to feel him up. One guy tried to pull Ryan's shorts down, and Dragon restrained him.

"Show some respect, dude. That's not cool around here. It's not a strip club."

"Sorry," the guy said to Ryan. "I can tell you have a pretty cock, and I wanted to see it."

Ryan stroked himself until he was hard—the shorts revealed every contour of his dick. "Now what do you think, sir?"

"Gorgeous. Can I get you off here?"

"No, sir. It's against the rules in the bar. And I don't think my sir would let us play in a room." Ryan glanced to Petrov's table.

Petrov was watching him with an eagle eye. He shook his head.

Ryan shrugged. "Sorry, sir. He won't mind a quick touch."

The guy grinned and rubbed Ryan a few times through the shorts. His friend glared at him until he stuffed more cash in there.

"Thank you, sir." Ryan made his way to Petrov's table. A few other customers called him over and pushed tips into his shorts. The clients tipped for hard-ons.

He presented himself to Petrov, who made him stand at attention while he played with Ryan's nipples, pinching one and tugging on the piercing in the other. It felt good. Ryan's cock swelled, and he felt heat rushing to his core.

"That man is right, you do have a lovely cock. I like to see how much you enjoy my touch." Petrov pinched Ryan's nipples harder, approaching the boundary between pleasure and pain.

Ryan's breath got shallow and his balls started to ache. "Sir." He didn't know how he could get so hard, so close to the edge, just with what Petrov was doing to his nipples. He closed his eyes, centering himself on the pressure morphing across the line into the beautiful pain.

"You've been such a good boy this week. Does my pretty pet deserve to come?"

"If that would please you, sir." The words came out of their own accord now, he'd said them so many times during the past week.

"It would. It would probably please everyone here."

Ryan opened his eyes. Everyone in the bar—fifteen or twenty people—was watching. He wanted to come because Petrov said he could, and nothing else mattered.

Petrov pointed to something. Ryan glanced across the bar without moving his head.

Dakota was coming out of one of the small playrooms. He came over to the table when Petrov beckoned. He wore a jockstrap made from the same translucent latex as Ryan's shorts. When he presented himself to Petrov, Ryan noticed his shoulders, back, and especially his ass were bright rosy red. He'd just been flogged.

"How may I please you, sir?" His gaze was on Petrov's feet, and he didn't even glance at Ryan.

"Dakota, do you like to give blowjobs?"

"Yes, sir. If it would please you, sir."

"Good. I would like one."

Dakota grinned like he'd won the lottery. "Yes, sir."

"For Rio." Petrov waved his hand in Ryan's direction.

Dakota's smile melted for a split second; then he recovered. "Yes, sir."

"Come here where everyone can see." Petrov led Ryan and Dakota to a pedestal in the center of the room. He put Ryan's wrists into cuffs hanging from the ceiling, after adjusting the height. Then he peeled Ryan's shorts down, and Ryan felt his cock spring free, heavy and throbbing. Petrov played with his piercing until Ryan's cock felt like a stone dragging him down.

"So hard, without anyone even touching it. So very, very pretty." Petrov touched Ryan's cock just enough to make it bounce a few times. Ryan couldn't help pushing against the touch, seeking friction, release, but Petrov had let go.

Murmurs of appreciation spread through the men in the bar.

"Dakota, come here." Petrov made Dakota kneel between Ryan's legs. "You be a good boy too. Make it last at least ten minutes. Don't let him come until then."

Dakota nodded. He looked up at Ryan, hatred blazing in his eyes as he opened his mouth.

"Rio, you have permission to speak or to make noise, express your pleasure."

"Thank you, sir."

Dakota took the head of Ryan's cock into his mouth and started sucking. He wasn't very careful with his teeth.

"Ow."

Petrov grabbed the back of Dakota's head and pulled him off Ryan. "You are to suck him like you suck me. Exactly the same. When you are sucking Rio, it is like you are also sucking my cock. Understand."

"Yes, sir."

Petrov let go of Dakota's head roughly. The hatred in Dakota's gaze smoldered into fear.

Dakota took Ryan's cock in again, licking it and sucking it as if savoring a delicious meal. Ryan moaned. Dakota was talented. He used his lips and tongue in creative ways, each stroke bringing Ryan close to the edge. He wasn't sure how he could last ten minutes. If he came early, who would be punished? Dakota for going too fast, or Ryan for not controlling his body better?

Probably both.

Ryan groaned and heard echoing moans from the men watching. He felt Dakota groaning too, the vibrations running up Ryan's cock and pooling at the base of his balls.

"Oh, good. So good."

"Rio, you can't see, but Dakota's cock is nice and hard. He likes sucking you. Two more minutes, boys."

Ryan was panting now—his whole body felt flushed, and the fire was spreading through his balls and ass. Dakota had lowered the pressure and gone back to gently sucking the head of his cock, making wet slurpy noises that suddenly sounded so fucking hot. Ryan heard himself moan, the sound becoming a gasp and a sob because it was just too hard to hold back the tide of pleasure.

"Not yet, sweet," Petrov said, his voice soft. "Dakota, you've been good. Made Rio feel very good. You may come too, when he does. No hands. Show me how you please me, boys."

Ryan couldn't help himself. "Please, sir, now? Now?" It had to be ten minutes by now. It was at least two from when he'd said two. Or was he teasing them? Was Ryan supposed to be paying attention to the time? Oh fuck, he wasn't going to get this one right.

"Time is up."

Ryan let go and spurted. Dakota was licking him, and some of Ryan's come went into his mouth, but the rest splattered all over his face and throat. Dakota let out a whimper and sank onto his heels.

Ryan's wrists were still secured. He felt his dick spasming, still spurting jizz on Dakota's hair and body and some on the floor. A little puddle of come spread on the pedestal between Dakota's knees.

Applause rang out in the bar. Ryan glanced around to see the crowd had grown to forty or fifty men. They must have come in from the other part of the club to watch.

Petrov unhooked Ryan's hands and pulled him into a tight hug, and Ryan melted against him. He was exhausted. But he'd done what Petrov wanted. The pleasure of that stood out in his mind, far more than the orgasm Dakota so skillfully drew from his body.

Petrov picked Ryan up.

"Luther, please look after Dakota." Petrov carried Ryan into one of the little rooms and laid him down on the couch. He gave Ryan water, then rubbed Ryan's wrists where they'd been in the cuffs. Then he stroked Ryan's hair and caressed his shoulders and the curve of his hip.

"Feel good, pet?"

Ryan nodded. "May I please you, sir?"

"You have."

"May I pleasure you?"

"You have done that too. I do not require anything else from you now."

"Yes, sir."

"Sleep, my sweet. It's okay." Petrov lay down next to Ryan and gathered him in his arms, kissing his neck and shoulders. Ryan snuggled against his warmth, feeling the whiskery brush of beard against his skin.

Petrov's soft kisses moved to his throat and chin. Ryan's heartbeat accelerated, and he pressed closer to Petrov's chest. He didn't want to receive Petrov's kiss, lest it erase the taste of Deke's kiss from his lips.

Where was Deke, Ryan wondered as he pretended to be asleep. He felt so close to Petrov right now, but something in his core was glad Deke hadn't been here to see him with Dakota, to see what he did to please Petrov.

DEKE SAT in the surveillance room at FBI HQ, watching the feed from the club.

"Jesus, Mary, and Joseph. I shoulda been fucking gay!" Brad Norris, one of the junior agents on the Petrov operation, was staring at the screen. "That was hot. Maybe I am fucking gay."

Deke was trying to get his breathing under control after watching Dakota and Ryan. The audio and video were excellent. Too good, and Deke had nearly shot his own load watching. He glanced over at Norris.

"You want me to do that to you?"

Norris furrowed his brow. "Uh, isn't that against regs?"

"Don't worry, you're not gay. If you were, you wouldn't care about regs, you'd be in my lap before I finished that sentence."

"How do—?" Norris stopped. "Oh…. Really?"

"Guilty as charged."

"Sorry, man, no offense." Norris sat up straighter and looked worried.

"None taken. But you are missing out." Deke grinned to put Norris at ease.

"Really?" Norris asked again. "I mean, you seem so…."

"What? Normal? Manly? Straight?"

"Kinda all of the above."

"I don't wear my pink lip gloss in the office." Deke grinned again. He enjoyed toying with some guys. He knew Norris hadn't meant to offend him. On his desk, the guy had a photo of himself doing an AIDS walk with a group of friends. It was Deke's ready admission that had put Norris off guard.

"I don't think pink's your color." Norris raised an eyebrow.

Deke laughed. "Probably right. I'll get your advice if I do start wearing lip gloss."

"Sounds fair."

Deke glanced up at the screen again. Petrov had carried Ryan into a room. He wasn't likely to spill any drug-dealing secrets in there. Any spills would be of an entirely different nature. He was probably in there fucking Ryan. So far they hadn't actually gotten any fucking on tape. Did Petrov know the surveillance equipment was there?

"Looks like there's nothing more happening tonight," Deke said.

Norris looked at his watch. "Eleven thirty. Would he be having a meeting after that?"

"Probably not. Go home."

"What about the summaries for Serah?"

"They can wait till morning."

"Thanks." Norris grabbed his jacket off the chair and left.

Deke took the DVD out of the recorder and labeled it with the date, location, and time before slipping it into a plastic case. He waited ten minutes, then put the case into the inner pocket of his suit jacket.

He was going to watch it a few more times when he got home.

CHAPTER 20

RYAN WAS working four days a week at the suit store and spending most evenings with Petrov. They'd had a discussion with Luke present to draw up an appropriate training plan, allowing Ryan full say in what he would and would not do and what control he would give up to Petrov. It was a part-time training contract, with Ryan having the opportunity to end the training relationship at any time by talking to Luke as a go-between.

Some nights Petrov let him work in the club bar before he arrived; other nights he gave Ryan at least as much money as he would have earned and brought him home for training.

They were working on bondage.

Petrov showed Ryan the different types of restraints, including cuffs and a few simple knots, and they discussed which ones Petrov would train him for. At first Petrov would restrain him for only short periods of time, staying close in case Ryan needed to be released. They worked up the amount of time.

Like everything so far, it was a mental challenge for Ryan to remain in the desired position or pose. He earned far more rewards than punishments. Plenty of hugs, caresses, massages, and orgasms. When Petrov gave Ryan his choice of reward one night after a perfect dinner service, Ryan asked for a flogging session.

"You want me to flog you?"

"Yes, sir."

"Now?"

"Please." Before he'd asked, Ryan hadn't known he'd wanted it. Of all the toys, the flogger was his favorite. Petrov had many floggers, and he let Ryan choose from the floggers on the bottom row on the wall. The others, Petrov told him, were too heavy, and he wasn't ready yet. Ryan selected the one with both suede and leather. He played with the soft strands before handing it to Petrov.

"A lovely choice. What a sweet pet you are." Petrov pulled Ryan into a hug and kissed his throat. Petrov's hugs were wonderful. Warm and comforting, but Ryan felt the power in the man's muscular arms. And they always got Ryan hard, though he couldn't say why.

Petrov let go of Ryan and tugged on Ryan's cock. "Already so hard, pretty one?"

Ryan kept his gaze lowered and smiled. He enjoyed everything Petrov did to him or asked him to do. Petrov still hadn't fucked Ryan, and now he wanted that so much some days he couldn't stop thinking about it.

Why hadn't Petrov done it yet? Wasn't Ryan good enough for him? The worry ate at Ryan for days at a time. It made him strive harder to please Petrov.

Petrov put Ryan into the cross and trailed the flogger across his shoulders and ass.

It felt good. The strands felt soft and silky against Ryan's skin. He felt goose bumps rise in the wake of the strands; then a heated flush set in from anticipation.

Petrov moved back a step and let the flogger come down on each shoulder. He started very slowly. Too slowly. Gradually, he increased the pace and force of each blow, varying the spot where the strands would strike. Ryan felt the flush blooming, and he went into the zone, floating in a sea of sensation that became almost no sensation. Someone else heard each blow and felt the sting. Ryan was at peace. His mind blanked, and he stopped worrying about Petrov and Gregory and suits and drugs and whether his feet were in the right place. He gave up conscious thought, let Petrov have complete control.

Everything felt just right for this brief period of time.

How long since he'd felt this good being out of control?

Since Agent Cowboy kissed him in the little playroom at Dungeon 69.

CHAPTER 21

THE NEXT night was Deke's first class at Dungeon 69. He was an official member, but he wasn't allowed into the member-only playrooms until he'd taken at least three classes, and he wasn't allowed to play with the club's subs until he'd had at least one class taught by Luke or Luther.

He'd signed up for the next three available classes.

Tonight was a spanking class. Serah had laughed her ass off when he explained Luther's demands. It sounded hilarious when she didn't know about Deke kissing Ryan in the playroom. She would never know.

So Deke showed up on time with an enthusiastic smile.

There were seven guys in the class, including two couples. Luther lectured in the front of one of the demo rooms on the members' side. He discussed the history of spanking and the definition of erotic spanking, including use as punishment or even as a reward.

By the end of the first fifteen minutes, Deke had decided there wasn't anything wrong with enjoying either side of a good spanking, and he was ready to bend over for Luther, despite the guy not being his type at all. But he was a good speaker and clearly really had a passion for spanking.

Then he brought in a sub for a demo—Phoenix, whom Deke had met on his first visit—to illustrate the basics of spanking, where to spank, where not to, and the effect of different techniques, then aftercare.

"Hands-on practice!" he said after the demonstration. Everyone chuckled at the double meaning.

There were three guys on their own and the other two looked at Deke, then chose each other. One was a saggy middle-aged guy with a receding hairline, and the other was a burly bear wearing just a leather vest and leather jockstrap. He had the saggy guy over his lap pretty quickly, and Deke was left standing alone, like the cheese in that kid's song.

Luther came up to him. "Hi, Dan. I'd offer to partner with you, but I don't bottom for anyone. Sorry. And I don't think you want a spanking from me, do you?" He grinned good-naturedly, and Deke chose to consider it a rhetorical question. "I'll find someone for you to practice on." He whistled through his fingers. "Everyone else hang on for a few minutes. We're going to do this one step at a time together. When I get back. Got it?"

Nods and a chorus of agreement rang out.

Deke stood around feeling like a loser while everyone else tried not to stare at him. A guy in one of the couples gave him a wistful look that cheered Deke up, as if the guy wished he could have Deke spank him instead of the guy he'd arrived with.

A few minutes later, Luther came in with Dakota following. Deke would have preferred pairing up with anyone but Dakota. But as the men got closer, Deke realized it wasn't Dakota after all.

It was Ryan.

Now Dakota seemed like a better idea after all.

"Your lucky day, Danny Boy. Rio's free. I know you like playing with him, and this way I can monitor. It's the only chance you'll get because his trainer is very strict."

Ryan knelt down in front of Deke and presented himself. "Good evening, sir." He didn't make eye contact with Deke and had clearly advanced in his training, a little too much in Deke's opinion.

"Hello, Rio."

Luther stood on a chair. "Okay, people, get started. I want to hear you talking safe words, limits, you know the drill, even if you are married. Let's go."

Deke selected a chair and called Ryan over. "No need to kneel. What are your words?"

Ryan stood. "Daffodil and carnation, sir."

"You don't need the 'sir.'"

"Okay."

Luther gave the next command. "Subs, strip down."

Ryan wore skintight gold lamé shorts of fabric so thin Deke would be able to see the veins on his cock when he got hard. At the moment he wasn't. He twisted slightly at the waist because they unzipped on the side. Deke noticed some of the other men watching him and Ryan.

By the time Ryan had his shorts off, he had a nice erection going. Deke took a deep breath and wondered how he'd ended up here on this investigation.

Luther got the room's attention again. "We're gonna use cock rings tonight so we'll have time to practice everything before your horny little subs lose their cool. Gentlemen, put your rings on."

Ryan handed Deke a leather cock ring, and Deke stared at it, then at Ryan's erection. How was he supposed to put this on that? Under any other circumstances, he would love this opportunity, but it felt like an invasion of Ryan's privacy, no matter how many other men had had their hands on his body.

"You're a little far gone for that, aren't you?" Deke asked.

"It unsnaps." Ryan took the leather from Deke's hands, unsnapped it, and put it back. His eyes danced with mirth as he watched Deke struggling with his conscience.

Deke felt heavy gazes on his back and realized just about everyone else was watching him—or more likely Ryan. He was the only one in the room with a hard-on. Unless they could tell about Deke's state. But the other men seemed to be admiring Ryan's pleasing proportions.

Deke handed him the ring. "Put it on." He was the Dom, wasn't he?

"Yes, sir." Ryan made a big show of playing with his cock and arranging his balls as he placed the ring on and snapped it.

Deke heard one guy suck in a breath. The ring made Ryan's cock stand even straighter and taller, the veins starting to show.

"Do I please you, sir?" Ryan asked, moving just enough for his cock to bounce close to Deke's face.

"You absolutely deserve a spanking, boy," Deke said.

Was it his imagination, or did Ryan's cock swell even more at the words? He liked to think it did.

Fuck it. He was going to enjoy this. At the moment, it was part of his job.

LUTHER CONTINUED to give instructions. "Subs, you should be allowed to talk during this, to let your Doms know how it feels, what you like or don't like. Doms, you'll get more out of the session if you give them permission...."

"I suppose I don't need to give you permission since you say what you think anyway," Deke bent down to whisper in Ryan's ear. Ryan was already sprawled over Deke's lap, on top of a towel.

"You say that like it's a bad thing."

"You must earn a lot of punishments."

"Only the ones I want, and there aren't many of those."

Deke smoothed his hand over each of Ryan's buttocks, exploring the shape. He hadn't been caned or cropped lately. Tonight his ass was pristine and pale. Deke found the spots that got a reaction out of Ryan—a moan or his cock swelling more—before starting to spank. Then, without warning, he brought down his hand in a loud slap. He could see he'd caught Ryan off guard, but the stroke was more sound than force.

They practiced different strokes, had the subs shift from nonstress to stress position. In between strokes Deke smoothed his hand across Ryan's ass. He felt the heat starting.

Another slap.

"Seven," Ryan counted.

Deke flattened his hand and slid it between Ryan's cheeks like he was slicing him in half. Ryan shuddered at the sensations.

Slap. "Eight." Deke smoothed the warm bloom. He felt Ryan's breathing change, becoming shallower. Deke was having some trouble catching his own breath. He was hard, his nipples tingled, and there was no way Ryan wouldn't know how much Deke was enjoying this. Ryan liked it too.

Another hard slap. "Nine."

When they were up to fifteen, Deke delivered a particularly strong one that knocked the wind out of Ryan.

Smack. "Sixteen."

Ryan gripped Deke's thigh as number seventeen came down.

On eighteen, Ryan pressed his hips into Deke. Time to ease off a bit. Luther was hovering. "Play with him some more between strokes. You want to make it good for him."

Deke slid his fingers down Ryan's crack again.

"Try playing with his hole, Dan. Just the outside."

Deke took a breath and traced around Ryan's pucker with a fingertip. He felt Ryan tremble beneath him and let out a little moan.

"Sub, is that good?" Luther bellowed.

"Yes, sir." Ryan's voice wavered as if he didn't have enough energy to speak. "Good."

"You got him in a good place, Dan. Try some light slaps and more fingering."

Deke almost replied with "Yes, sir." He followed instructions, and more shudders wracked Ryan's body. His ass was a dark pink, as were the tops of his thighs. He practically clung to Deke.

Deke played with his ass and balls as Luther stood on a chair again. "I think you've all got your subs in a good place right now. Go ahead and finish them off. Hard smacks will get them off fast, or keep rubbing and little smacks to make it nice and slow."

"Fast or slow, Rio?"

"Yes."

"It wasn't a yes or no question." Deke chuckled. He applied short quick slaps that made Ryan's ass bounce and sent vibrations through his core—or so Luther had said. Then he slid his fingertip down Ryan's crack and made rings around his hole until Ryan sucked in his breath and little tremors became an earthquake. Deke felt Ryan shooting against the towel for what seemed like a very long time.

Ryan's sounds of ecstasy pushed Deke over the edge, and he came too. He pressed his hips against Ryan's body and let the pleasure wash over him. He helped Ryan stand and took him onto his lap and held him tight, keeping him warm with his body heat.

"Good boy," Deke said. "That was very good."

Ryan melted against him, still limp and spent, and Deke smoothed his hair and pressed his lips to the back of Ryan's neck. Ryan tightened his arms around Deke's neck.

"Shhh, Ryan," Deke said against Ryan's ear, amazed how fast Ryan's heart still beat.

He had seen Petrov cradling Ryan after a session, and he pushed the images away. He leaned back so he could look at Ryan's face, caressing his cheek until Ryan opened his eyes. Their gazes met, and Deke knew Ryan felt it too. Then Ryan shut his eyes again, dislodging one fat tear, and burrowed his head into Deke's chest.

After this he'd have to give Ryan back to Petrov, because the bigger goal of the investigation was more important than anything that might exist between the two of them.

Deke glanced up to see Luther watching him. How had he and Ryan shared such an intimate moment with someone else looking on? Deke didn't understand it, but he'd enjoyed this class, being with Ryan. Then he remembered the discussion with Timothy and felt even more confused. The lines between work and play, pleasure and pain, connection and emotion, blurred worse than ever.

Had his relationship with Ryan changed after this? How could it not?

But had anything really changed for Ryan?

CHAPTER 22

THE FOLLOWING night Petrov had a long session with Ryan. Deke couldn't watch and left Norris in the surveillance room. Serah called as Deke was heading for the garage.

"Good job on spotting the Vancouver reference. We need to find out more about it, and get him to bring Ryan along. Make it happen. I'm authorizing a team to head up there to keep eyes on Petrov even if he doesn't bring Ryan. You'll get Brad Lim up to speed."

"Lim's taking a team up there?" Deke stopped outside the elevator in the garage.

"You've been seen by Petrov and any of his friends who have been to the club. You know you can't risk it."

Deke knew, but that didn't make it any easier to accept. "Got it. I'll talk to Brad tomorrow."

"What does Ryan know about the trip?"

"Nothing, as far as I know."

"Talk to him. And scour the latest tapes from Petrov's office." She hung up.

On the drive home, Deke simmered about not being able to go to Vancouver, but Serah was right. The good news was there were more audio files for Ryan to listen to. Deke got on the handsfree and left a voice mail for Norris to arrange a newspaper meet with Ryan for the next morning. Deke had an appointment with the shrink, but Norris could relay a message about the tapes. Ryan was smart enough to know what that meant.

AT NOON the following day, Deke got a phone call from Antony's that his suit was ready, and if he couldn't come in before the shop closed, it could be delivered that evening.

Deke grinned as he pictured Ryan making the call, pleased with the plan he'd concocted.

"I can't get out of work until at least seven thirty."

"Eight o'clock work for you, Mr. Daniels?" Ryan's tone was typically flirtatious.

"Perfect. Could I offer dinner as a thank you for going out of your way?"

"If it pleases you, sir." Ryan's impish grin came through loud and clear.

"Bad boy," Deke said under his breath, and the words made his pulse quicken.

"You know how to handle that."

"Kane?" Serah's voice echoed across the room, and Deke sat up straighter in his chair.

"See you later," he said and hung up. He had to compose himself before he went to see what Serah wanted.

AT SEVEN Deke came through his front door with a bag of groceries. He had some salmon and all the ingredients for his special pesto. He threw an apron over his work clothes, then went to work on the pesto and got the fish ready to toss on the grill. He'd get the water for pasta boiling and jump in the shower before Ryan arrived. He was just heating up the grill when the doorbell rang.

He checked his watch as he raced for the door: seven forty, twenty minutes early. A look through the peephole showed Ryan holding up Deke's new suit in a sturdy plastic cover.

Deke opened the door. "I should get you a better watch."

"Good evening, Mr. Daniels," Ryan said. He gave Deke the once-over and reached up and pulled his tie down from where he'd tossed it over his shoulder for cooking.

Deke took the suit from Ryan and folded it over a chair in the living room. The next thing he knew, Ryan was in his arms and their lips were pressed together. Deke couldn't catch his breath as he pulled Ryan in tight and pushed his tongue between Ryan's parted lips.

They stood there, enjoying a playful exploratory kiss, until Deke heard the timer go off on the grill. It broke the spell. Ryan stepped back half a pace and licked his lower lip, and Deke leaned down for another kiss, sucking the lip into his mouth to savor. Then he got himself back under control.

Ryan was wearing a suit and tie; clearly, he'd come directly from the boutique. At first glance he looked like any other professional, though he wore the suit better than most. It was tailored to accentuate his body, and Deke wondered how wool and silk could look so damn sexy. Maybe it was just Ryan.

"Are you going to say I look so different with my clothes on?"

"No. I was thinking how well it suits you."

"Do you want me to take it off?"

That was an odd question, and Deke didn't quite know how to respond. "Uh, I usually don't undress before dinner." Had he just insulted Ryan by not assuming they would have sex first? He wasn't sure what he was expecting tonight, but that wasn't it. "Do you want some sweats or a T-shirt to be more comfortable?"

"No." Ryan seemed surprised by the offer. He took off the jacket and laid it over a chair. Then he loosened his tie.

"I intended to hop in the shower before you arrived, but you...."

"Go ahead. I can help in the kitchen if you want."

"I was going to throw the pasta on while the fish is grilling."

"I'll do it. Go shower."

"That bad?" Deke was going to sniff but decided not to.

"No. I like how you look fresh out of the shower." Ryan gave a sultry smile and waved Deke in the direction of the bedroom.

Deke took a quick shower and put on his best jeans and a long-sleeved, burgundy Henley. When he got back to the kitchen, Ryan was just draining the pasta. A timer dinged.

"That's the fish," Ryan said.

"Got it." Deke retrieved the grilled salmon. It looked perfect, with dark grill marks.

Together, they served dinner and sat down. Ryan had opened a bottle of pinot noir and poured each a glass.

As Ryan glanced around the comfortably furnished room, Deke wondered what he was thinking. It didn't take long to find out.

"I wouldn't have expected you'd live over by Trendy-third Street." He used a local pejorative term for the upscale area where Deke lived, one neighborhood over from Petrov's penthouse in the even more exclusive Pearl District.

It had been Timothy who had chosen the location, but Deke wouldn't use that as an excuse. "I don't spend much time at home, so maybe the charm of the area is wasted on me." Once upon a time he'd enjoyed visiting the unique shops and restaurants in the area with Timothy.

Finding appropriate dinner conversation topics proved challenging. Deke couldn't exactly ask Ryan about where he'd grown up or what brought him to Portland. Petrov's shadow hung over the table too, so Deke avoided discussing the case.

"How's the boutique job working out?" Deke asked after discarding at least a dozen other questions. At least this had nothing to do with Petrov or potentially touchy topics.

"I like it. Most of the guys who come in are professionals. The high prices weed out almost everyone else. It's nice to work in a place where the clients aren't trying to scam you. Gregory's been a lifesaver for me and Gina."

"How's that?"

"He was a client at the Kiwi." Ryan glanced away for a split second, then went on. "He and I got to be friends too. One day he asked me what I most wanted to do."

"Which is?"

"Finish college."

The answer caught Deke off guard. "Really?"

"I dropped out when things went bad with my family—after my dad found out I was gay. Typical story, I know. But I got in some rough spots and didn't ask for help or support." He shrugged. "Anyway, Gregory offered me a job and said he'd start a college fund for me. One dollar goes into the fund for every dollar I make at the store. And he covers rent if I need it so I won't be tempted to earn it any other way. I hate lying to him, but technically, I'm not getting paid for sex."

"But he wouldn't approve?"

"No."

"He doesn't want you to be with anyone but him?" Deke bit his lip. Why had he asked?

Ryan shook his head. "I don't sleep with him anymore. It was another condition. He was a good guy, though, in that regard."

Deke didn't want to follow up on that tangent. He finished his fish and sipped wine.

"I haven't had sex with Petrov, Deke."

Deke's throat tightened. He could only nod. He was glad to hear it, but they both knew it was only a matter of time. Was this Ryan's way of saying he wanted to be with Deke? Deke was lousy at interpreting things like this. He wouldn't ask. He also wouldn't get his hopes up.

"Dinner was delicious. Thank you," Ryan said.

"Do you need to go?" Deke's heart pounded.

"No. Let me do the dishes."

"No. I have a maid."

Ryan looked around. "I hope her dishwashing is better than her general housekeeping skills."

"Yeah, I don't have a maid." Deke laughed, and Ryan joined in. "Let's finish the wine and then we can do the dishes together."

"Sounds good." Ryan stood and grabbed the bottle. "Let's sit on the couch." He made himself comfortable, and Deke sat next to him, thighs touching.

Why was this so damn awkward? The last time they'd been together, Ryan had been bent over his lap and he'd been playing with his ass. Now they were having the closest thing to a date Deke could remember, though this would get him in worse trouble with OPR than getting his CI off by fingering his hole.

The whole thing made Deke laugh.

"What?" Ryan took a sip of wine.

Deke took the bottle from him and filled up Ryan's glass.

"Just thinking about the class the other night."

Ryan gave a wistful smile that made him look ten years younger. Sweet and innocent. "I thought it was fun."

"Me too."

"You did say I was a bad boy when I called you at work."

"You were." Deke grinned. Ryan's teasing put him at ease. As much as he hated to do it, he had to talk to Ryan about Vancouver. He put his glass down on the table. "There's some business we need to discuss, then I won't bring it up again tonight."

"Okay." Ryan put his glass down and gave Deke his full attention.

"Did Petrov say anything to you about Vancouver?"

Ryan turned down one corner of his mouth at mention of Petrov. "Not directly. He says he needs to do some traveling for business. I asked about his business—casually, since he'd brought it up."

Deke waited, hoping Ryan hadn't blown it.

"He says he does different kinds of investing. I'd find it too boring. I just let it go there."

"Good choice. See if you can find out anything about the trip, carefully. If you can figure a way to get him to bring you along, that would help a lot."

Ryan nodded. His gaze darkened. They both had an idea how he might make himself more important to Petrov.

"End of business."

"Good. So will you be back to the Dungeon? I haven't seen you much lately, except for that class."

"I've got Luther's seal of approval to come back. He liked how I treated you the other night. I'm taking another class on Friday. Flogging."

"I should offer my services for that too." Ryan grinned. He picked up his wine.

"Oh, please do. Or I'll end up with one of the guys in the class. Or Dakota."

"Dakota. He'd love to play with you. Petrov and the other members take him only for really heavy sessions now. He would love to have you spank him. I heard him telling Phoenix."

"What?"

Ryan grinned. "Phoenix asked Luther about you after the class, and Dakota heard how you held me afterward. He said he'd pay to get treated like that now." Ryan started laughing and spilled wine on his shirt. He looked down. "Crap." The red wine seeped into the fine cotton, spreading out like a bad TV gunshot wound.

"Let me get some club soda. You can rinse it off in the bathroom."

Ryan got up and went into the bathroom. Deke brought the club soda and found him sitting on the countertop next to the sink. He was dabbing at the stain with a wet tissue.

"Let me." Deke meant to pour club soda on the tissue, but Ryan moved and the club soda went directly onto his shirt. The wet cotton was thin and clung to his body, the piercing through Ryan's nipple plainly visible. The sight of it triggered something, and Deke leaned down and put his mouth over the nipple, sucking it through the damp, wine-flavored cloth.

Ryan put his arms around Deke's neck and held tight, letting out a soft moan as Deke played with his nipple using lips and teeth.

Deke pulled Ryan's shirt up, catching his arms in the cloth so they were held over his head, both nipples now hard buds and at his mercy to take. Ryan arched his back and opened his legs so Deke could stand between his knees. He kicked off his shoes and wrapped his legs around Deke's waist as he worked his hands out of the shirtsleeves.

Deke could barely catch his breath as he took his fill of Ryan's plump nipples. He'd wanted to taste them for so long, and they were even better than he'd imagined. Heat and electricity raced through his body as Ryan slid his hands under Deke's shirt, first gliding along his back and shoulders, then around to Deke's nipples. He backed away for a second to pull his shirt off and take Ryan into his arms for a long, deep kiss.

DEKE'S HOT, hungry mouth on Ryan's nipples sent the temperature soaring in the bathroom. Ryan gave himself up to the sensations. Normally so restrained and in control of his emotions, Deke was like an animal finally uncaged, and Ryan loved it. Deke let loose, ready to take what he wanted from Ryan—and Ryan was eager to give whatever he wanted.

It had been there under the surface for so long, and finally, Deke was ready. Ryan was just as ready. Deke's passion ignited him further, so different from the calculated way Petrov touched him. Petrov knew just how to get Ryan to respond in the way he wished. There was no emotion in him. The pleasure he gave Ryan was completely different from what Deke could bring forth.

It would be a genuine pleasure to be with Deke. And so much better to be able to give himself to Deke before Petrov.

Ryan tightened his knees around Deke's waist and felt Deke's cock, thick and hard through his jeans, pressing against Ryan's. Deke groaned into Ryan's mouth and kissed more deeply. Ryan unwrapped his legs and began on Deke's belt. Deke stood in front of him, watching Ryan's hands unzip him. Deke was wearing pale blue boxers and his cock tented them. It was so very normal—and so very adorable—that Deke hadn't put on any special underwear tonight. Or gone without. Yes, that would have been sexy as hell, but Ryan found the boxers even sexier. He slid Deke's jeans and boxers far enough down his hips that they fell away on their own.

Deke's cock was beautiful. Ryan hadn't seen it this close before, and he couldn't wait to have it do marvelous things to him.

Deke took Ryan's hands in his and instead of putting them on his cock, raised them to his mouth and kissed them. Kissed the palms, the fingers, the wrists.

For the very first time in his life, Ryan understood desire.

He'd known about it, how to elicit it in others, and how to use it, but until this moment he'd never felt desire for anyone else. Ryan wanted Deke in a way he couldn't explain, and the knowing and wanting made his chest heavy and his heart pound. Ryan had never had sex with a man because he wanted to. It had always been a necessity, not a choice.

How would it feel to be with Deke? Could that much joy and pleasure be fatal? Ryan thought if he didn't feel Deke next to him, in him, very soon, he might burst from the wanting. Such ecstasy would certainly change Ryan forever.

And after Deke, how could Ryan possibly give himself to Petrov or anyone else? The thought of how that would pain Deke pulled Ryan back from the edge of desire. His brain calculated the repercussions his body couldn't yet understand.

Ryan had to stay with Petrov. He could become the center of Petrov's world, and only then could Ryan get the information Deke needed. Deke's passion was intoxicating, but he'd soon grow tired of a used-up whore, and that would crush Ryan.

No. Ryan could do much more for Deke by manipulating Petrov than by giving in to the desire Deke had awakened in him.

He pulled his hands away from Deke. The surprise and hurt in Deke's eyes felt like a dagger to Ryan's heart, but he had to do it now, before it was too late. Before Deke melted Ryan's defenses completely away.

"I need to go. I'm supposed to see Petrov later tonight." He grabbed his shirt and ran out of the bathroom. He couldn't bear to see the look on Deke's face. God, he was such a coward.

CHAPTER 23

RYAN HEADED for the alleyway, clutching his shirt and jacket. He made it around the corner before he vomited. He rid his stomach of the wonderful meal he'd shared with Deke. He heaved for several minutes before he could stand again and push the dizziness away.

He got on the motorbike and rode to the closest gas station. After he cleaned up in the bathroom, he bought a soda and guzzled half of it to get the acrid taste out of his mouth. He regretted losing the last delicious taste of Deke's mouth, but there was no other choice. In the morning Deke would admit to himself he was better off for not fucking Ryan. Maybe he'd go back to the guy who'd taken half the furniture when he moved out. Deke deserved the kind of guy who owned furniture worth taking.

Ryan drove home by the most indirect route possible. He wanted to put off the amount of time he'd have to lie alone in his bed.

But he didn't have to be alone. He didn't have to deal with this on his own.

He parked the bike in the underground garage and went upstairs. He walked past his door and knocked at Gina's new apartment. She opened the door and almost instantly pulled him into her arms.

On the couch he cried on her lap and her shoulder as he told her what had happened.

"Was there any other way, Gee?"

She stroked his hair, just like Deke had the other night. "I don't know. But if the feelings are that strong, maybe someday, after this...."

"I've never wanted anything—anyone—so much in my life."

She kissed his hair. "Doing the right thing can really hurt like hell. I think that's how you know it's right."

CHAPTER 24

AFTER RYAN left, Deke took a cold shower, hoping to gain some clarity over what had just happened. He'd come on too strong. Ryan seemed to be trying really hard to create a life that wasn't built around sex, and Deke had gone and stuck his dick right in the middle of it. He was no better than the men who'd paid Ryan for sex or who thought it was okay to put their hands all over him as long as they gave a decent tip.

Deke was just like the others. Worse, since he hadn't even offered to pay for what he wanted. What did Ryan want? He'd seemed so animated when he talked about the college fund his new boss set up. The guy seemed like just what Ryan needed. He was doing a lot more for Ryan's stability and future than Deke. Putting Ryan in Petrov's clutches was the worst thing for him.

As Deke washed dishes and cleaned up the kitchen, he realized how badly he'd been using Ryan for his own ends. Yes, the Petrov drugs and weapons connection was important, and stopping it might save lives. But was it worth ruining Ryan's life?

He was going to talk to Serah in the morning.

BUT THE next day, he didn't.

He'd stayed up half the night doing housework until he was so exhausted he could finally fall asleep. Two hours later he had shouted himself awake again. The nightmare was back.

By the time he got to work, he'd talked himself out of going to Serah again. They'd already had this discussion, and he knew what she would say. Worse, she'd start doubting him again, and he didn't need any more black marks in his file. The best thing he could do now would be to focus on every possible angle to get what they needed on Petrov. He'd be able to get Ryan out of the investigation and back to his safe new life more quickly.

And then Deke could get started on forgetting he'd ever met Ryan Griffiths.

TWO NIGHTS later, Deke watched Petrov move the flogger over Ryan's body. The color on the monitor was perfect. He saw the bloom spread across Ryan's skin, saw him relax against the wooden bars of the X-frame. He didn't flinch at all, like Dakota did when Petrov worked him over.

It was easy to see why Petrov played less frequently with Dakota. Ryan must be a Dom's dream come true. Someone for whom every experience was new and who could easily fall under his spell.

He certainly wasn't Deke's or the FBI's dream, though. Serah and her boss, Ward, the head of the Portland field office, had been increasingly vocal about the lack of progress in the Petrov operation.

On the screen, Petrov slowed his movements until he completely stopped. He went up to Ryan and spoke to him too quietly for the mics to pick up. Then Petrov helped Ryan off the wooden bars and lay down with him on the recovery couch, offering him water and caressing his hair.

"What a lovely session tonight, sweetheart."

"Thank you, sir."

"I have another reward for your performance and obedience."

"My cock" Deke nearly said out loud. He'd been worried when Petrov hadn't asked Ryan to get him off in any of their sessions, thinking Ryan had failed at getting Petrov to take him into his life.

"What, sir?"

"Next week I go to Vancouver for a business meeting. You will come with me?"

"Halle-fucking-lujah!" Deke stood up and did a few fist pumps.

"If that would please you, sir." Ryan's voice was stronger now.

On the screen, Deke could swear Ryan was looking directly into the camera when he said it.

PETROV AND Ryan were to leave for Vancouver the following Saturday morning. Petrov had him training in his penthouse every single night.

They didn't go to the club at all, and Ryan hadn't seen Deke since the night at his apartment.

Maybe it was a good thing. Ryan was so busy trying to meet Petrov's ever-increasing demands on his mind and body, he had little opportunity to let himself dwell on how much it hurt to push Deke away. Ryan forced himself to concentrate on being everything Petrov wanted or needed. Only then would he gain enough trust to get proof for Deke.

Ryan threw himself 100 percent into being Petrov's submissive. He could do it because it was for Deke, and it was the way to act on his feelings for Deke. As the week wore on, Petrov drove Ryan to exhaustion and his limits of pain and performance, both mentally and physically.

But he rewarded Ryan for every success, and Ryan found a new outlet for his energy and a surprising fulfillment in earning Petrov's praise and rewards.

BEFORE THE trip an FBI agent called Bradford Lim met with Ryan at the Starbucks and gave him a mic and a camera. If he had the chance to place them in order to listen in on Petrov's business, he was to do so. Otherwise, he wasn't to risk the tech getting discovered.

Two other agents would travel to Vancouver and keep an eye on him the best they could. Because Petrov knew Deke from Dungeon 69, the FBI couldn't risk sending him to Vancouver. Ryan knew it was best that Deke not go along, and not just because Petrov had seen him. It would be rough on Ryan to see Deke and not have some kind of reaction to him.

CHAPTER 25

Saturday morning
Portland OR

AT 10:00 a.m., Deke was at his desk waiting for the surveillance reports from the night before Ryan and Petrov left for Vancouver when the call came in.

"Kane, got a call from PD about a body a block from Dungeon 69. One of the boys from that club. No ID yet."

Deke's first cup of coffee rose toward the back of his throat. He calmed himself before he spewed up all over his desk. "Description?"

"White guy in his twenties. Light brown hair. Suffocated. Got those S and M marks on him."

Deke couldn't breathe. It couldn't be Ryan, could it? He shuffled through the printouts on his desk, looking for the last known whereabouts of Petrov and Ryan. The latest report ended at six the night before. Why was there nothing later?

"Keep me posted," he managed to say.

"Sure. I'll get copies of the photos and reports."

Deke hung up. He didn't want to see photos and reports. He raced up to the surveillance room assigned to his operation and flung open the door.

Agent Norris sat there staring at a video of Ryan with Petrov. "Hey, Boss. I'm still working on the transcripts. Sorry."

"What time is that one?"

"Nine o'clock, at the Dungeon. Wh—"

"Fast forward to the end."

Norris didn't ask any more questions and did as requested. The tape showed Ryan and Petrov leaving the bar area with another man, one Deke didn't recognize.

"Go back a couple of minutes, with sound."

Petrov was speaking. "Steven, come with us, we're going to—" Sounds of laughter obliterated what he said. "—see what my new sub can—"

Ryan stood in the now-familiar position at attention. Petrov put a possessive hand on Ryan's shoulder as he moved away from the table. The other man got out of the booth and slid a hand along Ryan's waist, then up to the piercing, and tugged at it.

Ryan didn't move or respond.

"Say thank you, boy," the man told him, twisting the nipple hard.

"Thank you, sir," Ryan said, voice tight.

Deke felt the pain Ryan didn't let on in his expression. He'd seen Ryan get turned on from nipple play, but this touch had moved past play. Petrov was out of the camera frame, and the man slid his hand up Ryan's torso to his collarbone, then along his throat. It was a menacing touch, not a sensual caress.

Then the man dropped his hand and walked out of the frame. Ryan turned and followed.

"That's it, Deke. We didn't have anyone in the club last night."

"Find me something with Griffiths—audio, video, anything—after this. Who collected the feeds?"

"Ortiz. He's off today—"

Deke glared, and Norris quickly followed with "But I'll call him. Right now."

Deke paced while Norris got Ortiz on the phone, then grabbed the receiver. "Where did Griffiths sleep last night? Did he go home?"

"Uh, no. He might have been at Petrov's. One of the relay transmitters was out of juice, and we don't actually have the—"

"Can't anybody do their fucking jobs around here?" Deke shouted to everyone within hearing distance. He smashed the receiver down and slammed his fist against the glass wall. The guys in the next room stared at him. He stopped himself before he flipped them the bird.

"I didn't think anything of it since Griffiths was flying out this morning. But what's the concern?" Norris kept his tone neutral.

"PD found a dead guy near that club, and he fits the CI's description. The last image we have of him is what you just saw. Petrov's friend doesn't play by the rules."

"You saw him for a minute, how do you know?"

"I've spent enough time there to know what's play and what's real. That guy wasn't playing. Find out who the fuck he is and call me."

"On it." Norris turned back to the monitor and started up a facial recognition program.

Deke headed for the garage, dialing Serah on his cell phone. He had to get over to the morgue.

"Cartier."

"Kane here. We have a problem."

"I heard about the DB. He our guy?"

"Not sure." Deke wasn't sure how he kept his voice from breaking. She was so matter-of-fact, while he was about to fall to pieces at the thought it might be Ryan. "I'm heading to the morgue. Can you check the flight information?" He gave her the Air Canada flight number.

"Not a US carrier, so it'll take another signature, but I'll let you know as soon as I have any info. Being a Saturday doesn't make it easier."

"I'll call if I find out anything at the morgue." He hung up as he exited the elevator and raced for his vehicle. He squealed out of the parking garage, leaving the security guy staring in his wake, and narrowly avoided another car entering as he careened away from the garage exit.

Ten minutes later he got to the morgue building and left his car outside with a special placard on the dashboard so he wouldn't be towed.

When he entered the morgue, the receptionist paged the ME handling the John Doe in question.

"Where's the fire on this one? Don't think he's on the most wanted list," Dr. Chen said, scratching behind his left ear.

"You print him?"

"Didn't they tell you?"

"What?"

"No hands. Or feet. Kinda weird. Whole fucking thing is weird, you ask me."

Deke followed him into the exam room, where two bodies were laid out on autopsy tables. The place smelled like Clorox on top of formaldehyde, mixed with blood and other odors Deke preferred not to identify.

"Here's your guy." Chen peeled back the sheet.

Deke wished he hadn't. The body had no hands and the head was smashed in. The mouth gaped, displaying broken teeth. There was a bloody scab where the left nipple should have been—someone had ripped out a piercing a while before the guy died. There were other extensive bruises and marks from restraints and toys Deke could now recognize.

He felt his gut shifting and ran for the trash can, where he emptied the contents of his stomach.

Jesus, had he sent Ryan in to that club and this is what happened? Had they discovered he was a CI? Deke steadied himself against the wall.

"Ugly way to go. They definitely tortured this guy. He was raped—or maybe not. Not sure what they used, but it did some damage." Chen cocked his head. "You know him?" he asked. He had a clipboard and was making notes.

Deke racked his brain, trying to remember if Ryan had any tats or birthmarks or moles. He didn't recall any, but with the bruising, they might be hard to distinguish. The sheet was pulled back just to the navel.

This might not be Ryan. The body type and size could be Dakota, Deke reminded himself. They had similar coloring. Without prints, how could he know? He edged closer to the body, trying not to give in to the revulsion he felt. There was only one thing he knew for sure would distinguish them. He prayed it would be there.

His cell phone beeped. "Kane." He turned away from the corpse for a moment.

"Norris here. I ID'd the dude with Petrov. He's a hitter. Suspected hitter. We know he's done a few guys who crossed the Russians and the Colombians. Not a speck of proof. Name's Handler."

The story Ryan had eventually shared about the bald guy outside the hotel room where his friend and their trick were killed bubbled through Deke's addled brain. "Thanks, Norris. See if you can locate Handler, and try to track down Dakota, another one of the guys working at Dungeon 69." Deke disconnected and turned back to the body.

If Handler recognized Ryan from the motel, or from Club Kiwi, he might have thought Ryan could connect him to the murders. If Petrov had ordered the hits, he might have asked Handler to clean up the evidence: Ryan. Deke stared at the body again.

Then he took a deep breath and pulled the sheet farther down the hips. The corpse's cock was mutilated too, but it wasn't very large. Ryan was bigger than that, wasn't he? And Dakota had one of those dick piercings, only in the current state, Deke couldn't tell whether this one did or not. He pulled up stored images of Ryan's naked body, hoping against hope this wasn't him.

Chen pulled the sheet back up. "You Feds are a bunch of fucking pervs. Don't tell me you're gonna ID him by his Johnson."

Deke's stomach calmed slightly, and he got his breathing under control. He was 99 percent sure this was Dakota and not Ryan. But he needed more proof than what he remembered about their cocks.

Vancouver, BC

PETROV HAD gotten them business-class seats, even for the short flight. They sat two across in the front of the plane, and Petrov kept his hand on Ryan's thigh the entire flight, reminding him not very subtly of his place.

"You will stay with me the whole time, pet. I may introduce you to my colleagues, but you will not speak unless I allow it."

"Yes, sir." Ryan glanced at the other passengers, wondering whether he'd be able to spot the FBI agents who would be watching from a distance.

They took a taxi from the airport to the Pan Pacific Hotel, right at the waterfront, overlooking Canada House and the impressive structure designed to look like the sails of a ship. Petrov had booked the Jade Suite, and the bellman eyed Ryan suspiciously as he took them to their room.

The suite was incredible. It spanned half the sixteenth floor, with floor-to-ceiling windows giving almost a 180-degree view of the bay and the distant mountains. There was an expansive living room, an office area, and a spacious balcony in addition to the large bedroom with a king-size bed. The bathroom was marble with a huge tub and a separate shower.

Ryan unpacked their clothes and hung everything up in the bedroom. Petrov had bought him some new clothes for the trip: a beautiful dark gray suit at Antony's boutique and several shirts and pretty ties, as well as two pairs of jeans—tight-fitting to show off Ryan's ass—and some other casual clothing.

Petrov hadn't packed any toys or fetish wear, and Ryan wondered whether there would be any play or training. Maybe Petrov would just treat him normally during the trip. He had no idea what to expect, but he'd agreed to be a full-time sub during the trip, within the limits they already had.

Petrov sat on the bed while Ryan put the clothes away. He'd wanted Ryan to wear the new suit on the plane, and Petrov also wore a suit.

"Take my jacket."

Ryan slid Petrov's jacket off.

"Hang up your suit, too."

"Yes, sir." Ryan started to take his jacket off.

"Strip slowly."

Ryan wasn't sure if Petrov wanted an actual striptease, so he just slowed down his movements, peeling the jacket off and hanging it in the closet. Petrov nodded and lay back against the pillows.

"Your tie."

Ryan slowly unknotted his tie and slid it off his neck. He kept his gaze down, not making eye contact with Petrov, so he couldn't tell if he was doing the right thing. He heard Petrov groan and took it as encouragement.

"Shirt. Unbutton slowly but don't take off."

Ryan followed directions. Petrov shifted on the bed and groaned again. Ryan tugged on his shirttails to flash first one nipple, then the other for Petrov.

"Good boy. Very pretty."

Petrov's voice was low and raspy, and the sound of it got Ryan excited. He wasn't sure if he was allowed to yet.

"Sir?"

"Yes?"

"May I get hard?"

"Of course."

Ryan relaxed and preened a little more for Petrov.

"Shirt off."

Ryan let the shirt fall away from his shoulders. His cock tented the trousers. He wished he could see Petrov's expression.

"Come here."

Ryan moved to the edge of the bed.

"Show me how hard you are."

Ryan undid his belt and started to unzip his trousers, slipping them down just until his cock pushed its way out. He wasn't wearing underwear. Petrov reached out and grabbed his cock.

"Why are you so hard?"

Ryan didn't know what to say. What did Petrov want him to say?

Petrov tightened his grip on Ryan and kept squeezing. It began to hurt. "Well?"

The pain started, but it wasn't the good pain. Ryan blinked. "Because it pleases you, sir?"

Petrov kept squeezing.

"Because it makes me happy to do what you want?"

"You don't sound sure." Petrov's voice was as rough as his touch. "Why?"

"I don't know, sir. I can't explain it. But I get turned on by not knowing what you will want of me and also by your touch and your voice." Ryan felt tears spilling down his cheeks. He didn't know when the pain in his cock would end or what would happen because he didn't have a good answer.

Then Petrov let go.

Ryan's dick flopped against his thigh. He wasn't hard anymore. He let out a sob, then tried to control himself.

"Take your trousers off."

Ryan nodded and slid them all the way, embarrassed he didn't have an erection anymore.

"Come sit on the bed with me." Petrov pulled Ryan next to him.

Now Ryan could see Petrov's cock pushing against the fabric of his pants.

"You can open my pants. Slowly."

Ryan nodded and sniffled. Through tears he unfastened Petrov's belt, then the button on the waistband. Only a couple of layers of fabric separated him from Petrov's cock. He'd never been allowed to touch Petrov or see him naked before. Why was he being allowed now after he'd just failed a test?

"Now unzip me."

Ryan did and saw Petrov was wearing silk boxers, bright blue with a yellow paisley pattern. He let his hand hover over the bulge.

"Push them down." Petrov raised his hips so Ryan could slide the boxers and trousers down until his cock sprang free.

It was swollen and purple, with lots of veins. It was also very thick. It was the kind of cock Ryan would like to fuck him. He wanted to touch it, taste it, spread himself open for it. He stared at it.

"I see you like it?"

Ryan nodded, feeling his own cock start to thicken again. "Yes, sir."

"Touch me. Hands only."

He hesitated. He'd never been allowed this much before. He didn't want to do this wrong.

"Now." Petrov's voice grew urgent, and Ryan put his hand on him.

He played with Petrov, gradually speeding up his movements and pressure. He took his cue from Petrov's breathing and groans. Then Petrov put his hand over Ryan's and took back control. Without warning he came, shooting all over Ryan's cheek and into his hair. The rest of the strands landed on Ryan's neck and chest.

Petrov reached out and smeared it into Ryan's hair and his chest, streaking it across the pierced nipple.

"Very good, pet. Get a wet cloth from the bathroom."

Ryan did as requested. Now his cock bounced with each step. He hoped Petrov would see that. He returned with the cloth.

"Clean me up."

When Ryan was done, Petrov pulled his boxers up and slid out of the trousers. "Hang these up."

After Ryan did so, he turned back to Petrov, waiting for another order. Wanting another order. He hated standing and waiting, not knowing how to please.

"Go clean up. Take a shower. Cool water, not hot."

"Yes, sir."

Petrov sat on the edge of the huge Jacuzzi tub while Ryan slipped under the shower spray.

He felt his nipples bud as the cool spray hit them.

"Can you stay hard the whole time, without touching your cock? I have a reward if you can."

That was enough incentive. He quickly shampooed his hair and washed his face and chest, shoulders and ass, trying to show himself off. He slid soapy hands up and down the curve of his ass, and heard Petrov's low chuckle.

"Very nice. Bend over and show me more."

Ryan did. It had been nearly two months, and this was the most interest Petrov had paid his ass.

"Make sure you are very clean. Wash everything."

Ryan made another good show of soaping up his hole and balls and using the showerhead to rinse away the soap.

"Lovely. Warm water now. Nice and warm as you like."

Grateful, Ryan adjusted the temperature. "Thank you, sir."

"Did you make sure your cock is clean? You may touch yourself."

Ryan soaped up a hand and gently touched himself. He was still hard.

"Show me how clean you get it. You have one minute, then you will come against the shower door."

For the next sixty seconds, Ryan soaped and tugged and played with himself as arousingly as possible. Then, when Petrov nodded slightly, he let loose and splashed pearly jets against the shower door as requested. He hadn't come for more than a day, and there was a good quantity of sticky white streaks when he was done.

"Leave it there."

He rinsed off and stepped out of the shower into the towel Petrov held for him.

"Hurry and dry off. We are going out. Five minutes. Jeans and the dark red shirt. Black boots."

"Yes, sir." Ryan was still out of breath, but he raced into the bedroom.

Petrov dressed himself, then watched Ryan slip into a pair of the new jeans.

He hadn't been allowed to pack any underwear, so Ryan pulled the jeans on and zipped carefully. They were tight, and his cock would be obvious to anyone who looked for half a second. He put on the rest of the clothing, then waited by the door to the suite, at attention.

Petrov rubbed the head of Ryan's cock through the jeans, smiling when he got a reaction. "So pretty. You deserve something special."

The concierge helped them into a taxi, and Petrov gave the driver an address. Twenty minutes later they stopped in front of an old Victorian-style home on the outskirts of the city. Petrov told the driver to wait, and then they went inside.

The walls were covered with whips, floggers, paddles, and other toys. There were half a dozen rooms, like a rabbit warren, and Petrov led Ryan through each one, then back to the entrance.

"What would you like? Anything you want."

AN HOUR later they got back in the taxi with several new toys. At Petrov's request, the driver waited at the hotel while they took the purchases upstairs.

"Put on this jacket." Petrov took a brown suede jacket from the closet for Ryan and selected one for himself. He stuffed two ties into his pocket.

The taxi then took them to a small, out-of-the-way restaurant: La Gavroche in the West End. It was intimate and dark. They didn't need the ties. The hostess seated them at a table with a lovely view of the bay, where lights twinkled on boats moving across the water.

"I may find some way to use these later," Petrov said, holding up the ties once the hostess had left them.

After they had ordered and the sommelier had brought them an old, expensive-looking bottle, Petrov cleared his throat.

"For this meal, we are not Dom and sub. Right now, we are just Maksim and Ryan. Understand?"

"Yes, sir."

"No 'sir.' Look me in the eye when you speak, as you would everyone but your Dom."

It took Ryan a moment to lift his gaze. "Okay." He looked into Petrov's eyes. They were twinkly blue, bright even in the flickering light of the candle between them. It was the first time they hadn't been Dom and sub since the day they had entered into their agreement for Petrov to take Ryan on.

"Do you want to ask anything, or say anything?"

Portland, OR

DEKE SAT waiting outside the morgue exam room until his head was clear enough to drive again. He sipped water from a paper cup and ignored the receptionist's judgmental stares.

He'd gotten over his initial panic that Ryan had been killed. The fact remained someone had died horribly. This was beyond BDSM and sadomasochistic pleasures. Whether the body was Ryan's or Dakota's, this was a ruthless killer, and he wasn't playing sex games.

If Ryan was alive, he was in far more danger than either of them ever suspected.

It drove home one more thing to Deke: his concern for Ryan went far beyond protecting a source or CI, or losing a way to get at Petrov. Deke had fallen for Ryan, head over proverbial heels.

And he was going to keep Ryan safe if it was the last thing he ever did.

DEKE WAS walking around the block in a light drizzle, trying to clear his brain, when Serah called.

"What did you hear?" he asked.

"Petrov and Griffiths landed in Vancouver this morning. We have two agents on them, but there's some fuckup with their cell phones. They have had visual contact on both men. Last location was a shop. Tiny place didn't even have a name on the door…. They are in there right now."

"Thanks."

"You ID the corpse?"

"I think it's Dakota, one of the other subs working the club."

"Why's he dead?"

"Not sure. There's a chance it's a hitter called Handler. I'm heading to the club now to—"

"No. Send someone else. Do not blow your cover there."

"Serah, we have to shut this operation down, at least the Dungeon 69 aspect. It's too dangerous unless we can get more coverage. My guys are spread too thin, and Ryan's falling through the cracks. Everyone dropped the ball last night—including me. Most importantly me. I shouldn't have delegated—"

"Pull yourself together. Dakota—if that's him—may not be connected to Petrov or Ryan. Let PD handle it. I'll stay in the loop with the Chief of Detectives, and if there is any chance they'll fuck up our operation, we'll take over. For now, focus on Petrov and Ryan. Got it?"

"Yes, but—"

"No buts. We have too much invested in this now, and we got Ryan where we need him. Focus on that."

"Got it." He hung up and jammed the phone into his breast pocket.

Curiosity got the better of him, and he googled the address of the shop the agent in Vancouver mentioned.

A sex-toy shop with Canada's largest selection of whips and floggers, according to the website. He accessed Petrov's financial transactions and discovered he'd purchased a deerskin flogger, a three-foot single-tail whip, and two very expensive glass dildos.

All while Deke was panicking that Ryan was dead and mutilated in the Portland morgue. The reality was Ryan was probably on the receiving end of another series of spectacular orgasms, thanks to Petrov's new acquisitions.

He did another lap of the block even though the rain had increased, and by the time he got into his car, he was soaking wet and shivering.

CHAPTER 26

Vancouver BC

RYAN SAT across from Petrov in the romantic restaurant, not sure how he should respond to Petrov's unexpected openness. *Did you have my friend killed? Are you involved in weapons trafficking? Who killed Jimmy Hoffa?*

"I was wondering about what you asked me before we went shopping. About why I get so excited with you even when you don't touch me."

"Go on."

"Why did you hurt me? It wasn't like the other pain. It wasn't play."

Petrov smiled. His teeth reflected the candlelight, and it made him look frightening, like a tiger about to pounce. "Because you didn't tell me the truth the first time. Or the second."

"I didn't lie."

"Not the same. You didn't know the reason, but you wouldn't tell me that. I demonstrated that I know when you are not truthful. Your body does not lie. Your eyes do not lie, even if your brain or your mouth does. Don't lie to me."

Ryan inhaled, then took a sip of wine. He needed a moment to process Petrov's words. Did the man know who he was and why they had met? What did he mean about Ryan lying?

He laughed. It was the only response that wouldn't make Petrov suspicious. "You use my cock like a lie detector?" Ryan grinned.

Petrov's smile widened. "It may be very effective. I should find other ways to use your cock." His voice turned playful again. The tiger had receded.

The food was delicious, the wine superb. Petrov held Ryan's hand through much of the meal, bringing it to his mouth and kissing it as if they were on a date.

By dessert he had Ryan in his lap, feeding him bites of chocolate mousse, oblivious to the stares from the other patrons.

"Ryan, tonight has been very special. I like spending time with you very much. You awaken something in here." Petrov touched his heart. "It is different from what I feel as your Dom, which is here." He indicated his cock. "And here." His head. "You are so very eager to please me in every way. But I find myself wanting to please you."

Ryan smiled and his heart pounded. He did want to please Petrov. He didn't know if it was out of fear or affection, or an inexplicable mixture of the two.

"Promise me, Ryan. Promise me you will never lie to me, and I will never lie to you about anything."

"I won't, s— Maksim. I won't ever lie."

Petrov pulled Ryan's face close to his, and as Petrov brushed his lips across Ryan's cheek, Ryan put his arms around him and held him tight.

Petrov kissed Ryan's ear and whispered, "*Ya lubl'u teb'a.*"

I love you.

CHAPTER 27

Sunday

Vancouver, BC

THE NEXT morning they had breakfast on their balcony, watching ferries and sailboats crisscrossing the blue-gray waters of the Vancouver Harbor. Cruise ships docked to the north, and passengers streamed off like multicolored ants.

"My guests will be arriving at ten. You will stay in the bedroom. They will not meet you, see you, or hear you. Understand?"

"Yes, sir." They were back to D/s. The moment they left the restaurant, Petrov was in charge again.

Ryan preferred it that way. He didn't have to pretend when he was under Petrov's command. There was no way for him to reveal his true intentions. He simply had to follow directions. It took all the pressure off.

A steward took their breakfast dishes, and they were alone again.

"Come inside so I can get you ready."

"Ready, sir?"

"You will see." Petrov led Ryan into the bedroom. "Strip down."

Ryan slid out of the silk boxers Petrov had let him wear for breakfast. He hadn't been wearing a shirt. Petrov had worn a hotel robe over silk pajamas while they ate, and the waiter stared at Ryan's piercing, then glanced at Petrov, smirking behind his back. He'd easily pegged Ryan as the rich man's toy.

Petrov grabbed a necktie and bound Ryan's wrists together, then slipped his wrists over a hook on the door to the bathroom.

"Today is a test for you. See how long you can stay here completely still while I am having my meeting in the living room. I will check on you every thirty minutes. If you need me before then, squeeze this ball." Petrov handed him a ball with a bell.

Ryan gave a test squeeze, and it made a soft tinkling sound.

"I will leave the bedroom door open so I can hear this. You will not speak or call my name unless you are unable to breathe. Anything else is not an emergency. Understand?"

"Yes, sir." Ryan glanced toward the door to the living room. He wanted to listen to the conversation, but this far away he would not be able to hear much. He looked at his wrists and realized he was not secured to the door. He could probably lift his wrists high enough to clear the hook. He'd try that as soon as Petrov left him alone.

"One last thing. To make sure you do not move." Petrov stuck his hand into his suitcase and pulled out a small velvet pouch. He extracted a nubby black butt plug and a bottle of lube. He drizzled lube on the plug and more on a finger; then he slipped the finger into Ryan's ass and slicked him up.

Ryan let out a sigh at the unexpected pleasurable sensation. Then Petrov pushed the plug in, and Ryan was rock hard almost immediately. He let out a soft groan.

"It's very good, yes?" Petrov stroked Ryan's back and ass, the slight movement creating incredible sensations inside of Ryan. "If you move too much, you will come. I do not want that. If you can stay still until my meeting is over, you will get a special reward. If not, you will sleep on the balcony tonight. Understand?"

Ryan nodded. The movement made the plug massage his ass, and his cock twitched.

"Ah, you see? You must not move at all. Now I must dress." Petrov moved away. Ryan couldn't see him, but he heard the rustle of fabric and the *zzzz* of a zipper. Petrov hummed as he dressed. Ryan couldn't name the song, but he recalled the tune, one his mother often sang as she did housework.

If he helped the FBI, he could see his mother. He wondered whether she still sang that song. He had to listen to that meeting.

The room phone buzzed.

"Yes? … Send them up to the suite. Thank you." Petrov hung up. "My guests are coming up now. You will be a good boy for me?"

"Yes, sir," Ryan whispered.

"Good." Petrov ran his finger along the length of Ryan's cock, sending fire to his core and ratcheting up Ryan's arousal about three more notches. He groaned. Petrov kissed his shoulder and chuckled, then left the bedroom.

Ryan heard the suite doorbell ring—an elegant three-note chime. Petrov opened the door and greeted his guests. Three men. Ryan couldn't hear any specific words.

The voices got louder and more distinct. The couch was not far from the bedroom door.

"I don't think we'll need your assistant," Petrov said. "You may wait in hotel lobby."

The reply was indistinct.

"This is no time for strangers." Petrov raised his voice.

Two men spoke in Russian, but Ryan couldn't make out what they were saying. He stood on tiptoe to get his hands off the hook, but the shift in position sent jolts through his ass and cock. He grunted as he tried to get control of his body. He took a step toward the door, trying to ignore the sensations from the butt plug.

He could hear a little better. "… I don't have any problems with him staying," Ryan heard a husky-voiced man say. "Let's just get down to business."

"… reconsider the property in North Africa…." Ryan didn't recognize the voice of this second man. He needed to get closer. Another step had him gasping and shuddering. He needed to make sure the ball didn't jingle. How the hell could he manage everything at once and still remember what Petrov and his guests talked about?

The bug was in his shoe. No way to get it in the living room. Petrov had been with him every single second from the time they'd arrived until now.

"The financial side of that transaction is ready," Petrov said. "When can you close the deal, *moy druk*?" *My friend.*

"Which property is this?" the man with the husky voice asked.

"The Middle Eastern one," the other stranger—Petrov's friend—said. "I can make the transfer next week. I'm on a shopping trip and can connect with the seller in Dubai on my way there."

Fuck. Ryan needed to get closer. He took tiny steps, trying not to pick up his feet, just slide along the carpet. The pressure inside continued to build, and he had to stop halfway between the two doors and catch his breath, trying to center himself.

He wanted to get Petrov's reward. Failure meant being pushed away, and he craved approval. He needed it. His breath came in short bursts. He moved back toward the bathroom. He couldn't let Petrov down....

But Deke was counting on him too. How could Ryan choose? If Deke got what he needed, Petrov was going to prison. The thought hit Ryan hard. How could he do that after everything Petrov had done for him, especially on this trip?

Ryan froze, listening, heart and mind pulled in opposite directions, with his body trapped somewhere in the middle.

"The coast is clear on a transaction next week," Husky said. "Don't move until Tuesday. I'll guarantee your safety between Tuesday and Friday."

"How many acres can you get for that price?" Number Two said.

"A thousand, maybe fifteen hundred," Petrov replied.

"Wait a minute." It was the third stranger, speaking for the first time. "Acres are automatic or semiautomatic?"

Petrov let out a loud curse in Russian. Ryan understood that loud and clear. "Excuse me for a few minutes."

Shit. Ryan remembered Petrov was going to check on him. He glanced at the door to the living room and the one to the bathroom. Only three feet, but how could he get there fast enough without shooting his load on the floor in a spot he wasn't supposed to be? If Petrov discovered Ryan had disobeyed he'd be punished. He really wanted the reward. With the next step the electricity inside him surged. Another step. He gritted his teeth. Nearly at the bathroom. He could do this. He *would* earn Petrov's reward. Moving slowly, Ryan got his wrists up to the hook, body at the bursting point.

What reward would he get? It might be a kiss.

Ryan remembered the last kiss he'd gotten: from Deke—the hot, wet kiss that had pulled Ryan in like delicious quicksand he never wanted to escape.

"*Kotnyonok*, how are you, my kitten?" Petrov opened the bedroom door.

Ryan recalled how Deke's arms had held him tight against his hard chest. Then Ryan's breath caught, and he came all over the bathroom door, body heaving and shuddering, pushed over the edge by the memory of the kiss.

Oh shit.

Petrov was on him in a second and hauled him off the door, then threw him onto the bed. Ryan couldn't brace for the impact with his wrists bound and crumpled into a heap, pulling his knees in for protection. The butt plug shifted and made him squirm with another burst of pleasure as his cock attempted to drain him dry.

Petrov put a hand over Ryan's mouth and yanked the thing out of him. He roared against Petrov's palm and felt tears spilling down his face. *Fuck, that hurt.*

"I'm sorry, sir," he tried to say.

Petrov pulled his hand away. "I asked you to hold on until the end of my meeting. You barely lasted twenty minutes."

"I know. I failed you. I'm so sorry. Please don't punish me."

"What happened?"

Ryan blinked a few times and sniffled. "It was too good. Felt too good. I couldn't control myself." He sobbed again, expecting more pain, knowing he deserved it.

Petrov laughed. "My precious little slut. You did fine." He brushed tears from Ryan's cheeks and stroked his hair, then planted a kiss on the top of his head. "It's okay." He pulled Ryan into his lap and called him beautiful in Russian.

Ryan melted against Petrov's chest.

"I gave you a difficult task. Impossible task. I simply wanted to see how you reacted. You did well. I will reward you later. For now, have a nap. I will bring you food after my guests have eaten."

"Thank you, sir."

Petrov slid Ryan off his lap and stood, then walked out of the bedroom. He left the door open a few inches, as before.

Ryan listened to the men talking about real estate transactions. Now he understood they were code words for weapons. He also knew when the next purchase would be made and where.

This would help Deke and the FBI.

Ryan rolled over and laid his head on Petrov's pillow. It smelled like him. Like lemons and good pipe tobacco. He thought about Deke's kiss and about all the hugs and caresses from Petrov, and how good a sir Petrov was to him. How this trip had been so wonderful and they'd gotten so much closer.

Petrov had let Ryan touch his cock for the first time, and then at dinner he'd said "I love you."

No one had ever told Ryan they loved him, unless he included a few tricks with their cocks up his ass. And to Ryan, that didn't count.

He snuggled up against the pillow and wondered about his reward.

Then he remembered why he was here in the first place. For Deke.

Ryan slid off the bed and scooted toward the open door. He could see a little bit through the crack. The back of the couch and Petrov's head. He changed position but he couldn't see any of the other men, just their coats draped across the back of a chair. A dark blue one, a gray-green one, both good quality, and a cheaper light tan jacket. That would be the assistant's. The gray-green coat had a tear on one arm and pale fluff peeked out from beneath.

Ryan concentrated on the conversation. Now that he understood they were talking in code, suddenly everything made sense.

PETROV ORDERED room service for his guests, and Ryan got back in bed when he heard footsteps approaching. Petrov brought a plate of food for Ryan and fed him before going back to the living room.

There was a loud argument at that point, and Petrov had closed the door, so Ryan couldn't hear what they were shouting about. He'd been cuffed to the bed after eating and couldn't get to the door to listen.

He liked being restrained. He wondered what Petrov would do to him when he got back. Maybe he'd come in and play while the guests were out there. It would be fun to do that.

After the guests left, Petrov took Ryan for another special dinner, and when they got back to the room, he got his reward: Petrov bent him over the desk in the living room, slicked him up, and fucked him with one of the brand-new glass dildos.

CHAPTER 28

Sunday afternoon
Portland, OR

"NORRIS, WHY don't I have any reports from Vancouver? What the fuck is happening up there?"

"Our guys haven't seen Ryan since they came back from dinner on Saturday night."

"And Petrov?"

"He had guests, but we couldn't see who. The suite he's in has a private elevator. The bug you gave Ryan hasn't been activated. Sorry."

"How do we know Ryan's okay?"

"I can try and get a guy into the suite with room service or maid service."

"Do it."

The security at the Pan Pacific was excellent, and the FBI agent was apprehended. Serah had to tap dance to avoid an international incident for not coordinating the operation in advance with the Canadians.

"But the local intelligence unit agreed to plant a bug on the next room service order, provided we let them have the feed too," Serah told Deke.

"That's better than nothing." It was late Sunday morning, and he'd been up for nearly forty-eight hours, much of which he'd been in panic mode until he verified the Dungeon corpse wasn't Ryan.

The bug had gone in on the lunch cart for Petrov. Deke and Norris sat in Portland listening to the feed of Petrov and his three guests eating and drinking and talking about skiing.

"So, if we have a green light for the Middle Eastern property, what's the schedule for acquiring the one in North Africa?" It was one of the guests. They didn't have visuals, and the only voice they recognized was Petrov.

"When was this room swept?" a husky-voiced man asked. It was the first time he'd said more than a word or two.

"After breakfast. It was clean."

"Do it again," the man said.

"Shit," Deke and Norris said simultaneously.

Twenty seconds later a loud screech pierced their ears and they pulled off the headsets.

Their bug had been detected.

"Petrov sounded calm, though," Norris said.

"Meaning?"

"If he'd just killed or seriously injured Griffiths, he probably wouldn't be so relaxed—or have three guys to his room for lunch and chitchat."

"I'm not convinced. If he was involved in Dakota's death, a few hours later he was on a flight with Ryan as if nothing had happened. We have no idea what this man is capable of." Deke stared at the headset. How had Petrov managed to elude their agents nearly the entire visit?

You'd almost think he knew they were following him.

CHAPTER 29

THE FLIGHT back was uneventful. Ryan slept at his own place for the first time in a week and the next morning found the second page of his newspaper ripped. He was expected to be at the Starbucks by 10:00 a.m. He was supposed to work at ten. He called Gregory's cell. It went to voice mail.

"Gregory, it's Ryan. I have to come in a little late today. Eleven o'clock, I think. I'm sorry. I'll call the store too."

He hung up and showered and made coffee. He needed caffeine before ten. He stared at the newspaper headlines, not taking in the words. The featured photo was a town in Iraq where a car bomb had gone off outside a US government office the previous day. He turned the paper over and wondered if he could get out of the meeting that morning.

He played his fingers across the kitchen table, barely noticing the movement. It calmed him. He got dressed in one of the suits he used for work. What the hell was he going to do?

Deke would send someone to meet him at Starbucks and ask what he'd learned over the weekend. If he told Deke, they might have enough on Petrov to arrest him. Ryan wasn't sure he could survive if that happened. He still wanted desperately to help Deke, but was there a way to please both men?

He could lie and say he hadn't heard anything. Until he'd met Petrov, he'd been a good liar. A great liar. You can't make money turning tricks without some acting skills. "Oh, that's the biggest one I've ever seen," "I don't think it's going to fit," and the ever-useful "Oh God, that's so fucking good."

Or he could postpone the decision. Just a few more days with Petrov. Maybe Ryan would learn something even better. That's what he'd tell Deke. But not today. Not yet.

He blew off the FBI and went to work on time. Let them come after him if they were so interested in whatever he had on Petrov. He wasn't ready to pass on the information. They would have to do more than threaten him this time. They'd have to fucking arrest him for something. He knew Deke wouldn't do that—not unless his boss forced him to.

After this past weekend, Ryan felt so close to Petrov. It had been wonderful. Ryan needed Petrov, and when Petrov said he loved Ryan, it meant Petrov needed him too.

DEKE SAT in the Starbucks, sipping his second cup of black coffee. He'd arrived early, and now it was nearly eleven and Ryan hadn't arrived. Deke's initial excitement and anticipation over seeing Ryan after the horrible weekend scare with Dakota's body gradually turned to anger, then panic. He needed to see Ryan in the flesh, talk to him directly to make sure he was okay. And then he was going to pull Ryan from this operation. What kind of stupid fucking idea was it to let a CI go into a bondage, S&M situation? He should lose his job if this turned into another clusterfuck.

He couldn't suppress the shudder at the thought of the way his last operation had ended. He was not going to let anything happen to Ryan.

Monday. Ryan would be at the clothing store. Deke could pretend to shop for new shirts today. He tried to slow his pace as he walked the six blocks, but it took conscious effort. He was slightly winded when he arrived.

Ryan and the redheaded woman—Julianne, was it?—were both there. Ryan was helping a client, and the woman greeted Deke.

"He was helping me." He motioned toward Ryan.

Ryan looked over, an initial flare of concern in his eyes; then he turned his attention to the customer.

"I can help you," the woman said. "What were you interested in today?"

Deke glanced at Ryan. *Calm down,* he told himself. *Ryan looks fine. No visible marks.* He had to play it cool or the woman would get suspicious. "I recently purchased a suit, and I'd like to check out a jacket too."

"Right this way."

He followed her and killed time trying a few on. Ryan's client left without making a purchase.

"I hope this won't sound rude, but I'd like to get his opinion on which of these two looks better," Deke said.

She grinned and a light must have sparked somewhere in her brain. "Oh, I remember you now." She nodded with a knowing grin. "Ryan? You have a return client...." She spoke in a teasing sing-song.

Ryan came over wearing an expression like Deke might breathe fire. "Mr. uh...?"

"Daniels. Can you help me?"

The woman made herself scarce, leaving Ryan and Deke alone on the sales floor.

"You stood me up, Ryan."

"I didn't want coffee this morning."

Deke stared down at Ryan, looked into his eyes, and knew something had changed. A wall had come down in him, shutting Deke out. The man who'd teased and flirted and kissed him back with genuine passion was gone. This was more than just running off after dinner. This was a complete shutout that went beyond deciding to get physical. What had happened to him?

"We need to talk. Alone."

Ryan shook his head and started to step away. Deke reached for him and grabbed his elbow. At that moment the woman came back and Deke let go. He took off the jacket he was trying on, handed it to Ryan, and left.

TWO HOURS later, Deke closed the folder holding the Dakota murder investigation file and stood in the observation room watching Ryan.

Ryan's jaw was set, and his lips were just a thin, pale line in his face. He narrowed his eyes at the one-way glass wall.

Deke sighed and went inside. Best to start off neutral, keep Ryan from getting defensive.

"Hey, thanks for coming down."

"Your minion threatened to arrest me."

Deke sat down and put the folder on the table. He leaned forward. "Ryan, is everything okay?"

"Everything's fine. Except that I'm here. I don't want to do this anymore. How do I cancel our agreement?"

Any other day and Deke would be thrilled to hear those words. But Ryan's behavior and his refusal to say if he'd learned anything in Vancouver worried Deke. The interview was being recorded, so he had to watch himself.

"I'm not sure what the process is. I'll check with my boss. Hang on." Deke left the room. He'd barely closed the door when he slammed his fist against the wall in the hallway. What the hell had happened to Ryan to shake him up? Deke paced the hall to calm himself, then went back to Ryan.

While he was gone, the level of anxiety in the room had escalated. He felt it emanating from Ryan, who looked shaken and had started his invisible-piano playing.

"She'll be down to discuss the agreement," Deke said casually.

"Good." He peered at Deke and opened his mouth but apparently decided not to say anything.

Deke knew it would be counterproductive to try to get Ryan to change his mind. He would play this another way.

"Did the agent who picked you up explain why I wanted to talk to you today?"

"No, but I assume it's about Vancouver."

"Actually, no. We need your help in another matter."

"Oh." Ryan didn't look relieved.

"You been to Dungeon 69 since you got back?"

"No."

"Then you haven't heard." Deke moved to open the folder and Ryan flinched. He'd definitely looked in the folder while Deke was out of the room. Good. Deke flipped the folder open and watched Ryan shy away from the gruesome crime scene photo of Dakota's mutilated corpse.

"You recognize him?"

Ryan blinked and shook his head, holding out a hand to shield himself from the image.

"Found him near the Dungeon Friday night." Deke had been using his authoritative Special-Agent voice, but seeing the photo made him relive the moment. "I thought it was you, Ryan." Deke couldn't help the emotion in his voice, the mixture of relief and concern.

Ryan looked up at him, and their gazes locked for a moment. A split second of connection. Tears formed in Ryan's eyes, pooling but not falling. His breathing accelerated.

"It's Dakota. The only lead we have is that he was seen with you, Petrov, and the shaved-head guy who was rough on you Friday night," Deke continued with his regular voice, and he noticed Ryan flinched again when he mentioned the bald guy. "What?"

"I don't know. Petrov did a scene with me and Dakota in one of the main rooms. The guy watched, and afterwards he wanted me for the night." Ryan glanced away and colored slightly. "Petrov said that wasn't an option. They had an argument about it. The guy left. I don't know what time it was."

"Who was the man? Had you seen him before that night?" Deke watched for Ryan's reaction. Could this be the same man Ryan had told him about, the one who'd killed his friend?

"No. I'd remember if I had. He had kind of piggy eyes...." Ryan's breathing sped up and he stared down at the table, as if trying to steady himself.

"Talking about him seems to be getting you upset. Why? Is this the guy who killed Rocco?"

Ryan jerked his head up. "No." He relaxed a little. "No. That guy moved differently, like a cat. The guy the other night was more like a...." He seemed to be searching for the right word.

"Pig?" Deke chanced a smile.

Ryan shook his head and didn't return the smile. "Elephant, maybe."

"So what got you so spooked?" Because hearing that another guy you work with got murdered wasn't enough?

"Besides the obvious." There was still no humor in Ryan's voice. "I just don't like bald guys. They remind me of that night."

Deke decided to let that topic go. "You were with Petrov the whole night?" Deke's throat tightened when he asked. Seeing Ryan with Petrov was getting more and more difficult.

"Yes. No. I was at his place, but slept in a different room."

"Did he go out during the night?"

Ryan thought for a moment. "I heard doors opening and closing. I don't know if it was the front door." He paused. "Hang on. You're not suggesting he was responsible…." His eyes took on that defensive cast again.

"No. We don't have any reason to, but it would help to rule him out." Deke looked at Ryan. "I'd feel better about you being with him if we could rule him out."

Ryan's eyes teared up again. Deke fought the urge to reach out and touch his hands, his face, pull him close and keep him safe from Petrov and murder and having to look at pictures like Dakota's.

"I was really worried about you. I still am."

"Petrov would not do that. He's very kind. He doesn't hurt me that way."

"But he does hurt you."

"It's different."

Deke exhaled, calming himself. He hated seeing Petrov hurting Ryan and Ryan thinking he wanted that. Deke didn't trust himself to respond to Ryan's insistence. "How was Vancouver?"

Ryan's eyes lit up. Deke wished he hadn't seen the flash of excitement. Apparently, it had been memorable. All he could think about was Petrov finally fucking Ryan in a king-size bed in a luxury hotel.

He had to head off any chance of the conversation going there. "Specifically, what about his meeting?"

"I wasn't at the meeting." Ryan stopped talking. He looked at Deke, something working behind his eyes. "I was in the other room."

"Did you see the others or hear anything they said?"

Ryan shook his head.

"Anything, Ryan. Any word or sound or even something that doesn't sound important." Deke closed the file folder and moved to slide it back toward him, his fingers brushing Ryan's as he did so. He had to reconnect with Ryan, bring him back from wherever he'd retreated. The same electricity between them in the playroom at the club sparked again, and Deke suppressed a gasp Ryan couldn't.

"What did you hear?"

RYAN FELT the residual tingle of Deke's hand, and it knocked the breath out of him despite being so gentle and so quick.

"What did you hear?" Deke's voice was low and soft, like a caress. It rumbled in his throat, and Ryan imagined the vibrations if Deke's arms were wrapped around him. Again.

Did Deke really worry about him? Ryan glanced at the closed folder, wishing he could unsee the image of Dakota. How had Deke felt when he thought Ryan was dead? The emotion in Deke's voice surprised Ryan. Could he be such a good actor? Maybe it was a skill FBI agents picked up, just like rent boys learned to act.

But Ryan couldn't get Petrov into trouble yet. He wouldn't say anything against Petrov.

"They talked about real estate."

"Real estate?" Deke exhaled loudly and shook his head. "Fucking waste of time," he muttered.

"In the Middle East."

That perked Deke right up. "Go on."

Ryan hesitated. He wasn't really hurting Petrov, and he could make Deke happy too.

"One of the guys was going to Dubai to handle a payment. This week."

Deke made notes on a little pad he pulled from his shirt pocket.

"Anything else?"

"The next one is in North Africa, but I don't know where or when."

"Do you have any idea who the other men were?"

Ryan shook his head. "Oh, one of them spoke Russian. The other had a deep voice. No one said any names the whole time."

"Good. Good stuff. I can work with this."

Ryan liked seeing Deke's smile. He had some color in his face now too. When he'd walked in, Deke had been so pale and drawn, Ryan thought he looked like he had seen a ghost. In essence, he had: Dakota. Ryan shuddered again.

"Thanks, Ryan. I think this is going to help a lot."

Now Ryan wondered if he should have said anything. He didn't think Deke could put it together that quickly. He didn't know that the men had been talking about guns. Part of Ryan was impressed with Deke's quick intelligence. And the other part—the part that wanted to love and protect Petrov—wished he'd kept his mouth shut.

Deke grabbed the folder and stopped before he stood up. "I'm glad you want to get out of this now. I'll be back with the forms to dissolve the agreement, but I'm going to keep some protection on you. I'll feel a lot better when you get away from Petrov. It's too dangerous."

Ryan stared at Deke for a moment. "I don't want to get away from Petrov. I'm staying with him."

Deke's eyebrows shot up and his eyes widened. "What? But-but…."

Ryan put his hand out on Deke's and looked into his eyes. "Don't worry. He won't hurt me. He loves me."

CHAPTER 30

DEKE HADN'T seen that one coming. Ryan thought Petrov loved him? What had happened in Vancouver? He nearly stumbled out of the room, then went directly to Serah's office.

"I got something good from Griffiths."

"'Bout fucking time. What?"

"Do you want me to write it—"

"No. Right now. Tell me." She came around her desk and sat on the edge. She was wearing a slim, dark blue, skirted suit today. It made her look like a banker instead of a flower child.

"All those useless dinner conversations about real estate…. They were talking about guns or money laundering all along. One of his men is going to make a payment for something in Dubai this week."

"You got all that from the little whore?"

Deke decided not to respond to her disparaging description. "Uh, yeah. Gonna have Cyber work on flight manifests, including Portland, Vancouver, and Dubai."

"How do you know the guy is from Portland?"

Deke sat up. "You're right. I don't. I'll have them start here and widen the search to every known associate of Petrov's."

"Alert a team in Dubai to stand by."

"I thought I'd go."

"Deke, if the guy left directly from Vancouver, he's already there. We don't have time. I'll consider letting you bring him back if they nab someone."

He nodded. She was right.

"Let me know if I need to bump it up…. Ward is out of town and I'll have to go to a Deputy Director in DC."

"Will do." Deke went back to his desk. He'd left Ryan in Interrogation, waiting to be released from his agreement. Deke picked up the phone and dialed. "Norris, go down to Interrogation 2 and tell Griffiths we need a few days to draw up the paperwork, and we'll call him when it's done. Drive him home and sit on his place. I'll arrange backup."

Ryan was in danger while they worked on apprehending the money guy, and even more after they did. This was no time to let him out of their sight. Whether Ryan wanted it or not, Deke was going to protect him from Petrov—and himself.

Love!

What the fuck did Ryan know about love from a drug-dealing sadomasochist?

IT TOOK Cyber less than six hours to narrow the search down to three suspects, men traveling to Dubai with connections to Petrov and access to international bank accounts. One of them had also been to Vancouver over the weekend. An FBI-Interpol team brought the suspect in and notified Serah. They also seized all of the suspect's accounts in every country, including the U.S., to the tune of nearly ten million dollars. Undoubtedly, there was more they hadn't found.

"I can't believe it. We never suspected him," Deke said, sitting in Serah's office. "Ryan's in more danger now."

"Try and get him into protective custody."

RYAN WASN'T at home or at Dungeon 69. He wasn't at the men's boutique. Deke couldn't just visit his regular places to look for him and let on Ryan was working with the FBI.

Deke's phone buzzed. He was parked across the street from Ryan's apartment building in a fake FedEx truck. The back was filled with boxes, and he was wearing a FedEx jacket so no one walking by would pay him more than minimal attention.

"Yeah, Norris?"

"He's at Petrov's. They're eating dinner. Well, Petrov is. Everything looks and sounds normal. Well, normal for those two."

"Be back in ten."

Deke started up the truck and raced off, taking the next corner too fast so the packages in the back tumbled from racks and slid around. He'd clean it up later, once he knew Ryan was okay. He wished they still had the van near Petrov's. Once the surveillance equipment in Petrov's was functioning properly, the mobile unit had been dispatched to another operation. Now Deke could only watch in the Federal Building. Too far to help if Ryan needed it.

Norris had all the cameras in Petrov's penthouse up on the big screens when Deke got back.

Petrov was still having dinner. Ryan was serving, wearing a tiny pair of leather shorts with the back cut out. What was the point, really? Ryan stood by Petrov's chair while Petrov squeezed his ass and slapped it now and then, occasionally giving Ryan a bite of food after a particularly loud slap.

Ryan looked fine. Looked like he was enjoying the attention.

Petrov started working on Ryan's piercing, tugging at it. Ryan moved, and Deke saw something shimmer. He zoomed in slightly and noticed the original bar now had a ring dangling from it adorned with something sparkly. Crystals? Diamonds?

"Clear up, boy," Petrov said and got up, leaving Ryan in the dining room.

Petrov went into the dungeon. Norris watched that screen while Deke stayed with Ryan.

"Just setting up for one of their sessions," Norris said as Deke watched Ryan put dishes in the dishwasher.

Everything looked calm and domestic. A little too domestic. Deke felt a pang in his chest he didn't want to identify, but it felt a lot like the one he'd had when Ryan announced that Petrov was in love with him. Any emotion for Ryan was ridiculous. The guy was a prostitute. Who knew how many guys he'd been with? What did Deke see in him besides sexual attraction?

But Ryan had come to the FBI with information, and he'd agreed to get into this relationship with Petrov, putting himself in a dangerously vulnerable situation. Ryan looked to be enjoying playing with Petrov, and something significant had happened in Vancouver, but Ryan had impressed Deke with his willingness to take a chance to stop Petrov.

Even if he stopped informing, they'd made major progress in shutting Petrov down. Soon Ryan would be caught up in the aftermath. The money guy they'd caught in Dubai would help as soon as they got him to Portland.

"Boy!" Petrov summoned Ryan, who came in from the kitchen and presented himself to Petrov in the dungeon.

"Yes, sir."

"Let's get started. Strip for me."

Ryan made as much of a show as he could getting out of the miniscule shorts, and Petrov smiled in enjoyment. "Very nice. I should have put more clothes on you to start. Next time." He chuckled, then motioned to the bench. Ryan bent over, and Petrov fastened his ankles and wrists.

"Okay?" Petrov asked.

"Yes, sir. Fine."

Petrov stood behind Ryan and caressed his ass, squeezing the fleshy globes and playing with his balls. Still business as usual.

Norris yawned. "This is getting kind of old. Too bad the other one's dead. I liked watching the two of *them* together."

Deke turned his attention to Norris for a minute, wondering how to respond to that remark. He would have found it amusing, even intriguing, if Dakota wasn't a tortured, mutilated corpse lying in the morgue. The thought took the edge off Deke. The play between Ryan and Petrov often got him going a bit more than he felt comfortable with. But now he wasn't aroused at all, just worried.

Petrov gave Ryan a few spanks with his hand, leaving prints he examined closely and massaged. He picked up a red flogger with dozens of falls, then started working Ryan over, moving from ass to back to legs.

"I wonder how that feels," Norris said. He was in a particularly talkative and confessional mood this evening. "You ever done that? Let someone hit you?"

"No. I had to spank a couple of guys over at that club to keep my cover." Deke didn't know why he'd said that, but Norris chuckled.

"This job. You never know what you'll have to do. Never thought I'd be watching this sort of thing. Didn't know half this stuff even happened."

On the screen, Petrov had picked up a black flogger, this one heavier looking than the other. He put the first one in his left hand and went back to his original pattern, alternating hands and target body parts. He was surprisingly ambidextrous. He threw in a swat now and then with the heavy flogger. Each time it came down, Ryan twitched or flinched. It appeared to be far more painful than the little red one.

Petrov put the floggers down and went up to Ryan, smoothing his bright red flesh, speaking too quietly for the mics to pick up. Deke saw Ryan nod, then shake his head. Petrov said something else, and Ryan nodded. Petrov retrieved a bottle of water from under the bench and gave some to Ryan, then picked up the floggers and started working again.

Then Petrov's cell phone chirped. He grabbed it and turned it off, muttering something in Russian. He turned his attention back to Ryan. After a few strokes he moved close again.

"You doing okay? You had enough for tonight?"

Ryan shook his head.

"I need you to speak to me, boy."

"I'm fine, sir."

"You want to try the new single tail again? I'll give you something special if you do."

"Yes, please."

"Very good." Petrov got the thin whip and had gotten two lashes in when his landline rang. He ignored it, but the phone kept ringing and ringing. He threw the whip down to the floor and stormed out to the living room.

The ringing stopped before he reached the phone. Deke expected him to unplug it, but Petrov glanced at the handset, then said something in Russian. He glanced back toward the dungeon, where Ryan was still restrained, and pushed a button on the phone.

"What the fuck is the matter? Why you call me four times tonight?"

They had the phone bugged, so they heard the caller: "We had a problem in Dubai, or didn't you hear yet? The mortgage broker was arrested."

Petrov sat with a thud on the couch. "Say that again?"

"Interpol intercepted the transfer."

Deke recognized the husky-voiced man from the Vancouver meeting.

Petrov sneered. "How did that happen? You are supposed to—"

"The orders went out while I was in Vancouver."

"How much did they get?"

"Only ten mil. I'm having the other accounts relocated."

"Shit."

"Why didn't you tell me about the dead boy?" The man paused. "Hold on." There was silence for a moment. "Did you sweep your apartment lately?"

"Perhaps a week ago."

"Fool. Sweep now. And make sure to use the signal jammer on frequency 2 and 17. Make sure to do both." He disconnected.

Petrov slammed the phone down and glanced toward the dungeon again, then back at the phone. He still held the flogger but tossed it onto the couch and went into his office.

"Shit, Deke, he's going to find the bugs. Who's this caller who knows which freqs to jam?"

"Good question." That wasn't the only thing the man had said that worried Deke. But he couldn't focus now, not with Ryan still in Petrov's and the place about to go dark.

RYAN HEARD Petrov moving from room to room and muttering in Russian. With his wrists and ankles restrained, he couldn't venture a look, and he wasn't sure he wanted to. Sounds of heavy items crashing to the floor carried all the way to the dungeon. When Petrov raised his voice, growling out Russian obscenities, Ryan realized he was looking for the FBI's surveillance cameras and microphones.

Fear prickled along Ryan's skin. Was Deke listening now? Did he know Petrov had found the bugs? Ryan tugged his wrists, but the padded cuffs were locked to the edge of the bench. There had to be some emergency latch. He felt around with his fingers, breath coming in gasps as Petrov came back into the room.

Please don't let him find the cameras in here.

Then Petrov stomped toward Ryan. He had a bottle of vodka in one hand and a glass in the other. Until now he'd never drunk while they played. He only allowed himself a few sips of wine with dinner. But now he drained the glass and poured more, draining that too.

Ryan tried to look at him out of the corner of his eye, heart pounding. At least Petrov hadn't picked up any of the toys. Maybe he was done for the night and would release Ryan's restraints.

Petrov was a little unsteady on his feet, and he nearly tripped when he grabbed the heavy black flogger and pulled the falls through one hand while he paced. He nodded a couple of times, then moved toward Ryan.

"Sir? Are you okay?" Ryan ventured.

"Fine. Just a little problem. Sorry. I forget my English." He put the glass down on the table holding a variety of dildos. "You ready to continue?" Petrov's voice was thick. He came up close and smoothed a hand on Ryan's hair.

The gentle touch calmed Ryan, and he leaned into the caress. "Yes, sir." He spoke loudly, hoping Deke or his team would realize he was okay.

Petrov brought the flogger down, hitting only part of Ryan's back and the sensitive flesh along his side—a mistake that experienced tops like Petrov rarely made.

Ryan cried out in pain, and the resulting sound echoed in the dungeon.

"Rio?"

"Yes, sir?" Ryan hoped Petrov would stop now, realizing he wasn't in shape to continue.

Petrov flicked the edges of the flogger over and over on Ryan's right buttock. This was more like it, though Ryan couldn't stop his hips bucking. He was close to his limit.

"I called you at lunchtime. Where were you?" Petrov's voice was high, cracking with emotion.

Ryan's throat tightened.

"At—ow!"

Petrov had brought the flogger down hard. Ryan had never felt pain like that before. He could barely breathe as he let the sting ebb away. He could handle this. Petrov wouldn't ask more of him than he could handle.

Taking this was Ryan's way of proving himself worthy of Petrov's love. He wouldn't use the safe word. That would offend his Dom.

"Where? I called the suits boutique."

"I had to talk to the cops." Ryan forced the words out in a rush of air. He expected another lash with the flogger, but none came. He closed his eyes to center himself again.

"Cops? *Mussor!*" Petrov's roar morphed into a sob. "Why?" He moved to Ryan's head and stroked his hair. "Why? You were my good boy."

"Yes!" Ryan nodded, grateful for the tender touch. He relaxed a little more.

Petrov sobbed again, then brought the flogger straight down for another vicious blow.

The pain radiated throughout Ryan's entire body, stunning and crippling him. Why was this happening? Petrov never hurt him before. Said he loved Ryan. Didn't he?

Blinking back tears, Ryan struggled against the restraints. He was ready to give in and use the word. "Daffodil." This should stop the flogging, or bring Petrov to his senses.

"What did you tell *cops*?" He struck Ryan again. Then grabbed the vodka and drank from the bottle before bringing down another crushing, stinging blow.

Oh, God, no more. "Carnation." It was part shout, part sob. "Please, no more." The scene was over; now Ryan was afraid.

"Answer me!"

"Dead-dead club boy." Ryan gulped. "Asked me what I knew about him."

"What did you say?" Another blow.

"Carnation. Carnation. Please?" Ryan begged and tugged at his wrists, trying to move as far from Petrov as possible.

"Tell me first." Another blow.

"Didn't know anything. Told them that."

"Did you say anything about Vancouver?" Petrov's face was inches from Ryan's, and his eyes were like glowing coals. He stank of sweat and alcohol.

Ryan could barely think, barely remember what Deke had asked or what he'd said. He fought for breath. He'd told Deke that Petrov loved him. It had seemed like the truth at the time. Ryan sobbed, wondering if it had ever been true.

Petrov grabbed a handful of Ryan's hair and yanked his head up. "Well?"

"No." Ryan choked out the word. Had he finally seen the real Maksim? The one who had people killed. Would he kill Ryan himself, right here? *Is this what happened to Dakota? Oh, God.*

Petrov dropped Ryan's head and tossed the flogger away. He knelt down and stared face-to-face at Ryan. Then he started muttering in Russian and crying. But he uncuffed Ryan.

Ryan fled, grabbing at the first thing he saw to cover himself, and kept going until he was out of the penthouse.

DEKE WAS on his feet. "I'm going to get him out, Norris, even if it blows the operation. Keep watching and let me know what happens. Call an ambulance. No sirens or it may put him in more danger. Got it?"

Deke was out the door before Norris could respond.

The drive to Petrov's from the FBI building should have taken twenty minutes. Deke made it in thirteen.

He arrived at Petrov's building before the ambulance and raced inside, using the copied access key to reach the penthouse. He found Ryan crumpled in a heap outside Petrov's front door, wrapped in a tablecloth. The door was half-open, but Deke didn't see or hear Petrov. If he had he might have gone in and strangled the man. Ryan was semiconscious and didn't recognize Deke when he carried Ryan into the elevator. On the way down, he pulled the cloth away, thankful there was only a small amount of blood where the skin had broken. But the welts and abused flesh were still serious. He'd never seen this many marks on Ryan, on top of heavy bruising before tonight's session even started.

The paramedics met them on the ground floor with a gurney, got Ryan inside the ambulance, and took off for the hospital. They examined him carefully on the way and found no major damage. At least Petrov had avoided his spine and kidneys, except for one blow to the lower back.

They'd have to do X-rays at the hospital. Thankfully the Good Samaritan Hospital was only a few blocks away.

"Was he hurt in any other way?" Deke asked, heart still racing from the close call.

"If you mean sexually, there is no evidence of forcible penetration beyond typical, uh, vigorous sex. The skin lesions, heavy bruising, and shock appear to be the only concerns."

Rough sex? So Petrov finally decided Ryan had "earned" that in Vancouver?

Deke paced outside the ER exam room while the doc was inside. As soon as she came out, he flashed his badge.

"Agent, he's going to be fine. He's recovering from shock. We're giving him fluids and some pain meds. Sleep and some anesthetic cream will probably be enough. The bruising will last a few days. It's not the worst I've seen from practitioners, but I can tell he's not used to this level of heavy play from the base level of bruised tissue. We can keep him here—"

"No. I'll take him home."

"He needs someone to watch him overnight, in case the shock is worse than I think. I strongly suggest leaving him here."

Deke shook his head. There was too much risk in the hospital. Too big, too exposed, too many people Deke couldn't keep track of. He collected the meds, and a nurse wheeled Ryan to Deke's SUV. He put the backseat down to make a comfortable place for Ryan and snapped him in with seatbelts.

Ryan began to struggle, mumbling, "Carnation. Carnation."

Deke saw the nurse eyeing him warily.

"Let's try the floor so he won't need to be restrained. Can we get some blankets? Just add them to the bill."

She nodded, and they made a comfortable place for Ryan for the fifteen-minute drive to Deke's apartment.

Deke carried him inside and carefully laid him on the bed in the master bedroom. Ryan didn't wake, but he slept fitfully. Deke stayed at his bedside the entire night, except when he went into the hallway to call Serah with an update.

"Deke, this is not protocol. I want a report on my desk first thing."

"Something's fishy. Are you at home?"

"Of course I'm at home. It's 2:00 a.m. And I'm not happy to be talking to you at this hour."

"There's more to this than what's on the surface. Someone told Petrov something. The husky-voiced guy. He told him about the bugs, and he is somehow connected to the Interpol arrest."

"Come on, that's a load of horseshit."

"I don't think so. Who signed off on the raid?"

"The Deputy Director. I told you, with Ward away…."

"Right. You did." Deke's brain was on overload, and combined with the lack of sleep, he couldn't put his finger on what precisely bothered him. Something was there, out of reach. "Serah, do me a huge favor."

"Jesus fuck, Deke, what do you want next, a blowjob?"

"Humor me." His voice was deadly serious. "Don't report this whole thing tonight. Wait twenty-four hours. Just give me that long to figure out what's going on, or to at least get some proof you'll believe."

"And what about Ryan?"

"He's with me. He's getting medical treatment, and he's safe from Petrov."

"Twenty-four hours. Keep in touch."

"Thanks."

Deke sat in a chair at the side of the bed, making sure Ryan was comfortable during the night, giving him water or just stroking his hair or cheek when he was in distress, until he calmed and fell back into fitful sleep.

"MORNING, COWBOY."

Deke blinked in the pale morning light and smiled at Ryan. "Told you, I'm not a cowboy."

Ryan was pale and looked small against the pillows, but his eyes were bright and alert. Deke's heart tightened at the sight. "I knew the day I met you that you wanted to get me into bed."

Deke let out a soft laugh. "I originally expected to be in there with you."

Ryan patted the spot next to him. "Plenty of room." He lifted the covers and glanced underneath, then back at Deke.

Deke shrugged. "Yeah, it was easier putting on the cream if you weren't wearing pants...."

"Last night's a little hazy. I just remember Maksim went crazy, and I blacked out. How did I get here?"

"Petrov beat you severely. More than play. Do you remember that?"

"We had a hard session." Ryan glanced toward the ceiling. "The phone call. He got a call and then went crazy. He was drinking. He never drinks when we have a session. But the second call."

"Second call?"

"He talked to someone, hung up, and then got mad. He found the bugs. I remember now. Oh shit."

"You could say that again."

"He called out on the landline. He went berserk after that. I don't know what the caller said. That's when he started asking about the cops."

"You said you were with cops, not FBI. Thanks for trying to keep things going, but we're shutting this down. I want to keep you in protective custody." Deke waited for Ryan's response. The previous day in the interrogation room, Ryan had insisted Petrov loved him and wasn't a danger. He'd been wrong, but it wasn't Deke's place to mention it again.

"Do you have what you needed?"

"We made some progress, thanks to you. We'll crack the syndicate eventually with this."

"What else do you need? Let me know."

"I need for you to be safe, Ryan. You don't still want to stay with Petrov, do you?"

Ryan glanced away, eyes full of pain. "No. You were right. He's dangerous."

"How are you feeling?"

"Like I got hit by a truck. Everything aches. But my back doesn't hurt."

Deke held up the tube. "Anesthetic cream and some pain pills. Ready for more of either?"

"Cream. No pills. My stomach feels shaky. You have any food around here?"

"I can rustle up some breakfast after the cream."

"Thanks, Cowboy."

Ryan lay on his side near the middle of the bed, and Deke sat at the edge where he could work easily.

This morning the skin looked much less swollen and red, but it must still smart from any contact. Under the red were extensive dark bruises on his thighs, front and back, and both buttocks. Deke put lotion on his hand and started on Ryan's shoulder with the lightest pressure possible, dabbing with the pads of his fingers.

"Is that okay or am I hurting you?"

"It's fine. It stings a little, but—"

Deke pulled his hand away.

"No, it doesn't hurt. It's the good kind of sting."

Ryan's voice rumbled through his body as Deke gently applied cream to his shoulders and back. The skin was a little warm to the touch.

"I don't see how there could be a good kind of sting, Ryan. This is far beyond a spanking." Deke's gut tightened at the memory of Petrov hitting Ryan the night before. Didn't he remember any of it? They would never agree on this issue.

"You have to experience it to understand. And I know not everyone likes the same thing."

Deke moved down Ryan's back, just grazing the swell of Ryan's ass. Here the skin still showed welts on top of the massed bruises. He lightened his touch, fingers skimming over the mounds of flesh that were very warm to the touch. Ryan really did have a perfect ass. At least according to Deke's standards. It wasn't flat or an overly round bubble butt. Deke remembered having Ryan squirming in his lap as he spanked, then caressed, the curves.

Bad idea. Deke tried to keep his body from responding to the memory and the sensations channeling up from his fingertips. He was spending too much time on this particular part of Ryan's anatomy.

Ryan shifted under Deke, then reached for the sheets. From Deke's angle above Ryan, he realized Ryan had used the sheet to cover up an erection. Odd for someone so used to parading around naked to suddenly be embarrassed.

"Sorry," Deke said. He moved his fingers lower, to Ryan's thighs. In this position, he couldn't get to the sensitive skin where Ryan's ass and thighs met.

Ryan glanced up and back at Deke, and their gazes met. Ryan knew Deke had seen, but after a second the embarrassment faded to acknowledgement. Deke glanced away.

"I need you to roll onto your stomach so I can get the tops of your thighs."

"Okay." Ryan's voice was strained and low. He shifted, and Deke hurried to finish the job. Ryan moved beneath him.

"Am I hurting you?"

"No." Ryan didn't have to say more. Deke remembered how first Roy and then Ryan reacted when he'd hit them there. They had both enjoyed it. The area was very sensitive, and once Deke figured it out, he'd made sure to give them both some pleasure in his touch.

Now it was merely awkward, but if he could provide any comfort or pleasure to Ryan, he wanted to. He deserved it. It would be so easy to lean forward and pull the sheet away and give Ryan more real pleasure than he'd gotten from Petrov's heavy hand. Deke waited a moment, trying to decide if it was the right thing to do. He put a hand on Ryan's hip to roll him back to his side and then reached past his hip.

"I'm dying for breakfast now," Ryan said.

Deke pulled his hand back slowly. Maybe Ryan hadn't noticed what he'd been about to do. Or had he?

"Sure thing. Let me go see what I've got. Stay here."

Deke stood up and quickly moved into the hallway to adjust his jeans for comfort. In the kitchen he opened the refrigerator. Half a carton of milk, and that was for coffee. He didn't even have bread for toast.

"Looks like the cupboard is bare, Mother Hubbard." Ryan laughed.

Deke turned around to see Ryan wrapped in the sheets as though they were a toga, the pierced nipple visible with the sparkly ring dangling from the bar. "Let me go to the store."

"Don't you have to go to work?"

"You are my job today. Got to arrange a safe house for you. Till then you should be safe here."

"Unless I starve." Ryan gave one of his old flirtatious smiles.

"Go back to bed."

"My fridge is full. Let's just go back there for breakfast."

"Are you nuts? Of course you can't go home."

"Yes, Deke, I have to."

"Are you still trying to convince me that you really want to be with Petrov and he won't hurt you because he loves you?" Deke hadn't meant for the words to sound so petulant, but it was too late to worry. Or to take back any of the worry and emotion Ryan stirred in him.

"No." Ryan looked at the floor for a moment, then back at Deke. "You were right, and I was wrong. He has the potential for great violence. But that's not what I'm talking about."

"What then?"

"You said you don't have enough to nail him. Now I want to make sure you have all the proof you need. I can go back because now he trusts me completely."

"You're fucking crazy." Deke shook his head. "No way. I couldn't get approval for this if I wanted to. And I do not want to." His chest tightened, and he couldn't breathe at the idea of Ryan with Petrov again. He couldn't stand to see Ryan hurt or frightened.

"It's not up to you." Ryan went back into the bedroom.

Deke pulled himself together and calmed his pulse before following Ryan.

The sheet was on the floor, and naked and still half-hard, Ryan was at the chest of drawers looking for something to wear.

"There's some hospital scrubs in the bathroom."

Ryan glanced up and then walked into the bathroom, not bothering to cover himself or his arousal this time. He pulled the loose-fitting clothing on while Deke watched, then came back into the bedroom.

"Take me home. I'll give you the car ride over to try and talk me out of my plan. Then we'll just get some of my clothes, and I'll go hide in your safe house. Okay?"

It was as good as Deke was going to get. "Okay."

But on the ride to Ryan's, Deke didn't say anything. He had no better reason to stop Ryan from going back than anything he'd already said. At least nothing he was willing to admit to Ryan.

How could Deke admit he'd fallen in love with Ryan? It was crazy and unprofessional, and even if it weren't, Ryan would never want Deke. Ryan wanted to live life on the edge. Wanted danger and pain, and Deke's way of loving was completely the opposite. He wanted to keep Ryan safe, wrap his arms around him, and protect him from worry or danger. Wanted to take away his pain.

Ryan couldn't accept Deke's kind of love, and Deke couldn't give Ryan the "good" kind of pain.

Deke had to let him do what he wanted to do.

He hoped like hell he wouldn't lose another life all in the name of the operation and the goal.

Ryan glanced over at Deke; then, as if sensing Deke's resignation, he put his hand over Deke's on the armrest between them. He left it there but didn't look at Deke again. Instead, Ryan stared out the window through the raindrops and windshield wipers.

Deke took what he could from the comforting touch and blinked away a tear. Or maybe it was just the rain.

CHAPTER 31

DEKE PARKED behind the building, and they used the back entrance. He'd gone once around the block and hadn't seen Petrov's car or anything suspicious, but he still didn't think this was the right thing to do. He'd stay until Ryan threw him out.

Ryan unlocked the door, and Deke stooped to bring in the newspaper. He dumped it on the table in the nook between the kitchen and living room. He'd only been in Ryan's place once before, and he fought the urge to look around at everything in order to understand him better. They didn't have that relationship, and it would just hurt worse when Ryan pushed him away or rejected him.

Ryan was pulling fresh eggs and milk out of the refrigerator. The kettle was already on the stovetop.

"Ryan, why don't you lie down while I make breakfast?"

"I want to cook for you this time."

"I can make breakfast." Deke frowned.

Ryan shook his head.

"Okay. Can I make coffee?"

Ryan chuckled. "I better do that too. I've had your coffee...."

"Are you up to it?" Deke didn't need to ask. If Ryan could tease him, he was probably on the road to recovery, even if his body still looked abused.

"Yes. I'm feeling a lot better. I just needed a good night sleep and your healing touch." Ryan reached out and held Deke's hand in both of his own, then ruined the moment with a sardonic wink.

"Stop joking for ten seconds and be serious."

"Really, I'm okay. I bounce back pretty fast."

Deke made coffee—to Ryan's specifications—and toast, while Ryan made bacon, then fried eggs in the bacon fat. Breakfast was delicious and filling.

"What's your big plan, Ryan? With Petrov." Deke cleaned his plate with the last piece of toast and chewed. "He could hurt you worse next time."

"The thing is, Deke, he really does love me."

Deke let out an incredulous sound.

"Hear me out. Last night when he was interrogating me and he started to cry, he was still saying he loved me. In Russian. He hasn't said it directly in English, but I think that means it's really true. I can't explain why."

"But that didn't stop him from hurting you."

"Now I know what he is capable of. And the triggers. I can make sure to keep safe or have an escape. And I won't let him restrain me again. It's part of our contract that I get to set those limits, or change them. I will tell him this before I play again. Do you feel any better about the situation now?"

"Not much, but I don't want you over there until we get more surveillance tech installed. And you are not going to be bringing it. That's too risky. He knows someone is on to him because we arrested his associate in Dubai."

"What do you need from me, then? What can I find out?"

"There was a man in Vancouver. I know you didn't see any of them, but he had a husky voice. Can you remember anything about him? Have you heard anyone with that voice before or since? Someone at the club, maybe?"

Ryan shook his head, then stopped. "Hang on…. No, it's gone. I can't remember what it is I noticed about him. Something, in the back of my brain."

Deke did the dishes while Ryan took a shower. He came out of the bedroom in a towel, the jeweled chain hanging from his nipple glittering in the sunlight streaming in the window.

"Could you put some cream on before you leave?"

"Sure." Deke followed Ryan into the bedroom and watched as he lay on the bed. Ryan's back was almost back to normal. "Anywhere in particular this time?"

"Here?" Ryan skimmed his fingers over his ass.

Figured, Deke thought. He was as sensitive to Ryan's ass as Ryan was. He started to apply the cream.

"Thank you, Deke." Ryan turned to look at Deke sitting behind him on the bed. "I mean that. Thanks for worrying."

"You know you don't have to do this thing with Petrov. I hate that I put you there. I didn't understand what I was sending you into. I will never forgive myself for that, even if he ends up in prison for the rest of his life and we take down the whole ring. It's not worth risking... you."

Ryan didn't reply right away. "Except for last night, I didn't mind. I was scared, but the rest of the time I knew I could handle it. He really did want to take care of me in his way."

Deke stopped rubbing, his hand resting on Ryan's ass. "You know you don't have to give up so much of yourself to get love and affection. Or even to get laid, if that's all you want. There's someone out there who wants to treat you well, even for a quick fuck."

"Deke, those fairy tales are for people like you. Love and sex just don't work like that for people like me. I don't get your happy endings. I learned that a long time ago."

"Why not?"

"I spent most of my adult life earning money by fucking total strangers. For money, for food, for a roof over my head, for a new shirt. I can't reinvent myself now. To Petrov I'm just a body, not the sum of my past. Can't you see why that would be a nice change for me?"

RYAN WONDERED why he'd said those things to Deke. They should make Deke run away and stop being so fucking nice to him. Ryan didn't want nice. Nice either turned nasty or disappeared. Nice hurt much worse than mean, by the end.

But Deke didn't leave, and he didn't take his hand off Ryan's ass either. His hand felt good. He was trying so damn hard not to hurt Ryan, but every single touch of Deke's hand stirred something deep inside, not just Ryan's body, but his spirit. If he listened to Deke's pretty words long enough, Ryan might talk himself into believing them.

"You're more than just a body or your past. *To me*." Deke said the last words in barely more than a whisper, but they sliced through Ryan's heart all the same. "You volunteered to go back to Petrov even after he hurt you. Don't you see that's more important than the other things to show who you are inside?"

Ryan rolled toward Deke. "You wanted me to start up with him. Now you're only worried because you don't want something to happen to me, like those kids who got killed. I know it's not about *me*." Ryan saw Deke's face crumple. He'd purposely said the worst thing he could think of to break through Deke's delusions.

"You're wrong." Deke swallowed and visibly pulled himself back from the edge.

"No—"

Deke put a finger over Ryan's lips to silence him, and Ryan was shocked by the electricity that shot through his body at the touch. He must have shown that in his eyes because Deke was looking back at him as if he'd suddenly felt the same thing.

Thankfully, Deke didn't pull his fingers back. Instead, he gently traced Ryan's mouth with his fingertips, following the contours and eliciting a multitude of emotions Ryan couldn't fight off. His lips fell open slightly, letting Deke know he enjoyed the touch, inviting more. Fast enough to knock the breath out of Ryan, Deke pulled him in, arms circling him, and pressed his own lips to Ryan's.

Until it happened, Ryan had himself convinced he didn't want this. Couldn't handle this. But here in Deke's arms again, Ryan wondered how he'd handle it when Deke finally let go.

Ryan wasn't quite sure what had hit him, but he was sure he'd never been kissed quite like this in his life. It was even more incredible and intense than the first time in the room at the club or those few exquisite moments he'd allowed himself in Deke's bathroom.

Deke was practically extracting Ryan's life force through his mouth as his lips and tongue began seeking and finding, probing, and it felt so amazing Ryan was prepared to be consumed entirely by Deke, wanted desperately to give himself up completely to the overwhelming intensity of Deke Kane, even if it killed him. In fact, Ryan couldn't think of a more pleasant way to die than in Deke's arms, held tight against the hard wall of muscle, as Deke's body took away Ryan's ability to think or breathe or move, or do anything other than let Deke have everything and more.

Ryan had never felt so out of control, and that alone was intoxicating. It was far more dangerous to give in to Deke than to submit to Petrov or any of the other Doms at Dungeon 69. That loss of control was temporary, exhilarating, but ultimately left everyone untouched when it was over.

Ryan was freefalling now, knowing Deke would catch him, but that he would never be the same again. It was the most dangerous thing Ryan could possibly do, but with Deke's arms around him, he felt safer than he had since he'd left home. It had nothing to do with Deke being an FBI agent and everything to do with the look of wistful longing Ryan had seen in Deke's eyes as he'd tried to warn Ryan to give up the operation and run for safety. Deke wouldn't hurt him or let him be hurt. Every fiber of Ryan's body was now thrillingly aware of just how much Deke wanted to protect him, please him, shelter him, and Ryan wanted it as much as Deke did.

Deke's arms felt like hard steel, pulling Ryan closer, tighter, as his lips opened, mouth crushed to Ryan's. Deke seemed to be breathing through Ryan, and every single breath or moan or shudder was magnified through Ryan's body. He was on fire, flesh seared by Deke's touch, cock so hard it hurt just thinking about it, but so pleasant because Ryan knew there was the promise of infinite pleasure from Deke.

Deke would be just the sort of lover to take everything, but give back even more, leaving both of them exhausted and shattered and incoherent afterward, relying solely on the other for mere survival. Ryan had never wanted anyone more than this in his life, and he let Deke know that as he returned Deke's passion with equal fierceness and longing.

Buttons popped free, seams ripped, and finally Deke was naked, too, in a wonderful blur as they melted together on the bed. Deke kissed and licked his way down Ryan's body. Every inch he traveled was almost torture—Ryan's cock wanted all the attention, but Deke was taking his time, exploring with hands and mouth and eyes, pleasure evident in even the simplest touch or caress or glance. Deke slowed and lingered on the marks that Petrov's beating had left on Ryan's pale skin, kissing them gently as if loving away the pain that he'd allowed to be inflicted on Ryan.

Deke's tenderness nearly brought tears to Ryan, not just because of the affection that was evident in the touch, but because it brought home to him that these past weeks Deke had seen everything Petrov had done— had made Ryan do—and it hadn't stemmed the feelings Deke had for him. His initial shame at that knowledge washed away as Ryan realized exactly what Deke was offering him: unconditional acceptance.

Petrov might have brought them together, but nothing Ryan had done with Petrov was enough to push Deke away. The idea of emotion that strong and accepting was a new concept for Ryan, and it frightened him. He forced memories of Petrov from his mind and concentrated on the way Deke was sucking at his navel, one hand on Ryan's thigh, long, thick fingers wrapped around his leg with just the fingertips occasionally teasing their way toward the base of his balls and sending shockwaves and tremors through Ryan's entire body. It might be physically possible to come just from the thought of Deke touching his cock or pushing inside of him.

As much as Ryan wanted Deke to touch his cock—stroke it, lick it, suck it—he was terrified that first touch of Deke's fingers or mouth would send him over the edge. He couldn't decide which was worse, not having Deke touching him, or coming in two seconds like a horny virgin.

He didn't have to contemplate for long. Deke's lips brushed along Ryan's sac, stubbly chin scraping the skin of his inner thigh, as Deke kissed Ryan tenderly, audibly inhaling, breathing in Ryan's essence. Slowly, Deke caressed his way up Ryan's cock with lips and tongue, lowering a hand to fondle his balls and tease at his hole. Ryan was aware of a loud, deep moaning and was surprised to discover it was his own voice betraying the pleasure building inside as Deke teased and explored his body.

"What took you so long?" Ryan asked.

Deke raised his head, giving Ryan a beautiful view of the smooth, muscled expanse of his chest, and the even more beautiful dark, swollen cock just bobbing against his thigh. Ryan might have gasped at the sight of that and the thought of how good that cock would feel inside of him. And he wanted that sooner rather than later. His question had been for himself as much as for Deke.

"It wouldn't have meant anything before now," Deke whispered. "I would have been another trick to you."

It hurt that Deke was mostly right. Ryan had been attracted to him physically from the first time they'd met. He'd have done anything Deke wanted in those two encounters at the club, and he'd wished Deke had wanted more from him. But that day they'd kissed, Ryan knew then that being with Deke would peel away his layers of protection.

"Does sex have to mean something to you?" Ryan asked.

Deke stopped sucking and looked up at Ryan.

"No. But when it does, it's the most incredible thing in the world. And addicting." Deke grinned.

"Show me." Ryan let himself be swept away in Deke's passion, and Deke went back to lavishing attention on Ryan's cock.

Ryan's world fell away, narrowing itself to just what Deke was doing, where and how he was touching Ryan. Nothing else in the world mattered or existed as long as Deke was naked and hard, cock dripping as it dug into Ryan's leg while Deke moved his mouth over Ryan's cock. Instinctively, Ryan's fingers threaded themselves in Deke's soft, lush hair, taking even more pleasure from the contact, and Deke smiled and groaned his own delight at Ryan's touch.

Agonizingly slowly, Deke licked his way up and down the shaft, tongue tip probing at the slit, lapping up the pool of precome. Then even more slowly he began to take Ryan deep, devouring him inch by inch while Ryan watched, fascinated at the display of pleasure evident on Deke's face as he provided even more pleasure to Ryan. And Deke's mouth was hot and wet and skilled, his tongue eager to explore, soon discerning the most sensitive spots, those that caused Ryan to shudder or groan or squirm. Deke had one hand on Ryan's hip, pinning him in place, not allowing him any respite from the aggressive and overwhelming pleasure that Deke offered.

Deke hummed and groaned around Ryan's cock as he sucked, still playing at his hole or tugging at his balls, and the combination of sensations was more than Ryan could resist. He didn't want to fight the pleasure, the heavy ache at the base of his cock, the heat and pressure of Deke's mouth. He wanted all of it, wanted more of it, wanted it forever. He just didn't want it to end, and he struggled against his orgasm until finally Deke slid a spit-slick finger just inside and Ryan lost the battle, feeling his orgasm crash over him like a tsunami, leaving no survivors. He couldn't help the way he shouted as he came, shuddering beneath Deke as he pumped hot and strong, filling up Deke's mouth. Deke made little encouraging moans as he used his hands to prolong Ryan's pleasure, gulping down Ryan's come and not spilling a drop.

When the world stopped spinning and exploding, Ryan opened his eyes to see Deke grinning down at him. He reached up to pull Deke down next to him and leaned over for a kiss, enjoying the way Deke's strong arms encircled him, lending him strength and sharing his energy, his life force. Finally, Ryan's breathing returned to a more normal cadence. He let his hand travel down Deke's body and took loose hold of Deke's cock, hard and thick and hot to the touch.

"I certainly hope your next feat of magic would be to fuck me," Ryan groaned.

Deke pressed his lips together and frowned. "I don't really want to fuck you. I want to make love to you," Deke said softly.

Ryan hoped Deke made love the way he kissed, as if he'd die without Ryan and only Ryan's body could save Deke's life.

"That sounds even better," Ryan said and meant it. He couldn't remember the last time anyone had made love to him or the last time he'd even remembered that such a concept existed. Now, in the space of less than an hour, Deke Kane had once again turned Ryan's world completely upside down, lying next to him with that beautiful dimpled smile that lit up the room like summer sunshine. Ryan felt warm and safe basking in the glow that Deke shared with him, though that mind-blowing orgasm Deke had just given him probably had something to do with it. At the moment, Ryan would do anything Deke asked of him, and it scared him. Not because of what Deke might expect, but the acceptance of Ryan's own longing and vulnerability.

DEKE LET Ryan roll the condom down over his cock, watching Ryan's skillful fingers. He tried not to think of how many other men those hands had touched, how many times Ryan had been in this same situation with other men. He'd drive himself crazy thinking like that.

When Deke reached for the lube, Ryan beat him to it and prepped himself so quickly Deke didn't even get a chance to help. Ryan did look damn delectable flat on his back, legs wide, with a finger pushed inside, but Deke knew it was just a performance Ryan had perfected. He didn't want to use Ryan the way other men had.

"How do you want it?" Ryan asked, finger still inside.

"What do you like?"

"Whatever you want. Just name it." He finger-fucked himself again, then threw Deke a daring glance as he withdrew the fingers.

Deke lay down next to Ryan and pulled him close. "Okay. I want whatever *you* like. You name it."

"You really are a natural Dom, you know that?" Ryan flashed his flirtiest grin.

Deke frowned.

"It was meant as a compliment, Deke."

"So, what would you like me to do?"

The cocky, confident gleam in Ryan's eyes vanished, replaced by an expression of doubt, of vulnerability. He glanced away from Deke and then looked up again and shrugged in a way that ripped at Deke's heart. "I never... thought much about it."

"We'll figure it out—together." Deke gazed into Ryan's eyes and felt an even stronger desire to protect him from everything and anything. To make him forget pain and fear and darkness.

Deke leaned across for a soft kiss and wrapped Ryan in his arms again. The kiss deepened and Deke let his desire take over. Carefully, he rolled Ryan onto his back and moved to kneel between his knees. Ryan looked so much younger, so exposed, his emotions laid bare for perhaps the first time in years. Deke wouldn't take advantage of him.

He pushed in slowly, watching for cues from Ryan before moving. A gasp of pleasure told him all he needed to know, but he waited a moment then gathered Ryan in his arms. The tight heat felt amazing, but this was as much about Ryan's pleasure as Deke's, so he took his time, trying different speeds and angles, letting Ryan's reactions signal him.

Occasionally Ryan sucked in his breath sharply or squeezed Deke's arm in obvious delight. At other times a low moan told Deke what Ryan didn't enjoy. After the first few minutes of overstimulation, Deke was able to control himself, hold back his own pleasure as he sought to unlock Ryan's.

Eventually Ryan let himself relax, let Deke make love to him, and then Deke lost himself in Ryan, thrusting faster, deeper, as Ryan's arms and legs pulled him in and pleasure began to overwhelm every one of his senses.

Ryan looked up, gazing into Deke's eyes, and smiled, gold-flecked eyes twinkling. "Wow," he said. "Just... wow."

Deke inhaled, breathing in Ryan's scent, mingled with the medicinal salve, and let go completely, ecstasy shooting through every inch, every pore of his entire body. When it released him from its grasp, he rolled onto the bed and wrapped Ryan in his arms. But only when he saw the expression of equal joy on Ryan's face did Deke feel true satisfaction.

CHAPTER 32

THEY'D JUST gotten out of the shower, and Ryan had a towel wrapped loosely around his waist in a charming display of belated modesty. Deke really wanted to pull it off of him and devour him again, but they were both sated and exhausted.

"Don't take this the wrong way, but you know he's going to come looking for me," Ryan said.

Deke nodded, following him out of the bathroom with its steamed-up mirror and hot, foggy air. "I've got a tail on him. Norris is supposed to call me when Petrov leaves his place."

"Then maybe we have time to do whatever you're scheming," Ryan said with a smile that got Deke hard again just watching Ryan's lips part, thinking about how they'd felt on his body, how they'd feel again soon.

"How do you know I'm scheming?" Deke asked, trying to sound coy.

"Your cock can't keep a secret," Ryan said, reaching down to stroke Deke gently through his own towel, now tenting in a very unsubtle way.

Deke laughed as they sat down on the edge of the bed. Ryan flicked off the lamp on the table, and just as he was about to climb into bed next to Deke, there was a loud pounding on the front door.

Deke instantly sprang up, all his senses alert, at attention to potential danger. He tried to remember where he'd left his gun—and his clothing. In a pile near the foot of the bed, he recalled, as Ryan headed for the front door, the damp towel wrapped around his waist again. Deke stayed in the bedroom, lights still off, and watched Ryan peer through the peephole. He spotted Ryan's surprise right away, but Ryan waved at him to disappear back into the bedroom, and Deke immediately sensed something had gone wrong with the surveillance.

"Maksim, what are you doing here?" Ryan asked, just the tiniest hint of apprehension in his voice. Deke could tell that despite Ryan's professed lack of concern about Petrov's temper, he was terrified and trying hard not to show it, and it made Deke want to jump out and put a few bullets into Petrov's chest.

"I need to see you. I owe you apology. Please let me in."

"You can say what you want from outside."

Good, Ryan, Deke thought.

"I can't. I need to make sure you are okay. I did terrible thing last night. I am so sorry for that. For not trusting and for...."

Deke couldn't hear the rest of it. His heart flew into his throat when he heard Ryan open the door. He'd always wondered what the phrase meant; now he knew.

"Oh, my sweet, sweet boy, let me see you. Turn around."

A silence.

"Your back is recovering. Take off towel." A pause. "Towel."

Deke imagined Petrov's hands on Ryan's body, shoulders, ass. He felt the weight on his chest again.

"Poor little pet."

"Maksim, I'm not sure I want to be your pet anymore."

"What? Why not?"

Silence.

"Of course, you are right. I am fool. We could have new contract."

"Thank you."

"Come here, *moi krasavitz*, my beauty. I should have taken care of you. I don't remember much, but I remember hurting you. Something bad happened and *ment*—that cop—said you.... But how could I think you were involved?"

"What happened?" Ryan's voice had gone soft and worried. Was he pretending, or did Petrov still have some power over him? Deke felt a chill run down his spine.

"Business. Not your concern. I should not worry you."

"I want to be more than your boy. Let me help."

"I know. And that's why I'm here. You are so much more to me, and I couldn't let you get away without telling you. You know I am hooked on you."

"You are?" Ryan asked. He was relaxing and starting to sound coy.

Oh shit, Deke thought.

"You will give me second chance? You will still be my good boy? My Ryan. Not Rio. Not just my pet."

"I just need a break. A day or two?"

"Oh, please no. Please don't put me away. Let me make this better. Show you."

Deke thought he heard kissing. Wet sounds and soft groans he knew were Petrov's.

"Come here," Petrov said.

Deke couldn't see anything. He couldn't see, but he could hear: Petrov made more wet groans that made Deke feel sick in his gut.

"What's wrong, Ryan? You don't seem happy with kissing," Petrov said, and his voice had shifted dangerously quickly to a threatening tone that worried Deke.

"I'm just tired and—"

"There, how do you like that?"

Silence, but Deke imagined what was going on: Petrov had his hands on Ryan.

"Ah, you like. Let's go in bedroom."

"Maksim, no."

"You are still my boy, right?"

"Yes, sir."

Deke heard them coming and ducked into the closet, but he didn't have time to shut the closet door without being seen. He crouched and moved closer to the crack in the door. Now he could see Petrov on the bed with Ryan. The bed he'd shared with Deke less than an hour earlier.

"What's this?" Petrov leaned down to pick something up from the floor.

Deke hoped he hadn't left any clothes in the bedroom.

"Condom wrapper?" Petrov put his hand under Ryan's chin. "Who was here with you? I smell sex."

Deke coiled his muscles, ready to spring out of the closet if Petrov started to hurt Ryan.

"It's old. I was cleaning before you arrived. And I masturbated this morning."

"Oh." Petrov took his hand away, but Deke didn't relax. "Poor boy. I wasn't here to make you come. I will do now. Something you like. Something you always ask."

"I'm okay now."

"I want to make my boy happy. But you are more than just boy. I know I told you that you must wait to earn fucking. But now I give you to show you are so special, you do not have to earn. I give you."

Great. Deke couldn't watch or listen to that. Not now. Maybe last month or last week. Maybe even last night. But not now. Not after he'd shown Ryan how beautiful sex could be between people who share an emotional bond. He stood up slowly. Should he stop this?

"Sir, can we save that for a special night? Will you take me to a restaurant like in Vancouver? Take me on a date, and then it will feel more special."

"Yes, my sweet. It's good idea. I like that idea." Petrov kissed Ryan long and deep, pulling at the piercing at the same time. "Then you will still have nice reward today. Suck me, then I do you. You will like."

Ryan closed his eyes and nodded slowly.

Petrov stood up, and Ryan started to unzip his pants. "Thank you, sir. I want to do this for you."

Deke knew Ryan was telling him to let it go. He closed his eyes. He couldn't look. But the sounds were almost as bad because he could imagine how Petrov looked each time he grunted. Deke could picture what Petrov was doing, where his hands were, the moment when his cock pushed its way down Ryan's throat—Ryan made that now-familiar little sigh, sounding just like he had when Deke had pushed into his welcoming heat.

Then he heard a rhythmic banging sound and had to see.

Petrov had moved Ryan away from the bed and had him on his knees in front of the closed bedroom door. He was ramming his cock down Ryan's throat, pushing in hard and fast as Ryan's head banged against the door. Then Petrov pulled out and stroked himself a couple of times until he painted Ryan's lips, throat, and chest with come.

A cell phone burred. Deke swore under his breath before he realized it wasn't his, though he hadn't turned his off. It still could ring at any moment.

Petrov pulled a phone out of his pocket, his other hand still pointing his dick at Ryan.

"Yeah? … This is not good time." He squeezed a few more drops out and wiped himself in Ryan's hair.

Deke wanted to rip the dick right off his body. This was the special treatment?

Petrov listened to the caller, then said, "Half hour." He hung up and looked down at Ryan.

"I am so happy you are still mine." There was a pause. "But I am a little glad you know I can hurt you too. I need to be certain you always tell truth and never talk to anyone about me."

"Of course I won't."

"I want to make you my very special pet. But I must know you will always keep my secrets."

"Yes, sir."

"I hope so."

Petrov gripped Ryan's throat and banged his head against the door so hard it shook Deke to the bone. "No lies." He took his hand away and brought it back in a hard slap that left Ryan with blood dripping from the corner of his mouth and staining his teeth. And then Petrov left.

Deke was out of the closet before the front door shut.

"Not yet," Ryan mouthed.

"Boy?" Petrov shouted from the other room.

"Yes, sir?" Ryan rushed toward him.

"I will call you about dinner date." He paused. "Your lip is so pretty like that, soft and swollen. I would like to fuck your mouth again with the bloody lips. Perhaps later."

The door shut, and Deke heard Ryan lock it, but he didn't come back into the bedroom.

When Deke went out to the living room, he found Ryan slumped against the door, tears streaming down his face, body wracked by silent sobs.

Deke knelt down and pulled Ryan into his arms, stroking his hair. Now he had Petrov's semen all over him, but Deke didn't care. He was going to get that bastard if he had to kill him.

"Please leave, Deke. Just go away."

"No. I should never have let that happen. I should have stopped him. I'm sorry he hurt you."

"He didn't hurt me. And I didn't mind the other part." Ryan looked away.

"Then why are you crying?" Deke wiped tears away with a thumb.

"I never cared what a trick did to me—within reason—until today. Because now you've seen what a whore I really am."

"I don't see it that way."

"You will."

Deke kissed Ryan, hoping to kiss away the taste and memory of Petrov, but Ryan's tears kept flowing.

"Let's get cleaned up," Deke said and went to start the shower.

He washed them both again, then put Ryan to bed, where he fell asleep almost immediately. Deke watched him for a few minutes, wondering which side of Ryan was the real one. He'd been so many different people today: Petrov's victim, Deke's new lover—seemingly overwhelmed by tenderness—then Petrov's property yet again, giving in to his owner's wishes.

But what did Ryan want from Deke? He'd wanted to get Petrov rather than let Deke take him to a safe house. Was he risking himself to help Deke, or was there something else going on here?

Deke needed time to work through the unraveling threads of this case before Serah's deadline ran out.

Deke scribbled a note, then changed his mind. Petrov might come back; it wouldn't be safe. He crumpled the paper into his pocket and left.

For the time being, Ryan would be safe. There was a car out front, and they still had cameras in here. Deke stopped in his tracks. He'd completely forgotten about the cameras, including the one in Ryan's bedroom.

CHAPTER 33

DEKE WENT back to the Federal Building. He didn't care if he was wearing jeans. He had two things he had to do before he could talk to Serah, and they both started with Norris up in Surveillance.

He balled his hands into fists as he rode the elevator. He must have said something unintentionally, something inappropriate, because the other two people moved to the far side of the car.

Pull yourself together, Deke.

He was barely two strides out of the elevator when Norris arrived in the hallway.

"Deke, I—"

"You fucking dropped the ball on Petrov this morning."

"Give me a—"

"No, you don't get—" Deke stopped when Norris held up a DVD case with a shiny new disk inside.

"Take it, Deke." Norris looked around, then pulled Deke toward the men's room. "It's this morning at Ryan's."

Deke stared at the disk, knowing what was on there. He let out a puff of breath and looked at the floor.

"It's the only copy, just in case," Norris whispered, then continued in his normal voice. "I'm afraid I lost most of the footage from this morning rebooting the system because of a malfunction. I'm sorry. I lost almost an hour of surveillance."

"Is this why you didn't catch Petrov leaving?"

Norris nodded. "I am so fucking sorry about that. But I have the attack on Ryan. No malfunction."

"Okay. Keep watching." Deke would have to thank him later for making sure his encounter with Ryan didn't end up in the evidence box when—if—they ever got this case to the prosecution stage.

DEKE WENT out for lunch. He wasn't hungry, but he had to get rid of the DVD. It wouldn't do just to stick it in his car. Someone might see that, and he'd have to explain what it was. He moved at a leisurely pace through the mist that hadn't quite decided it was a drizzle yet. His hair and clothes picked up moisture, but he liked this weather. It cleared the city, cleaned the air, and kept the sidewalks fairly empty.

Four blocks away he turned into a copy shop that rented mailboxes. He rented one in Timothy's name and paid for six months in cash. Then he bought an envelope and put the DVD inside, addressed to Timothy at the new private mailbox, along with a hastily scrawled note:

> *Just in case this comes into your possession, don't watch it, unless I'm dead.*
> *—DK*

He bought postage and left the shop, going up two more blocks before putting the DVD in a street mailbox. Getting it off his person let him relax a little. He still wasn't out of the woods. Norris hadn't deleted the video off the transmitter relay. Chances were that no one would ever look there for it, but until Deke could figure out how to do that, he could still get in a hell of a lot of trouble.

Back at his desk, he worked on his report covering the events of the past two days for Serah. He didn't want to relive the memory of watching Ryan being abused as Petrov interrogated him, but it was the key, Deke was certain of that.

Petrov had gotten so angry at him, accused Ryan of saying something after Vancouver. How had Petrov known? Ryan actually hadn't said anything that directly connected Petrov or any of his friends to the money, the drugs, or the weapons. But Ryan had been smart enough to put the pieces together and tell Deke just what he needed.

Something else got Petrov's suspicions up.

Everything had started with the phone call. The husky-voiced man who had warned him to search for bugs.

Bugs the FBI had installed.

Was there a connection?

Who was the man, and how did he know about the listening devices in Vancouver and at Petrov's? And why had he somehow directed Petrov's anger at Ryan?

Timelines and facts swam in Deke's head, and he couldn't get them to form a coherent picture. He was too worried about Ryan now. If Petrov wasn't the one behind everything, the other man might want to get Ryan out of the way before he could bring anything concrete to the case against Petrov and the drug money.

Deke stood up so fast his chair shot out behind him and banged against the next desk.

"Someone should give you a ticket for that," Red Quinn shouted.

"Sorry," Deke said, grabbing his jacket as he took off for the door.

He took the stairs to the parking garage to save time dealing with the elevator jam at the ground floor, then raced to Ryan's apartment. He parked around the corner despite his temptation to get close. He still needed to keep to protocols.

He ran down the hallway to Ryan's apartment and found the door slightly ajar.

Deke pulled his weapon and held it out as he flung the door open. If Petrov was here and he blew their cover, so be it.

"Ryan?" Deke moved methodically through the rooms, but the place was empty. The open door had him on high alert. He moved back through each room, looking for any sign of what had happened.

He found it in the kitchen. An overturned carton of milk on the counter and blood. Blood on the counter, mixed in with the milk and on the floor. A heavy chef's knife lay there, blood glistening on the blade.

Had Ryan used the knife to ward off an attacker, then lost control of his weapon? Now Deke noticed a blood trail on the floor, leading to the front door. He'd missed it before on the dark carpet. He raced down the hall, following the blood. It stopped in front of apartment 4, where Ryan's friend Gina had moved for the operation.

Now there was the chance of two victims or hostages.

Deke kicked the door in at the knob and entered, gun leading.

A scream and the sound of a shattered glass brought him back from Special Agent autopilot mode.

Gina and Ryan sat at her kitchen table. Ryan had a bandage on his left hand. Gina had her hands up in surrender; a broken glass lay at her feet.

"Deke, what the hell?"

"Ryan, what happened?"

"I cut my finger on a damn knife. Calm down."

"No. As long as you don't need medical attention, I need you to come with me."

"What's wrong?" Gina asked.

"Better not to explain—for your safety." Deke nodded to Gina, whose eyes were still wide. She had a hand to her throat, and her fingers shook. "I'm sorry, Gina. We'll call you later. You should probably clean up that blood in the hallway. If Petrov does come back I don't want him finding you. Ready to go, Ryan?"

"See how popular I am?" Ryan joked to Gina, but he went with Deke. "Where are we going?" he asked when they were in the hallway.

From behind, Deke rushed him along to the back entrance without answering. Once they were in the car, Deke took off and got on the freeway.

"You gonna tell me where we're going?"

"Not sure yet. But we have to get out of this vehicle." Deke headed for downtown, fighting the urge to speed down the tree-lined street full of low-rise apartment buildings and trendy eateries. They got out of the car, and Deke led Ryan to the MAX light rail stop. They got on the next train. It was crowded, and they didn't get a seat.

"You gonna tell me—"

"Soon. In the meantime, tell me if you heard from our mutual 'friend' after I left."

"Yes. He called to apologize again. He wants me to go to the club with him tonight. One of his friends wants to meet me."

"Who?"

"I don't know, but maybe it's one of his—you know, the guys I'm supposed to…." He didn't finish the sentence after Deke glared at him.

"Considering what happened to Dakota last time one of his friends met him at the club, I hope you weren't considering going."

Color drained away from Ryan's face. "I forgot about that." He looked like he might be sick.

That's how Deke felt too. What if he hadn't come back in time?

They rode the MAX for about twenty minutes, then got off near Madison in Goose Hollow—a mostly residential area but only a couple of blocks from a busy street of shops and cafés. It was starting to get dark, and the restaurants and houses were putting their lights on.

Around one more corner and Deke went through an alley to the back of a beautifully restored Victorian fourplex and opened the back door to the building.

"Not even fucking locked," he muttered. Up a flight of stairs and then he found a key on the molding near the ceiling in the darkest part of the hallway, fifteen feet from the door he wanted to open.

"Where are we?"

"A friend's place. Let's get you changed and pack up some clothes." He found a suitcase in a hall closet and went into the bedroom. "Get some shirts and jeans and things. Warm clothes. Nothing that will draw attention."

Ryan put on a pale gray button-down shirt and a pair of tweedy trousers. He pulled a sweater vest out of a drawer and shook his head. "The only people who might notice us dressed in these would be at an accounting convention." Ryan continued to joke as he started packing.

Deke pulled his phone out of his pocket. *No. Not safe yet.* He could still be tracked or traced.

"Who is this friend?" Ryan had picked up a framed photograph from the dresser and pointed it toward Deke.

"I'll explain later." Deke took the photograph of himself with Timothy hiking in Peru and threw it into the suitcase. He couldn't leave evidence of their connection, just in case. No time to ponder that Timothy still had it on display in the bedroom.

"Let's go." In the kitchen, he grabbed a set of keys from a hook near the refrigerator and pulled out a carton of orange juice.

"Oh, yeah, I'm parched."

"We'll get something soon. This is a message." Deke put the carton on the entrance hall table, and they left with the suitcase. He locked the door and put the key back where he'd found it.

Behind the building was a garage, and Deke used the keys on the door, then to unlock a late-model dark blue Lexus. He tossed the suitcase in the backseat and hit the automatic garage-door opener. Then he backed out of the garage. He pulled to a stop, went back in, took a backpack off the wall, and tossed it in the spot the car had occupied. He'd bought the pack for Timothy for the Peruvian trip. He hoped the message was clear. Finally, he got back in the Lexus, gunned the engine, and raced down the street.

Twenty minutes later they were sitting at a hole-in-the-wall Greek restaurant on Columbia, near the university. Ryan had some color in his face by the time he was halfway through a huge gyro and had eaten half of Deke's fries.

"Now what?"

Deke opened his phone and texted Serah. Those couldn't be traced.

Need a safe house off the grid. Someone on our team involved.

Serah texted back:

I'll arrange a private house.

Deke replied:

Hurry.

Before they had finished eating, Serah had texted an address and

This place is off our grid. Call me when you get there.

"Time to go."

CHAPTER 34

TWO HOURS later they drove through the tiny hamlet of Rhododendron at the base of Mount Hood. The air was fresh and clean here. Neither of them had brought coats, so Deke stopped at a sporting goods shop and bought heavy waterproof jackets, decent boots, and some camping supplies. Then they went to a small mom-and-pop grocery store off Highway 26 where Serah had told him to pick up the keys from the caretaker who owned the grocery store and a local real estate/property management company.

They stocked up on food; then Deke located the house Serah had arranged. He drove by without going inside. It was dark. He drove two miles back into town and called Norris from a pay phone. Only a safe, homey town like this would still have a pay phone—complete with an intact phone book. Deke wondered what it would be like to live in a place where no one stole the phone book or spray-painted obscenities on the side of the booth or any of the shops in town.

Just a crazy idea. He'd be bored to death in a place like this, no matter how much his inner soul craved the concept of peace and safety.

He picked up the phone and punched in Norris's number.

"Norris."

"It's Dan. Don't say my nickname."

"De-Dan, what's up? I hav—"

"Norris, I need a fast favor. Take down this address and tell me who owns it. I'll call you back in five minutes."

He did.

"Owned by a property management company called Lake Properties for the past seven years. Before that, by a Mrs. Beryl Wilson for twenty years. No flags in our system on the address or Lake Properties."

"Okay. Thanks." Satisfied, Deke drove back to the house, and he and Ryan brought in the bags.

The property was a distinguished-looking old hunting lodge two miles outside of town, renovated and gentrified, with every appliance known to man and a few more besides. It wasn't large but had two bedrooms and thick carpeting everywhere but the front hall and the kitchen.

Ryan put food away while Deke turned on the heat. There was a nice fireplace in the living room, and he started a fire. It soon took the chill out of the place. He started looking through drawers but couldn't find anything that revealed the identity of the owner. But Serah had said she didn't trust anyone as much as this person.

Deke wandered through the cabin while Ryan curled up on a thick rug in front of the fire like a cat.

A set of hunters' crossbows hung on one wall and a collection of rifles on another. Deke couldn't tell if they were working models or for display only.

He pulled one down. No ammo, but everything was oiled and in smooth working condition. He located the ammo cache and loaded two rifles, as well as his own service weapon.

"Deke, don't you think you're overreacting a little?"

"No. Ryan, these guys are arms dealers."

"I thought they were drug dealers."

"If they aren't personally dealing in arms, they are friends with people with very dangerous toys."

"Okay, I believe you."

"Can you shoot?"

"What?"

"Have you ever shot a gun? A shotgun, a BB gun, anything?"

"No. I've played video games, but I don't really like the shooting ones."

"Close enough." Deke showed Ryan how to load the rifle, aim, shoot, and reload. "I'd have you practice, but I don't want to draw any extra attention here."

"Won't you protect me?"

Deke stopped and looked at Ryan. Bundled up in Timothy's sweater and the new jacket, he looked so different from the guy wearing nearly transparent shorts and parading around at Dungeon 69. He wasn't a kid anymore, but his smooth city rent-boy facade had been brushed aside, and he looked lost and afraid.

Deke stepped forward and pulled Ryan into his arms. "Yeah. I'll protect you. I'm going to make sure you're okay."

"I really hope you're overreacting."

"Me too."

Ryan looked up at Deke. "But keep holding on like this. Okay?"

"As long as I can." He brushed his lips against Ryan's hair and remembered how it felt making love to him that morning. It seemed like a hundred years ago.

"I'm tired." Ryan sighed against Deke's chest.

Deke remembered he'd spent the night before at the hospital and then slept fitfully in Deke's bed before he'd been attacked again by Petrov.

"Let's find the bedroom."

"No. The fireplace. Come lie down with me here." Ryan heaped some quilts from the couch on the floor and pulled Deke down with him. Deke couldn't remember the last time he'd relaxed. He'd been on constant alert, a state of vigilance, since before Dakota's body had been found. Four days? Five?

Ryan looked so warm and welcoming. Deke let himself fall into his arms and closed his eyes.

Ryan's lips were soft as he kissed Deke's eyelids. Deke felt fingers playing through his hair, and he could hear Ryan's heartbeat.

WHEN DEKE woke up, he couldn't remember where they were or why Ryan was wrapped around him. It felt good, but it couldn't be a good idea. Gradually, the situation cleared up. The fire was almost out. He got up and threw a few more logs into the fireplace.

"Let me warm you up," Ryan whispered. He slid a hand under Deke's sweater and started to unbutton his shirt. His fingers were warm, and the way he stroked Deke's skin got him heated up almost immediately. He pulled Ryan close and kissed him hard for a few moments, then backed away and enjoyed a longer, sweeter kiss while Ryan peeled away the layers of Deke's clothes.

The silence of the cabin was disturbed only by the crackling fire and their labored breathing, punctuated by soft moans. Deke kissed down Ryan's throat and neck, remembering Petrov's tight grip and wanting Ryan to forget it. He nuzzled Ryan's right nipple, pulling it into his mouth and enjoying how it felt as it plumped and hardened against his tongue. Ryan shuddered as Deke sucked.

Then he lifted his head to tug at the piercing. The nipple was already swollen and tight. "Are you going to keep this, after?"

Ryan raised his head so he could meet Deke's gaze. "Do you like it?"

Deke flipped the ring up and down. "I do. I didn't think I would, but I like how it looks, and you said it feels good."

"Mmm."

Deke put his mouth to the pierced nipple and played with the metal using the tip of his tongue. Beneath him, Ryan squirmed and groaned. Yes, he could get used to this. He slid a hand down to wrap around Ryan's cock, but Ryan rolled away. He shifted so now Deke was on his back.

The fire flickered and a log cracked, sending a little fireworks display toward the chimney. Ryan lay next to Deke, leaning over to play with his cock, then taking the crown into his mouth and using his tongue to incapacitate Deke.

Ryan straddled Deke, ass nearly in Deke's face, then moved back until his cock dangled over Deke's mouth.

He'd never successfully managed a 69 from this angle, but Ryan knew just what he was doing, and Deke opened his mouth and licked at Ryan's cock, hard and so perfectly accessible. Above him, Ryan dipped his hips. At first Deke tried to chase his cock, then moved his head so Ryan's cock plunged in and out.

Deke had never had his mouth fucked like this, and he loved the way it felt. He used pressure and suction on Ryan and paid little attention to whatever Ryan was doing to Deke's cock. Deke used his hands to cup Ryan's ass, stroke his balls, or push a finger inside. Soon Ryan began to shudder and lost his rhythm. He groaned, and Deke intensified his actions.

"Deke, gonna come. Slower, slower, please not yet."

Deke ignored him and a moment later, Ryan came, shooting into Deke's mouth, down his chin, and somehow a few splashes went up his nose. He started laughing. Ryan wiggled his ass and backed up so his balls were right in Deke's face. Deke licked and sucked them, enjoying the way it made Ryan squirt and dribble come onto his face.

Ryan sat up and turned around to face Deke. "You don't follow directions, do you?"

"No. It's one reason I'm still alive." He pulled Ryan down for a kiss.

Ryan licked Deke's face clean.

"Good puppy. I have another spot you can use your magical tongue."

"Is that what you'd like? I had something else in mind."

Deke didn't even try to guess what Ryan had in mind. There was little chance he'd figure it out. "Whatever you want."

Ryan got up and turned around. "Just lean back against the couch."

Deke sat up and scooted up to the couch. Ryan sat in his lap and kissed him, hands moving low to Deke's cock. One hand encircled it while Ryan rubbed the other thumb along the underside and across the slippery slit. Then Ryan moved backward. He stuck one hand under the quilts and produced a condom and a packet of lube.

"Seriously? You really plan ahead."

Ryan shrugged. "Occupational hazard." He gave Deke a completely unsupportable coy look and slid the condom on before Deke even heard the wrapper tear. A slathering of lube and Ryan was back in his lap, sliding down onto Deke's very impatient cock.

Ryan lowered himself, and Deke felt tight, slick heat engulf him. Ryan rose and sank, the muscle in his ass working the length of Deke's cock while his hands and mouth continued the onslaught, adding layers of sensation to arms, shoulders, throat, and nipples. And still Ryan came back to Deke's mouth, lavishing long, deep kisses on him.

Deke closed his eyes as if that might protect him from the waves of pleasure already engulfing him. Every single touch felt so incredible he didn't know how he'd managed to last this long. At every second he expected to explode, but Ryan kept him just this side of orgasm, prolonging the ecstasy until Deke begged.

The intensity built so high that when Ryan finally brought Deke over the top, he could barely catch his breath. It wasn't like riding a wave or racing a downhill ski course or skydiving. It was like everything happening at once, only fifty times better because Ryan kept whispering his name until Deke had given up every drop he had.

He pulled Ryan close and held on for dear life until the roller coaster slowed to a halt.

Then Ryan cleaned him up and laid him back in the quilted cocoon before wrapping himself around Deke again. As Deke lay staring at the ceiling and stroking Ryan's hair, he understood why politicians, megachurch preachers, and even presidents threw their lives and careers away for sex. Why guys with wives and kids got hung up on strippers and hookers and spent all their money, lost their jobs and families—or worse.

This feeling was so overwhelming, no one could make a rational choice. No one could survive sex like this on a regular basis, could they? Would any lover ever be enough after a few nights with Ryan?

There couldn't be any more nights like this, for so many reasons. There wouldn't be any more. Deke might spend the rest of his life having boring, mediocre sex, but he couldn't let himself believe there was anything more to this than a necessary and convenient outlet for their desire and their stress.

But until the sun came up, Deke could imagine he was the luckiest man in the universe.

CHAPTER 35

THE AROMAS of fresh coffee, crisp bacon, and eggs hit Deke's brain before he even opened his eyes. Ryan was kneeling next to him, holding out a mug and balancing a plate on his lap.

"Morning, Cowboy."

Deke took the coffee and sipped carefully. He'd burned the roof of his mouth too many times. Then he took a huge gulp and sighed. Breakfast in bed. Or on the floor, served by an even more delectable Ryan. The perfect morning.

Then Ryan turned as he served the plate, and Deke noticed the swollen face and bruises from Petrov's anger the previous day. His stomach shifted, and he lost his appetite.

"Not hungry."

"Of course you are. I heard your stomach rumbling. You need energy." Ryan winked. The glittery nipple piercing twinkled in the sunlight.

Deke tried not to stare at Ryan's body or remember how he'd used it the night before. "Maybe later."

"Should I wake you up again?" Ryan slid a hand between Deke's legs, but Deke pushed him away, with difficulty. It would be too easy to lie back and let Ryan do things to him.

"No. I need a shower." Deke pushed himself up, surprising Ryan, who dropped the plate. Toast, eggs, and bacon splattered to the carpet. "Oh, fuck. I'm sorry. Let me—"

"It's fine," Ryan said, but his voice was tight. "Take a shower. I'll clean up." He went into the kitchen, and Deke stared at his ass, still marked from Petrov's ill mood, the only blemishes on its perfection.

Shower! he reminded himself and took the coffee along with him.

When he came back out, wrapped in a towel, Ryan was dressed. It was quite a difference from the skimpy, sexy outfits he wore at Dungeon

69. Now he sat there in Timothy's somber pants and dark shirt: a lawyerly version of Ryan, or maybe the opening scene to a legal-themed porno where within two minutes his pants would be around his ankles while the judge bent him over the railing in the courtroom.

Ryan kept his eyes averted as Deke pulled on clean underwear, his jeans from the previous day, and one of Timothy's luxurious long-sleeved cashmere sweaters. It felt gorgeous against his bare skin.

"Now what?" Ryan asked, while Deke pulled his boots on and fastened his holster.

"I have to report to Serah, but first, I'd like to go over some more details with you. About the husky-voiced guy. Everything you can remember about him. Anything he said, the kind of words he used, how he sounded."

"What do you mean?"

"Who was in charge of the meeting?"

"Petrov, I th—" He paused. "Oh, wait. Maybe it was Husky. He let Petrov talk, but yes, it seemed he was getting a report, rather than Petrov explaining the plans to his subordinates."

"Okay, that's good."

"What are you thinking?"

"Not sure yet, but every little bit helps."

"Oh, there's one more thing I do remember. He was wearing a nice coat, one of the brands we sell at the shop—"

"Great, so he's got lots of money. We've already established that."

"No, more than that. There was a rip on the arm." Ryan rubbed a spot between the shoulder and bicep of his right arm. "He was growling at the other guy's assistant, something about ripping it in the elevator."

"That's the only other thing you remember?" Deke didn't want Ryan to sense his disappointment, or it would block any other memories.

"Sorry." Ryan knitted his eyebrows and looked like he might cry. "I wish I had seen or heard something."

"If you try too hard, you won't remember. Just think about something else for a while and another memory may surface. Text me if it does. No calls."

"Text you?"

Shit, he had intended to tell Ryan another way. "I need to meet someone. I won't be gone long, but I have to check on a few things. I don't trust anyone now. I have to do it myself."

"Let me come with you. I can be your driver, lookout. Whatever."

"You're safer here. No one will come looking for you here, but the people I'm after know what I'm doing."

"Then it's not safe for you either."

"Ryan, this is my job. I don't have the luxury of playing it safe if I'm doing it right."

"When will you be back?" Ryan wrapped his arms around himself, but he was shivering.

Deke grabbed another sweater from the suitcase, a thick cardigan with a cabled fisherman-style pattern. He sat next to Ryan and wrapped it around Ryan's shoulders with a squeeze and a kiss to the top of his head.

They sat together, Ryan wrapped in Deke's arms for a while. Ryan smelled like coffee and the peppermints Timothy liked to crunch when he read in the living room till all hours of the morning. There was an undernote of sex from the night before. Ryan smelled of everything good and comforting and worth coming home to in one piece at the end of the day.

"Don't let anyone in. If you hear anything outside, grab the gun. I'll text you when I'm back, before I knock, so you'll know it's me. You'll be fine. I know you can handle this."

Ryan nodded and sat up straighter, but he didn't say anything. He followed Deke to the door and held out his arms for a last hug and kiss before Deke needed to leave. He shut the door.

"Lock it."

"Okay."

Deke heard the bolt slide home; then he went around the corner to where he'd left Timothy's car and drove back toward the city.

CHAPTER 36

RYAN CLEANED up the kitchen and the living room floor after Deke left. He threw more logs on the fire and sat on the couch reading one of the books from the bookcase along one wall of the lodge. The books ran the gamut from *The Iliad* to Tom Clancy, and he picked something in the middle, *Great Expectations*, which he'd started reading in college and never finished because he'd dropped out.

All the years in between and he'd never thought to pick up the book again to find out how it ended. He'd wondered, but he knew reading it would bring up memories of college—he'd loved it—and all the unpleasantness surrounding his leaving.

No. He hadn't left, hadn't dropped out. He'd been forced to quit when his dad stopped supporting him. Why was he still sugarcoating it now as if it had been voluntary? It made him think of his mother.

He'd wanted to call her over the years, but he knew she was better off thinking he was dead than knowing who and what he'd actually become. But if he could help Deke, be a witness and get his name cleared of everything else, then he'd be someone she'd want to see again.

He looked down at the sweaters and pants he was wearing. Deke's friend's clothes. The guy was wealthy, based on the quality of his clothing, and boring. He liked soft, neutral tones and natural fibers. He had good taste in clothes. Ryan had learned enough from working at the men's boutique to know that. He got up and looked at himself in the mirror in one of the bedrooms.

He looked respectable in these clothes. Was this the kind of man Deke wanted in his life? He knew the clothes, apartment, and car belonged to Deke's lover or boyfriend or partner, even if Deke hadn't mentioned the fact. He was too casual about taking the man's property for any other relationship, and the "message" of an orange-juice carton on a hall table spoke of a degree of intimacy. But there was no trace of the well-dressed man at Deke's house. And nothing of Deke's in the other place. Ryan wondered why they'd split up.

Ryan could get respectable again. He needed to stick things out at Gregory's boutique. This would all blow over soon, and he could go back to his new life, his 12-step program for former sex workers, and try to turn himself into someone who looked respectable on the outside. He wouldn't be unblemished, but he might be the kind of man Deke would want to know if they hadn't been forced together to stop Petrov. Would Deke be able to forget Ryan's past if he could clean up his act going forward? He seemed like the kind of man who understood second chances.

Maybe Deke would come by the boutique again, and they could get to know each other like normal people—with their clothes on.

Shit. He hadn't called the store to tell them he wouldn't be in for a few days. He grabbed his phone and dialed, but there was no answer.

It was well past opening, but someone always answered. The voice mail was full so he couldn't even leave a message. That was strange. He didn't have Julianne's number, so he called Gregory to apologize. No time to burn bridges; Ryan needed that job when this—whatever it was—blew over. Maybe Deke would come back later and say the case was over and Ryan could go back to his regularly scheduled life.

Gregory's voice mail was also full. Something strange was happening.

His last option was to call Gina.

"Oh, Ryan, I just heard this morning. Gregory left the other day for his buying trip in Europe and Hong Kong, and apparently, he's been arrested. All the stores are closed, and no one knows what's going on."

"Arrested? For what?"

"Dunno. You should ask your hunky FBI guy with the big gun." She snickered. "Is he *protecting* you?"

"Yeah. He's here." Ryan didn't know why he lied, but it seemed like the right thing to do. Make sure no one knew he was alone.

"Where are you guys?"

"Vegas."

"You have all the fun." She stopped. "Oh, sorry. I know you're over all that kind of fun."

"It's okay."

"You are okay?"

"I'm good. See you soon. Call me if you hear anything about Gregory?"

"Sure thing. He owes me almost two weeks' wages, 'course I wanna know where that bastard is."

"Gotta go, Deke's calling."

"Bye."

Ryan hung up and turned the phone off. It was almost out of juice, and he didn't have a charger. He threw another log on the fire and sparks flew, but it would take a while before he felt any warmer.

He hated lying to Gina. He could use her support right now, but he was afraid to tell her what was really happening. Something big was wrong, and Deke was heading right for the middle of it. Hopefully, he knew what the hell he was doing.

Now Ryan felt more alone than ever.

DEKE DROVE about twenty miles west on 26 and found a coffee shop in Sandy. The sign outside said "Best Cupcake's in Town." He cringed at the misplaced apostrophe, but went in anyway because it had a nice corner location where he could see traffic in both directions.

He texted Serah the address.

An hour later she arrived, bundled up in three layers but still wearing summery strappy sandals. She had a sour look on her face. Her feet were probably freezing.

"What's with all the James Bond shit?"

"Sit down. Please."

She slid into the booth and raised an eyebrow.

The waitress came over, pulling her pad out of a pocket as she greeted Serah. "What can I get you? You need a menu?"

"Coffee, please. And—" She looked at Deke's plate with a half-eaten red velvet cupcake. "One of those. You got any carrot cupcakes?"

"Got seventeen kinds," the waitress said as if announcing a child had just been accepted to medical school. "I'll bring the list."

"Oh, good coffee," Serah said with a satisfied groan once she'd taken a sip. "But this place makes me feel like I stepped into a *Twin Peaks* episode. Do you hear creepy music?" She flashed a grin.

"I wish I could laugh." Deke sipped coffee. It was cold. He got the waitress's attention and she refilled it with a smile. He took a fortifying sip before trying to explain. "I went over the tapes with Petrov and Ryan—the ones from the other night." His back started aching just thinking about it. "What Petrov said, that phone call. And I went back through the whole case file, from the beginning."

"I still don't think we have enough proof for a prosecution, Deke. Petrov's associate has been brought back from Dubai. He isn't talking yet, but you can question him. He's one Gregory Antony, born in the former Soviet Union, as was our buddy Maks. Was he on our radar at all before this?"

Gregory Antony.... Ryan's saintly Gregory was one of Petrov's accomplices. The fog was beginning to lift. "Not exactly. Not in connection to Petrov, until now."

"Great work identifying him. The cross-references you put together did the trick."

"He's in Portland already?"

She nodded. "He owns several grocery stores and menswear boutiques. Looks like he was in the dry cleaning business, only he laundered more cash than cashmere. And, he's also the owner of Club Kiwi, through three levels of holding companies. Probably that's where the majority of the cash got laundered."

A cold mass formed in Deke's gut. "Don't let Antony talk to anyone. Put him on suicide watch and keep everyone out but you and me. We can't risk him getting a message to anyone. Ryan and his friend Gina are still in danger. Can you get her to a safe house too? Her connection to Ryan puts her at risk."

She frowned and pushed the rest of her cupcake away. "Look, Deke. You need to explain who and what the hell you suspect here. I've gone to bat for you on this operation, backed you because despite the mess you made last time out, I still think you're a talented, valuable agent. But I am still your supervisor, not your mother. I won't automatically support everything you want. I need facts."

"Someone in the FBI is in on the drugs-for-weapons operation. I just don't have concrete proof."

"That's ridiculous."

"No. Ryan gave me more details about Vancouver. When he repeated the conversations for me, verbatim, it seems the husky-voiced guy isn't just a partner. I think he's running everything. Petrov handles the merchandise—the drugs—and the other guy—Antony we caught in Dubai—is just the money end. Laundering it and transferring it for their purchases. They called him the mortgage broker. But the third guy is the one they called Security. He's the inside man."

"What makes you think he's Bureau?"

Deke took a breath before answering. He was putting everything on the line here. If he was wrong, he'd be lucky to end up in the Cybershit basement. And he could be in far worse trouble. If he was right, he and Ryan could still end up dead.

"I went back through the Petrov file. Every single page since the beginning of time. Some of the pages were missing."

"Missing?" Serah's attention perked up.

"From last year, the year before. A page here and there. I went back into the database to see where the agents on the case were those days… and almost every one of the dates had been a failed raid or sting on one of Petrov's locations, drops, deals. Someone had to be tipping him off. Different agents over the years, good guys with solid leads. But still Petrov was at least a step ahead of them. From his file, they've never had a solid piece of evidence against him. I'd like to talk to the agents and see their personal notes." Agents often kept their handwritten notes and interviews, even after they transferred the information to the official reports and files.

"That's not conclusive." She picked up a piece of cupcake with her fingers and popped it into her mouth. "But it's intriguing. Worrying. The part about the pages missing. Who would cover that up?"

"Whoever is tipping him off."

"Why?"

"So no one would notice the pattern over the years. That's all I can think of. But it means it's someone who's been in the Bureau that long, and has access to the paperwork. Someone who doesn't have to sign the file out officially to alter it."

"I suppose you already have a list of suspects?" She gave a sour smile and ate the last piece of cupcake.

"I do. I cross-checked agents working on Petrov against flights to Vancouver, as well as absence around the time of any of the known out-of-town meetings of Petrov's group. I have three names that meet at least two of the criteria. The insider could be working with someone else who helped diffuse the pattern."

"Let's see it."

"One of the names is yours." He watched her face for a response.

She let out a snort. "You have to be joking." Then she sat up straight when she realized he wasn't.

"Why'd you put me on this case, Serah? Because I was already halfway through the Bureau's exit door, and you thought I wouldn't figure it out?"

"You think I assigned this to you expecting you to fail so my partners in crime and I would be safe?"

He nodded. He didn't think she was involved, but he had to know.

"I'm not the one who chose you for this assignment."

His stomach twisted again. He slid the list across the table, and Serah picked it up, furrowing her brow.

"Deke, this *is* a joke." She put the paper back down.

He tapped a name. "Serah, he was away the other day. He's been gone a lot recently."

"He just finished treatment for throat cancer. There's nothing suspect about that. Perfectly legit."

Throat cancer? "The husky voice…."

"What husky voice?"

"The guy on some of the tapes. He had a low, husky voice." It hit Deke: Serah never heard the tapes, just read the transcripts and summaries. Everything fit.

She shook her head. "No. I've worked with him since I started in the Bureau. I trust him with my life, Deke. And yours. He's not part of this."

The words rang in his ear. "With your life?" She'd said that the previous day.

Deke hurtled toward the door.

CHAPTER 37

RYAN STARED at the phone, willing it to ring or even spit out a text message. He desperately wanted to call Deke, but he knew he wasn't supposed to.

The country was so damn quiet. Ryan had finished *Great Expectations*. The ending had disappointed him. Just like the ending to everything he'd looked forward to. The irony of the title was not lost on him. Why had he expected anything different this time around?

He was too nervous to relax or start another book. He had energy to burn, but Deke would shit a brick if Ryan left the house for a walk. It was starting to get dark, so he put the lights on.

A few cars drove past, the first ones he'd heard all day. Then another one, slowing down. He fought the urge to race to the window and look for Deke.

A knock sounded at the door.

"Deke?" Shit, he wasn't supposed to answer the door.

"Ryan? It's Agent Norris. Deke sent me." The name sounded familiar. Deke must have mentioned him before. Norris held up his badge and ID to the peephole.

He looked safe enough. A middle-aged guy, slightly balding. The tips of his ears were red from the cold.

"Can you prove Deke sent you?" Ryan remembered Deke was supposed to text him. He looked at the phone again, and realized he'd turned it off. He flipped it on. Immediately, a notification for a text from Deke popped up. Without reading it he shouted through the door, "Okay. Come in." He undid the chain and the bolt and opened the door.

Agent Norris came in. "Deke hit on a lead he needed to follow up out of town. I'm supposed to take you to another safe location. He thinks this one's been compromised."

"Okay. Let me get my stuff."

"No time."

"It's actually Deke's friend's stuff. I can't leave it." He went to get the suitcase by the fireplace.

"Come on." The guy's voice rose, and Ryan turned to stare at him. "Okay. But quickly. This is for your safety."

"Less than a minute."

Ryan knelt down behind the couch, putting the clothes back into the case. The agent paced near the door, picking up a pile of unopened mail from the top of the table by the door. He flipped through the letters and junk, then took one letter and opened it.

Why would he do that? Ryan reached down and felt around for what he needed. How had it gotten so far under the couch? Agent Norris moved, and Ryan noticed a little spot on the sleeve of his coat.

"Fuck."

The guy glanced over and their gazes met, acknowledgment sparking. The man put his hand in a pocket, but thankfully, Ryan had been ready.

He swung the rifle and pulled the trigger.

DEKE DROVE like the devil. He wished he'd thought to bring the cherry light into Timothy's car. Lights and siren would have made a difference. He'd broken several laws trying to text while speeding, but he didn't give a fuck. Ryan didn't respond.

When he got to the cabin, the street was quiet. Deserted. No new cars visible. Maybe he'd gotten here in time…. Was there any chance of that? He halted the car, tires screeching. He pulled his weapon out of the holster as he exited the vehicle.

The lights were on and the door shut. The house looked fine, but Deke ran for the front door. He was ten feet away when he heard shots.

THE GUY went down, but he fired as he fell. Ryan didn't duck fast enough and one bullet whizzed past his ear and another past his shoulder. He wasn't sure where he'd hit the guy, but he wouldn't take time to look. Where to hide?

The door burst open.

Should he shoot the intruder or stay behind the couch?

Shoot first. Ask questions later.

Ryan sprang up, gun aimed at the door. He was already squeezing the trigger when he realized it was Deke.

"Ryan, stop!"

The bullet shattered the wood of the door. Ryan dropped the rifle, his shout morphing into a wail. He raced toward Deke.

DEKE WAS leaning down to restrain Ward when the door exploded. The sound startled him, and Ward grabbed his knee and pulled him off balance. Deke went down and lost his grip on the gun.

Ward lunged for the weapon, blood streaming from his face and what was left of his ear. Deke smashed a fist against his head, but managed only a glancing blow. They struggled for the gun, but Ward had Deke's shoulder pinned to the floor with a bony knee and he had the advantage of leverage.

Deke let his body go limp, using Ward's momentum against him and giving Deke a brief advantage. The gun went off, shattering the window. In the distance, Deke heard sirens. Would they get here in time?

Then he heard a loud thwack, and Ward crumpled onto the floor.

Ryan stood holding a heavy leather-bound book in both hands. He brought it down on Ward's head again until the man stopped moving, half sprawled on top of Deke.

Ryan held up the book, *Great Expectations*. "I like this ending much better."

CHAPTER 38

RYAN TOSSED the book away and knelt down next to Deke, helping him push Ward off his leg. "Are you okay?"

Deke was pulling cuffs out of the pouch on his holster and had them around Ward's wrists before he caught his breath enough to answer.

"Barely. Good thing I ducked or my brains would be all over the wall. Who taught you to shoot like that?"

Ryan shrugged. "Maybe I played more video games than I care to admit." He looked down at Ward. "That's Husky. He had an FBI badge. Said you told him to take me somewhere. Then I noticed the sleeve." He touched the spot. "He got it fixed, but they didn't do a great job. Thankfully."

"I tried to call you. Why didn't you answer?" He turned toward the door. The sirens were right outside, and he heard car tires screeching.

"I turned it off to save the battery." Ryan threw his arms around Deke's neck. "I'm sorry. I could have shot you."

"You could have been killed. At least you protected yourself."

"You're a good teacher."

What was left of the front door burst open, and Serah came in, weapon drawn, followed by Norris and two other agents. "Kane, you okay?"

Deke and Ryan stood. Ward still lay on the floor, cuffed, blood streaming from his head wound.

Serah looked down at him. "This isn't proof of anything, Deke."

"He tried to shoot me," Ryan said, still visibly shaking. "I thought Norris was okay. I shouldn't have let him in."

Norris piped up. "What did you say? I'm Norris."

Ryan looked at Norris, then back at Ward. "He showed me an ID that said Norris."

Serah reached into the coat pockets until she found the badge case. "His photo, Norris's name." She handed it to Deke, shaking her head. "I'm sorry I questioned your conclusions, Kane. There's no reasonable explanation for that."

Ward was coming to on the floor. Deke grabbed his shoulder and helped him sit up. "Foster Ward, you are under arrest."

CHAPTER 39

WARD WAS read his rights, and Norris took him back to Portland. Serah and Deke supervised the evidence collection while Ryan sat in Deke's car.

"Deke, I'll finish up here. Take Ryan back to town and feed him—and yourself—before we start taking statements. I'm going to need you at 100 percent for that."

He looked around at the forensics team marking evidence bags and still snapping photos and taking measurements.

"Don't worry, Deke. This evidence won't mysteriously disappear. I want to nail him too. I can't believe he could keep this covered up for so many years."

Deke nodded. He was exhausted, but the day was far from over. He felt hollow, but each step back to the car was a chore, as if he had lead weights attached to his feet. This wasn't how he wanted this case to wrap up. There was little satisfaction. And it wasn't over.

Serah had reported that the team dispatched to pick up Petrov hadn't gotten to him in time, and he'd fled his penthouse. They'd search for him and alert ports and airports, but Deke knew he'd be nearly impossible to catch. He wouldn't tell Ryan about Petrov just yet.

Deke opened the door and got behind the wheel. Ryan slid across the seat so he was pressed close. Deke took him into his arms.

"Let's get back to town."

RYAN NODDED against Deke's neck and planted a soft kiss on his cheek, even though his body cried out for more. He needed Deke's warmth and strength right now because the situation terrified him. Even though the guy had been arrested, it was only now Ryan realized how much danger there had been.

And all along, Deke had been there trying to keep him safe. Strong arms around him felt good, but Ryan knew everything had changed today. He wasn't the CI anymore, the one with the connections. He was just another witness, and all Deke needed was a statement and his testimony in court at some point in the future.

It hurt to let go. In the space of a few days, he'd lost the two men he'd come to rely on. Three, if he counted Gregory, who had been arrested, apparently part of Petrov's operations all along. Petrov hadn't been the protector Ryan thought he was, just as Deke had tried to tell him.

And soon he would lose Deke too. Had Ryan ever really had him? They'd shared comfort and physical release when they both needed it during the investigation, but like Ryan's role at the club, there was no substance beneath the surface. Just another temporary relationship, the kind Ryan was a pro at, literally.

He let go of Deke and slid back to the passenger side of the car.

Deke didn't say anything as he started the engine and put the car in gear.

CHAPTER 40

DEKE SAT across from Foster Ward in Interrogation. Ward's ear was bandaged, but other than that he was fine. Serah and the deputy director watched from the other side of the glass. A trickle of sweat ran between Deke's shoulder blades. He was under as much scrutiny as Ward was at this point, but Ward seemed cool as a cucumber while Deke could barely sit still. It took all his willpower not to throttle the man.

"Do you want to give a statement?"

"No."

Off to a great start, Deke admonished himself. Thankfully, his back was to the mirror.

"What's your connection with Maksim Petrov?"

"The same as yours. I'm trying to get evidence of his drug operation and connection to weapons dealers." Ward's voice sounded almost normal, not the husky tones he'd used to disguise his voice for his discussions with Petrov, the voice they had on the audio surveillance. He'd recovered from the cancer treatment, but Serah recognized the voice on the audio.

"And how did meeting with him in Vancouver aid the investigation?"

"I didn't meet him in Vancouver."

"You deny being there?"

"I took my wife for the weekend. But we didn't talk to Maksim Petrov while we were there."

"Deke, just wrap it up," Serah said into the comm. "We've got news on Petrov."

Deke pushed a pad of paper toward Ward. "Why don't you write down your movements for the last week, professional and personal. And you could explain why you were impersonating another agent to my CI."

"Your CI. Yes, it all comes back to your CI, doesn't it?" Ward gave a sardonic smile and leaned back in his chair like he was lounging at the seaside.

Deke took a breath and stood up.

Serah and the deputy director were waiting when he got to the hall. He didn't have half a second to compose himself after Ward's remark about Ryan. Deke was going to be in some hot water when Ward finally started talking.

"Deke, let's go to my office." Serah led while Deke and the DD followed her upstairs. She shut the door and sat behind her desk. "We've got Gina safe and sound. If we're lucky neither Antony nor Petrov had time to get to her. But we have to keep her away from Ryan for the time being."

That was one less thing to worry about. Poor Gina got caught up in the mess Deke had made of Ryan's life. He'd find some way to help her get a new job and back on her feet. "Thanks, Serah."

"We need to talk about Petrov's great escape."

"He had to have been warned."

"Yes." Serah handed him a tablet with photos from Petrov's penthouse. The only thing he seemed to have taken were items from his playroom.

"He had plenty of notice."

"Yes, Agent Kane. That's part of the concern." It was the deputy director.

"Sir, I…." Deke paused. "I should have sent a retrieval team immediately rather than checking on the CI."

"With both Petrov and Antony in custody, we would have a lot more leverage against Ward. Antony is not likely to be enough. Ward covered his tracks very well. Much of the evidence could point to someone else."

"I understand. I made a bad call."

"Think carefully about your report, Kane. It will be a key part of prosecuting Ward." To Serah, "Cartier, I'm going to grab a coffee and make arrangements to transport Ward and Antony back to Washington."

"Yes, sir." Serah nodded.

Deke stood until the DD had left. "I haven't exactly redeemed my reputation with this operation."

Serah shrugged, and a smile hinted at the corners of her mouth. "No one died this time, Deke. That's an improvement."

"Dakota." Deke felt cold lead in his stomach. It could have been Ryan. With Petrov and Handler at large, he still might end up dead. Ward could tip them off as to Ryan's whereabouts. He knew too much about Bureau procedure.

"PD picked up Handler. He had incriminating evidence in his possession. He won't walk away from this, and he might roll on Petrov."

"What evidence?"

Serah pursed her lips and waited a moment before replying. "One of Dakota's piercings. They've got a DNA match."

The room began to swim, and Deke grabbed onto the edge of the desk for support. *It could have been Ryan.* He just nodded; he couldn't trust his voice.

"Despite the hiccups in the investigation, you connected enough of the dots for the U.S. Attorney to bring a strong case. And Ryan's testimony is going to be a key part. That's good work."

"But I put his safety above bringing Petrov in. I should have dispatched the team right away. He'd be in custody if I'd done that rather than hiding Ryan." And Ryan might be dead instead. Would it have been a better outcome for the case?

"I don't want to see a comment like that in your report."

Deke hadn't expected her to back him up on his decisions. He nodded. "Where—"

"The DD has him somewhere safe. No one in this office knows where, including me. It's better that way."

Deke exhaled. It was better. Ryan was in danger around Deke because Petrov and the rest of his team knew exactly where Deke was. He was a walking red arrow pointing to their target.

"They're processing his WitSec paperwork. It'll take a day or two."

Then Ryan would disappear off the face of the earth, and Deke would never see him again, except possibly at a trial, unless Ward and Antony pled out.

"I'll make sure you get a chance to say good-bye, Deke. Promise." Serah's voice softened, and Deke looked up. "Now, get started on your report while everything's still fresh in your mind."

Deke nodded and stood, though there was really no hurry. He'd never forget a single thing that happened since he met Ryan Griffiths.

CHAPTER 41

DEKE PUSHED himself to stay late working on the myriad reports required. It took willpower not to break down as he elaborated his every movement and decision on the case, especially over the past few days. Ryan was part of every thought and decision, and it wrenched Deke's emotions to go over the events in minute detail.

He was a mass of raw nerves and emotions, with only the need to be formal and professional reining in his emotions. He began to understand why many of his colleagues took to drink or drugs to numb themselves to the onslaught of feelings. Just one more set of stressors. He'd probably never sleep another night as long as he lived, between the memory of those dead boys and his imagination of what might happen to Ryan, even in WitSec.

At 12:30 he could barely keep his eyes open at his desk, but he dreaded going home to be alone with his roiling emotions. His desk phone rang.

"Kane."

"Deke, get your ass out of there, and that's a direct order." There was a new level of compassion in Serah's voice. "Try to get some sleep. I hate reading reports written by half-comatose agents."

"Yes, ma'am."

"And don't ma'am me."

"No, sir."

She chuckled. "I never took you for a sub." The phone clicked as she hung up.

What does Serah know about Doms and subs? It was time to go home.

Weary beyond words, Deke let himself into his apartment, shocked to discover Timothy settled on the couch, face in a thick book.

"I almost gave up hope."

Deke stared at him, at a complete loss for a response.

"I don't suppose you've got my car with you?"

"Shit, Timothy. I completely forgot to call you." Deke let out a sigh. "It's in the Bureau garage. I'll have an agent deliver it in the morning. Unless you want it now?"

"I can wait."

"Then why—" Deke stopped. He owed Timothy apologies and explanations.

"I wanted to make sure you were okay. When I got home and found your trail of subtle evidence, I knew something big was going on. Then I saw the story on the news."

Deke nodded and settled onto the couch, grateful Timothy hadn't been angry, asked any difficult questions. "Thanks. Sorry."

"No problem. So, are you okay? Do you want to talk about anything?"

"No."

"How's your CI doing?"

Deke glanced up and looked into Timothy's eyes, the genuine concern evident in the narrowed gaze and tight lips. Deke shrugged. "Alive."

"Good to hear."

"He's heading for WitSec." Deke tried to keep his voice steady.

"How are you handling that?" Clearly Deke hadn't been able to hide the emotion.

"You really want to have this conversation, Timothy?"

"Yes. I know this case—this man—really affected you. How are you, really?"

Deke leaned against the couch so his head rested on the back and stared at the ceiling. How did he feel? He hadn't let himself explore the answer to that question. "I'm not doing too well. But you don't want to hear about that, do you?"

"Yes, I do. I still love you, Deke. Very deeply. I'm not in love with you, but I'll never stop caring about you and I want you to find happiness, even if it's not with me." He paused and glanced away for a moment. "I could have been more supportive after what happened, and I kick myself for not being more understanding. So, let me try and make up for that by helping you through this. If you want."

An amazing sense of relief washed over Deke, a weight lifted from his shoulders. "Thank you."

"I'll make some tea, then we can talk."

Gripping a steaming mug of tea in both hands ten minutes later, Deke tried to put his feelings into words. "Ryan is so different from me—from you—and I can't explain why I'm so drawn to him. In some ways he's so independent and other ways he needs me.... It's nice being needed."

Tim had never needed anything from Deke. He was so self-sufficient. It was part of the reason he'd easily kept his life and job together after Deke's career had tanked.

"He sounds like a good fit for you." Timothy's voice betrayed no emotion. He had always been good at hiding it. Another way he was so different from Ryan. Ryan was all emotions and excitement. Deke always knew just what Ryan was thinking or feeling.

"You think?" He paused, considering his words. "He touched a side of me that frankly worries me a little."

"The BDSM?"

"Yes." Deke looked Tim squarely in the eye. "Ryan really is into it. I think he needs it in some way and I really wanted to give that to him. I liked it too, when we were together."

"Then you should."

"He's leaving soon. They haven't told me anything about where or when, for his safety." And mine, Deke thought. If he saw Ryan again, he didn't think he could let him go.

"I'm always here for you, Dan, when you need to talk about this."

Deke nodded and sipped his tea.

When the debriefings and reports were finished, Deke refused the time off Serah suggested. He couldn't bear to sit around the apartment alone, reliving moments from his short time with Ryan. He remembered how Ryan had done the striptease on the bar in front of Deke, the way he'd eagerly gone to have his nipple pierced, how he felt curled up in Deke's lap.

And then there were those times when he'd lain across Deke's lap, eagerly awaiting a spanking, taunting Deke, teasing him. Deke recalled how he smelled and tasted. How it felt to wake up tangled in Ryan's arms.

Of course there was Ryan's insistence on helping Deke no matter the risk. His loyalty to Rocco was remarkable; his loyalty to Deke even more so. Ryan Griffiths was unlike anyone Deke had met or could possibly hope to meet in the future.

Ryan awakened so many emotions in Deke: the urge to protect him as well as the more confusing urge to dominate him. Deke had learned that being a Dom included protecting and giving the submissive what he needed too. Until he'd met Ryan, Deke had no idea he wanted to give or take so much from anyone else. But the thought of going to Dungeon 69 or another of Portland's clubs without Ryan would be completely unfulfilling.

Deke had no idea how it had happened, but Ryan Griffiths had come into his life and Deke would never be the same. Not that he wanted to be. He loved that Ryan had affected him so powerfully. Love should change you completely. That's how you know it's real. And that's why Deke understood that what he'd felt for Timothy had fallen far short of love.

How long could Deke last now that he understood just how much he needed Ryan?

CHAPTER 42

THREE DAYS later Deke sat with Ryan in the back of a U.S. Marshal's car as they drove to a tiny municipal airport seventy miles from Portland. Serah rode in the front seat, making small talk with the marshal driving, a blonde woman who looked tough and capable enough to take down the three of them with one hand tied behind her back.

Ryan kept his face in the shadows, and Deke avoided looking at him. He wouldn't be able to hold back his own tears, and that wouldn't do. Not in front of his boss or the marshal. He slid his hand across the seat to tangle in Ryan's fingers and felt the familiar zing of electricity and emotion as skin met skin. He blinked slowly, willing away the sting behind his eyelids.

"Is Gina okay?"

Deke was surprised that Ryan's first concern was his friend, rather than his own situation or needs. After the initial twinge of jealousy, he realized that only proved what a good man Ryan really was, no matter what his life had been the past ten years.

"Yes. She's fine. The marshals are taking good care of her too. They are looking to settle her near you if at all possible."

Ryan let out a sigh. "Not if she'll be in any danger."

"Don't worry. How are you doing?"

Ryan gave a small shrug and pressed his lips together, as if he might not trust himself to answer. After a long pause, he spoke.

"I'll see you at the trial?" Ryan whispered.

"Yes." Deke kept his eyes straight ahead, but he tightened his grip on Ryan's fingers.

Ryan squeezed back and sniffled. "They said I can go to college. You know, back to college. No one would look for me there, would they?"

"That's great." Deke knew Ryan felt college would make all the difference in his life. Now it could. He could be anything he wanted, and he wouldn't have the rent-boy past to live down anymore. No one would ever be able to find out about it unless Ryan told them himself. "Really great." His voice scraped over the words, and his throat constricted. A weight pressed on his chest, and he wondered if this could have had a different ending.

If he'd never found Ryan or used him as a CI, they would never have met. If Deke hadn't kept poking his nose into inconsistencies in the investigation, he'd never have broken it open. Could he have gotten Ryan out of it sooner?

The car entered the gate at the tiny airstrip, and they drove out onto the tarmac, where a small plane waited. Three government-issue sedans clustered near the stairway leading inside. The marshal pulled to a stop in the middle of the cluster.

Serah and the marshal got out; then Serah leaned back in. "Take a few minutes." She shut the door, and the marshal did too.

Ryan put his hand on the door release, but Deke pulled him into his arms before he could open it. He tightened his arms around Ryan's firm shoulders and pressed his mouth to Ryan's. The kiss started sweet and shallow, then salty as their tears flowed. Deke breathed in Ryan's essence, not wanting to forget anything about his taste or smell or the way he felt in Deke's arms.

Flashes of memory played across the backs of his eyelids. He opened his eyes for the last chance to see Ryan this close, still his, for the very last time. Ryan clung on tightly, and they simply held each other, neither speaking until a sharp rap on the window brought Deke back to reality.

"Time to go," Serah said.

Deke heard the emotion in her voice and knew it would be a mistake for him to try to speak right now.

Ryan whispered something in Deke's ear, in Russian, then let go and got out of the car.

What the hell had he said? Deke's heart pounded, and he debated whether to watch Ryan climb the stairs or not.

Then the meaning of the words came to him. Without conscious thought, Deke flung the door open and bounded out. He looked at Serah, then put a hand into his coat pocket. He handed her his badge and gun. Serah stopped him with a hand on his arm.

"Keep these. You'll need them." She handed the weapon and his ID back.

Deke nodded as he took them; then he raced up the stairs after Ryan. He'd figure the details out later. All he knew was he couldn't let Ryan Griffiths go.

Deke caught Ryan at the door to the plane, grabbed his arm, and spun him around. *"Ya lubl'u teb'a.* I love you too," he said, repeating Ryan's words. "And I'm not going to let you get away."

"Are you sure about this, Deke?" Ryan's voice signaled his own uncertainty and surprise.

"I'm sure. But you know it's all your fault." Deke smiled.

Ryan narrowed his eyes.

"I'm going to have to spank you—at the very least."

A huge grin bloomed on Ryan's face and he cocked an eyebrow. "Oh, really? I think I'd like that, sir."

Excitement jolted through Deke's body at that last word.

He reached out and pulled Ryan into his arms for an all-too-brief kiss. After all, Serah, the marshal, and several others were still looking on.

Then together Deke and Ryan stepped onto the plane.

EM LYNLEY has worked finance, the wine industry, and high-tech, though she'd rather be writing hot man-on-man romance. She spent 10 years as an economist and financial analyst, including a year as a White House Staff Economist, but only because all the intern positions were filled. Tired of boring herself and others with dry business reports and articles, her creative muse is back and naughtier than ever. She has lived and worked in London, Tokyo and Washington, DC, but the San Francisco Bay Area is home for now.

Visit her web site at http://www.emlynley.com,
her blog at http://emlynley.livejournal.com,
her Twitter page at http://twitter.com/emlynley,
and her Facebook at http://www.facebook.com/emlynley.

The Delectable Series from EM LYNLEY

Also from EM LYNLEY

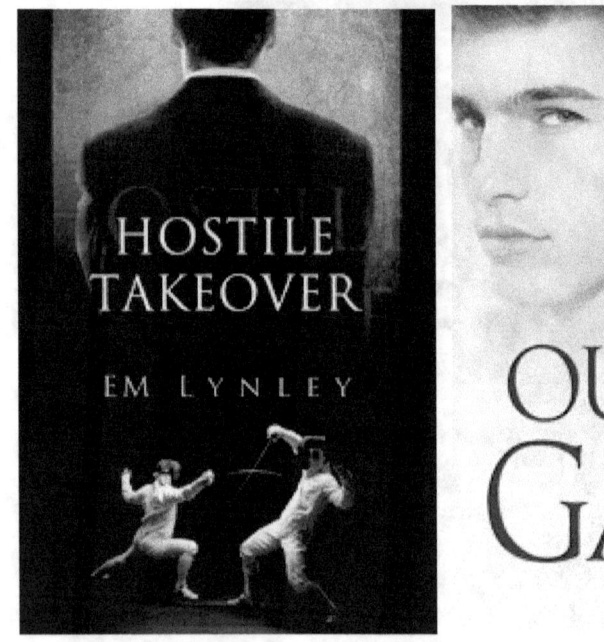

http://www.dreamspinnerpress.com

Also from DREAMSPINNER PRESS

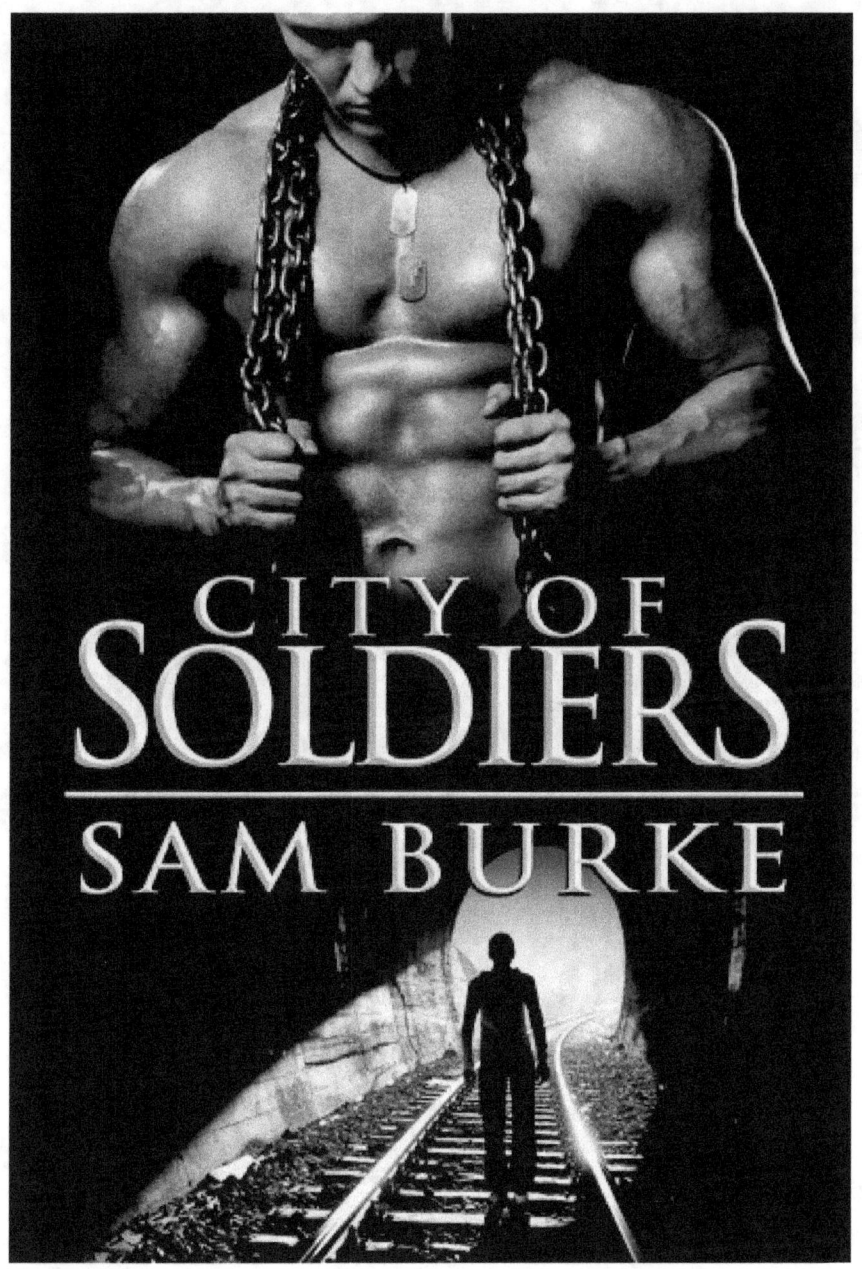

CITY OF
SOLDIERS

SAM BURKE

http://www.dreamspinnerpress.com

www.ingramcontent.com/pod-product-compliance
Lightning Source LLC
Chambersburg PA
CBHW051631260626
47170CB00004B/1134